The Handmaiden Legacy

A novel

G. A. Chamberlin

Titles by

G.A.Chamberlin

The Handmaiden Legacy
Cultural Attaché
Rare Earth Element
Outbound
Somma
Unintended Consequence
The Particle
The Kneeling Woman
Blackbird Secret
Exile

Kathleen The War Years

The Handmaiden Legacy
Printed in the United States
ISBN 978-0-9904027-0-1

Crown Eagle Publishing

Distribution by Ingram

Cover Design by Jennifer Chamberlin

Rare Earth Element

climate, culture, commerce...Too important to ignore, too well written to overlook. And too technically suspenseful not to wonder about...

* * *

The Handmaiden Legacy

The Handmaiden Legacy is a contemporary thriller full of corporate interests, beautiful seas and ancient legacies...
---*G.A. Chamberlin is an International Thriller Writer!*

"International Thriller Writers ...that will surprise "
--Agent, Thriller Fest, New York City

* * *

Cultural Attache

"...Amanda Wells is lecturing on the historical integrity of medieval works at the University when she is informed that the original manuscript of a major work...has been stolen from the vault.

* * *

* * *

The Handmaiden Legacy,
An International Thriller...

Amanda Wells responds to an act of terror
that takes her to the brink of destruction.
But it's a false alarm!

New to the Embassy staff in an area of
conflict, what began as an embarrassment is
a dead run extraction with rogue decisions
made in exchange for a hostage
... her boss.

*

The Handmaiden Legacy

A novel

G. A. Chamberlin

One

Abimelech spotted her in the marketplace and stopped. His companions, ambling beside him, bumped into him. He stepped into the shadows.

She stood with an erect stance, her head inclined. The vendor held captive her handmaidens. He had spices, roots and dyes. Here was mint, cumin, saffron. There, oils if they desired, and wait...
He pulled up a burlap sack and opened it up, grinning.
The white crystals gleamed in the sun.
Salt.
The girls laughed.
The young woman smiled, her linen garment draped down to silver slippers. She was tall, with a silhouette that suggested a slender body.

The girls listened to the vendor who must have delivered a compliment, his eyes dancing.
They giggled and looked back at their mistress.
Behind, a man in brown vestments took a step closer, perhaps to survey wares of the market.

They gathered around her, the handmaidens, and she examined their pouch of saffron for odor and color.

Stale?

How long ago ground into powder?

Here, where spice was the most coveted of commodities, she took in the aroma, revealing gold bracelets and gems of Mycenae at her wrist.

Good.

Abimelech watched them as if spellbound.

The young woman glanced behind her, catching the eye of the man in brown vestments.

Aye. She would buy more from the vendor, she told her handmaidens.

They cheered and rushed to inform him where he should deliver his basket, and from whence money would be paid.

The merchant grinned, pleased not only to be making his sale, he told them, but to such a *goddess.*

They giggled.

The vendor noticed the man in brown vestments and averted his eyes.

Abimelech angled himself closer, following her with his gaze.

They gathered around and she moved calmly forward. Her headdress, fringed with jeweled sequins parted at the peak of her forehead to reveal a long neckline. Then her garment reclasped around square shoulders.

Abimelech wanted to breathe freely, but he could not take his eyes off her.

She looked up.

Her eyes, incredibly, were arctic blue and her skin was a soft glossy olive.

He noticed her brows painted in the newest style of femininity, and her hair, such that peaked out, shone freshly in the sunlight.

He watched, recognizing the deportment of the highborn.

Then the man in brown vestments turned and proceeded down the marketplace. Slowly, they followed.

Abimelech hailed one of his servants.

"Find out! *Who*...is that household?"

His servant looked puzzled.

In this melee?

With his head the servant pleaded with exasperation: The world was converging upon them to buy food and grain. The marketplace was crowding with merchants, vendors, vagrants and performers all selling something - from human slaves to spices! Why would the Master wish to seek out anyone from this mess, he wanted to know. Rather better to ask about someone in this camp purchasing large-quantity orders, like the citizens who might be rich, *the very rich!*

Abimelech gave his servant a fierce look and beckoned his companions.

They gathered, clearly disdainful of the mob pressing upon them.

The entire northern territory was migrating because of drought, famine and distress. They were here buying up supplies, the rest left to die. They spat and stood apart.
Abimelech turned to his servant.
"*Go*. You stupid! And report to my Captain *only*!"
He spoke to his companions, adding "We must ask if we may pay our respects to the new arrivals with a visit!"
Abimelech watched her as far as he could.

* *

Beirut Lebanon

Whatever separated peoples thought Amanda, was not amongst the burnished beans, speckled rice, roots and green okra spilling from burlap sacks in the souk. Nor in stalls sheltering prickly pears, mangoes, tomatoes and tangerines stacked in pyramids.

She still could hardly believe that she was deployed on a tour in the Middle East...

The crowed moved like lava down a stone street that descended to the sea.

Amanda looked around her.

At the perimeter she observed smoke of barbequed lamb curling off grills which obscured her view. Then barrels of shivering brine coveting olives, cucumbers, onion and other uncertain elements. And it was hot.

Without air here you could choke, she decided. As she walked on slowly, Amanda dodged a cargo sack which appeared suddenly on the shoulders of a man emerging from shadows of chiaroscuro chaos. It surprised her, and she gasped for air.

Then a fresh wash of sea air swept up the ancient street, taming the souk with one breath.

She was relieved at the larger view, but she felt anxious. She and her companion had been separated in the crowd - if only a few moments ago.

This was not the place to lose sight of her charge. She could not see her... *Where was Lizzie?*

"Madam...See...Good?" said a woman, unclipping her veil to reveal a gold tooth that gleamed like a trophy. Amanda smiled, her nerves fraying.

Still no sight of Lizzie!

Amanda looked again. Could she spot Lizzie's head from thirty steps further down?

"Moving urgently and mincing down shops lined with brass, bracelets and straw hats, she felt sweat down her back.

"You like?" said a voice from beneath an awning of diffused sunlight. Amanda turned.

Three young girls stood grinning at her, their beads and bangles all swinging together.

No Lizzie.

Or. Was that her head bobbing in the crowd? A moving target?

Amanda sidled along carved Kashmir woods, goldsmiths and fullers. She paused.

Amanda stood besides medieval curtains sheltering shelves of fabrics, bolts stacked up against the walls like cordwood.

Within two men were talking and they broke off their debating, gaballeyha and tassels gone, but prayer beads in hand.

They would not talk to her, she knew. That was the prerogative of the shopkeeper.

Amanda stared.

Overhead canary-colored silks festooned the ceiling, walls lined with lightweight worsted woolens. Bolts of linen in shades of grey, charcoal, pinstripe, bone and black filled the light that penetrated shutters. Soft Afghan wools shimmered like black satin. This, Amanda realized, would be source material for Western tailors of men's wear from Paris to Brindisi. It was the heart of a trading legacy that originated with the silk route of ancient times.

He did invite her, the proprietor, to sit on the bench reserved for customers. She smiled and turned away.

Her priority was finding Lizzie.

Close now to approaching panic, Amanda stood on her toes, and thought she saw the familiar head a few dozen meters down.

Thank God!

Lizzie was standing behind a mass of cosmetics, perfumes, leather sandals, copper basins, silver ornaments and bicycle parts...

Amanda let out a yell. "Lizzie!"

She surged forward and she pressed too quickly against a kiosk which fell to the ground with a crash.

Amanda looked down at the wares splayed everywhere. Combat knives, swords and assault rifles spilled from straw crates. Landmines, ammunition belts and trays of grenades rolled to the ground.

"Oh...Excuse me! Sorry...I..." she began, anxious to not lose the girl in her sight.

She raised her arm waiving and made another shout out.

With her short hair and two white bobby pins, Lizzie looked up and waved back, nodding and grinning like a tourist.

Amanda reached her, panting and out of breath.

Lizzie was standing at a small jewelry shop with attendants not much older than herself. She had been showing them her accessories, including her tattoo, her sleeve all rolled up.

One girl, clearly animated with her discussion, had pushed back her burko to display green eyes, olive skin and a nose pierced with a jeweled diamond set in a small gold scarab.

"Lizzie..." Amanda pushed closer "You're on a celebrity tour?"

They laughed.

"You come tomorrow..." said the one with green eyes "I give you...for the nose, a *star!*"

"*Oooooh!*" they cupped their mouths and giggled.

With Lizzie firmly in her grasp Amanda led the way down the street.

"You'll never guess what I found" said Lizzie, patting her beach bag.

"What?"

"A choker that'll knock 'em dead-in-Amsterdam!"

"Oh yes?"

Amanda nudged Lizzie further downstream.

"Yeah... Take a look at this!"

Lizzie stopped dead and the mob flowed around them.

A work of art laced across her fingers in the form of a necklace. Tiny beads of silver filigree arranged with countless hooks shone in the sun with unabashed glitz.

"I'm impressed!" said Amanda.

"Trevor will like it...don't you think?" said Lizzie, her face capricious.

"Of course!"

They walked on with Amanda navigating the crowd.

"Oh! I almost forgot..." said Lizzie diving into a beach bag and pulling out a parcel. She unfurled it.

The dark shawl swung free and opened up a shawl of black and silver thread. In grand gesture she sashed it around her shoulders.

Amanda searched furtively for a gap in the pack of people to pass through.

"For the cooler evenings...from my brother to *you!*" said Lizzie, grinning.

If Amanda wished she could quell the hubris of the girl at her side, she did not show it.

And it did take her by surprise, all that dark muslin and shiny threading. She stared at it.

Clearly, nothing was going to dissuade Lizzie on adventure.

Amanda smiled. She accepted the brown paper parcel tied with butcher's string and stuffed it into her sling bag tucked under her arm, noting that her shirt was now showing stains of perspiration. She pressed forward.

Finally a break, and they stepped out into open air circulating.

"So. Did you find any colors?" asked Lizzie

"Err..." The noise surged.

"Tell you what..." said Amanda firmly gripping Lizzie's elbow "how about we take a break and go down a little further into the *French Quarter* where they have prints and fabric shops...and ice cold coffee!"

"Oh Yes. Please let's do that. I'm hot!"

They passed from ancient stone arches into wider streets of thinner crowds and glass fronted shop windows.

Inside one, they selected a fabric print of silk paisley.

"Perfect!" said Lizzie. "Can you sew that into a dress with an empire-seam cut like across here?"

Lizzie leveled her hand to her breast height.

"In less than two hours!" conceded Amanda.

"Whoa... you like your spindle Lady Amanda!"

Another parcel tied with butcher's string found its way into her bag.

They reached sea-level. The contrast was stark. A wide boulevard of sleek and chrome cars faced them like a cold splash of reality.

Chez Francois Café had crept it boundary well into the sidewalk, if wedged along the Cornish promenade.

Shaded by green awnings waiving tassels in the breeze, customers sat at tables between large terracotta-amphorae of bougainvillea.

Lizzie picked a corner table and they sank into their seats.

The waiter came over.

It was very hot, they told him, and they were happy to order something.

He smiled graciously, adding a few words of English to their menu.

Nothing better for the dry palate, he told them than citrus Greek salad and calamari ceviche...

Yes.

They added bottled-water; ice-cold Coca-Cola, *Cappuccino* coffee and a sweet desert.

 Amanda lounged back into her chair.
"My God it was hot in there!"
"I'm close to panting!" Lizzie's wet bangs stuck to her face.
The sea surged against coastal rock with thundering fury, then dissipated into a voluptuous display of frothy lace. Back and forth, unleashing its force against the stone jetty like a breathing assailant.
It wasn't intended, the feeling that came over Amanda. Sheer wonder at the natural beauty of the ancient world by the sea, lands of legend. Air stirred by the ocean turbulence refreshed them at their tables.
"Maybe we could go swimming some time..." she mused.
Lizzie's eyes grew wide with excitement. Amanda recalculated the need to show mature restraint. She was on chaperone duty for her boss, Trevor MacDonnell.
Trevor's sister was visiting and Amanda was asked to play tour guide until his own schedule eased up.
Amanda didn't mind at all. Her desk was relatively clear, and she felt comfortable with the task. During her college years, she had spent many a summer as Camp Director. Besides, there was little not to like about Lizzie.

A powerful wave sent a thrush from its perch on the vine trellis.

"This is great! I haven't had this much fun in ages!" said Lizzie set to sucking on her straw.

"The shawl, it's perfect..." smiled Amanda.

"Yes?" Lizzie was speaking over a thundering roar of the sea "...call me *Your New York Fashion Consultant*"

Amanda nodded, her hair now springing free from a hair-tie soaked by perspiration.

The waiter presented a second cappuccino and Lizzie looked up. He slew her a delicious look reserved for his best customers.

Lizzie giggled and twirled her spoon on her thumb, enjoying the playful eyebrow on Amanda's face. Then she itemized a continuous stream of stuff she'd have to wear.

"So..." she finally said "where did you go to school?"

Amanda had to laugh at the disjointed conversation.

"Well..." how to cram a life in a beach-sized sentence?

"I...err...went to school in the UK, then Washington for a graduate program."

Lizzie was listening.

Amanda told her of days in Washington DC where on hot days in May, she had to compete with tourists for a table at Dean and Delucca along the Rock Creek Canal.

"So. You went to Georgetown?"

"Yes!"

"How come?"

"It was exchange arrangement with the London School of Economics...and I grabbed it, along with a tour in the US Military Reserve Service."

Lizzie stared, then sucked on her straw, pensive.

They lapsed into silence, captives of a cerulean sea.

 "It's beautiful isn't it?" Amanda sighed, her elbows loose over the cane tabletop.

Lizzie grinned, her youthful features flushed and dreamy, as if at a carnival theme park.

Amanda thought that for a college student, this was a remarkable experience. Summer in the Mediterranean; visiting her brother serving in Beirut on the staff of the Embassy, followed by a stop in Cyprus before flying back to New York. She was about to ask if Lizzie was keeping a Journal when the waiter presented the check.

Amanda shaded her eyes with her hands to look up at a dark form eclipsing the sunlight. She glanced at the bill and plunged into her bag to pull out her wallet. She was fishing around.

Nothing could have prepared her for the shock.

Amanda froze, her smile falling off, and her face draining of color.

 It surprised her at first, the feel of the object as she traced around it. When her fingers detected that sharp angular shape she stiffened.

Hard threads, at the top end, into which her fingers had now laced themselves... *like a book made of metal with wires at the top.* She remembered her early training in counter-terrorism.

Once you disturb the detonation wires..

"Amanda..." began Lizzie

"Wait. I..."

"No! No! Trevor said I must pay for everything. Here's the money!"

Amanda wasn't listening, cold calculation seeping slowly up her arm. She wanted to rise abruptly, remove her hand from her bag. But a program took over.

To Lizzie, her mind was telling her, she was a liability...

Move away!

Amanda looked about frantically and got up slowly.

Her mind was fixed.

She began to make for the sea-jetty, her feet firm. Traffic passed,

Her breathing was shallow, she could imagine her steps; Quicken, over beyond pedestrians, children, mothers...

Move away!

She spoke.

"Lizzie, don't move and stay there!" her voice was detached.

Oh God.

She shut her eyes briefly and saw her surroundings as clear objectives, like digital robotics. She saw herself now in motion, steady at the torso. *Move away down the jetty and leave the safety of land ... get out over sand.* Amanda resisted the urge to hasten, only a few steps, the solid shape at her fingertips unmoving. But she was thinking. Oh yes, with deadly, methodical clarity.

She reached the stone wall, then moved carefully, stepping over the barriers and saw herself walking out...unhearing.

"Amanda!" screamed Lizzie. Even the waiter was waiving his arms.

Out beyond the sandy waterline ...where the waves dissipated on the jetty over open water. Out to where the waves heaved and rolled, out, out, slowly now, to where they crashed into boulders of mounting sea spray. There she must go. She moved carefully, over spongy rocks, wanting to push herself into a dead run, until she could reach the isolated extremity of the man-made promontory. There Amanda would stop, alone at the very end, as far away from people as she could go, and wait.

Sea spray was soaking her clothes and tears now streaming down her face. There, she decided, she would remove her hand from the trigger and wait to die. Careful now.

She had climbed 100 meters along the rocks beyond the stonewall. She was on the jetty when she slipped. She lay there, calm, one hand firm.

"Amanda!" she heard Lizzie calling.

"No!" she waived "Stand back!"

Amanda got up with the smooth motion of a performing contortionist, her eyes aflame and afar.

One slip of her fingers from the solid shape in her bag and they would all die in a blast.

Sea spray drenched her shirt. How far out she went, she wasn't aware. She stood on the large boulders like seaweed about to be buffeted by wind or wave.

The bomb never exploded.
At low tide, and the sea calm, the basalt rocks were still black, their glossy surfaces quickly drying in the open sun.
Someone grabbed her elbow.
"Got her!" yelled a voice.

 Lizzie had summoned her brother Trevor MacDonnell.
 Lizzie was pacing along the stone wall, shrieking for Amanda to stop. Two American MPs fanned out to the perimeter. She was told to stand back...
Yusuf the driver was behind Trevor when he lost his footing on a boulder reaching for Amanda. Trevor regained his footing. Then it was Yusuf who held them both steady, his legs astride.
"Amanda!" he said.
The sea, now surging in growing swells, had not yet breached the boulder line.
Amanda was dazed when Trevor thrust himself forward and pulled her hand away from her bag. She screeched with alarm.
"Are you alright?" he demanded over the closing roar.
Amanda looked at him, nodding in bewilderment.
Except for her waterproof bag, she was soaked. Not just from the salt spray, but from her own perspiration.
She stumbled, whimpering, slowly over the spongy surfaces. Yusuf had placed a blanket around her shoulders.
Soft sand brought her back to sure footing. She could not stop shivering, her eyes unfocused.

"Amanda" bellowed Trevor, holding her face in his hands "*Look at me!*"

His voice was a million miles away.

She stared at him, trying to speak. She was a bomb carrier.

"The...package. I...I"

"It's OK. It's alright. It's... You are safe!"

"I'm sorry...really sorry. Lizzie? I'm sorry!"

He held her.

"She may be going into shock" a voice was saying.

The MPs, nearby and inspecting her belongings, received an All-Clear by their Sergeant, and began to stand down. They nodded to Trevor MacDonnell: No one in sight who might be a threat. She was clear of danger. And just as suddenly as they appeared, they vanished, not wanting to draw attention.

Trevor held her by the shoulders. Scowling fiercely, he inspected her like a stray animal, then wrapped his arms about her and whispered in her ear.

"The crisis is over. There is no-one trying to hurt you. Nothing to be afraid of..."

She nodded blindly, teeth shattering like a steam engine.

Yusef dispelled a crowd of onlookers with a shrug. A beach incident! *Nothing more...*

A news journalist snapped a photograph.

Trevor instructed Yusef to drive Lizzie back in the Embassy car. He would deliver Amanda to the AUB Medical Center for a check over, and stay with her...

"*Really*. I'm fine, now...thank you Sir".

It was a ridiculous explanation, later in the car. Except that.. they were had been *briefed* to respond to acts of terrorist assault at all times? The clear markers, identifiers. She thought...

Trevor believed her, he said.

He agreed not to write up an official report on the incident. It was, he explained, a false alarm and a dreadful experience for her. *That would be the end of it. Promise!*

He walked with her up to her apartment, circling the front room to draw the curtains and turned down the air-conditioning. He plugged on the kettle and brought her a cold glass of ginger ale which she consumed immediately.

When she emerged from a hot shower twenty minutes later he was holding a mug of tea.

"Here!" he said, procuring two sedatives. "Doctors orders! Get some rest. I'll have Janice check in on you later this evening with some sandwiches. Then give me a call in the morning and we'll have a talk. You OK with this?"

She nodded obediently, turned and walked into her bedroom and sat on the bed.

"OK?" he asked from the door.

She nodded, looking down at her hands, then moved to the bed to turn back the covers.

He left.

Sleep came slowly as she gazed up at the ceiling, the ebb and flow of the sea a distant hum.

The sedatives were beginning to have their effect. Yet she remained aware of one thing. Even as they searched her belongings for items of hardware, she never explained which contents in her bag had been the source of her scare. *Souvenirs* she said, owning everything.

 The thought of a bomb squad inspecting her silly parcel brought both hands up to clutch the bed cover. She had decided, at some point, not to make a big deal out of it...

Her eyes closed.

By the next day, things had returned to normal. That is, Amanda felt as if she were once again in control of her life. Alone in her apartment she looked carefully at all the articles in her bag.

She observed the offending bundle for almost an hour, like an intruder in her life.

She resolved she would unwrap it.

Finally, when the outer tissue wrapping came off, she observed something alien and she lay it down, shrinking back.

It wasn't hers. It wasn't the fabric parcel. She left it where it lay. She never saw it before.

More importantly, why had she *lied* about it when they asked?

She didn't touch it.

There it lay, a leather bound pouch of some kind, tied about with trailing leather thongs visibly brittle with age.

Not the parcel of fabric with the butcher strings...

Idiot. Idiot. Idiot... she muttered.

* *

London

The black Jaguar pulled over.
The driver sprang into action and held open the door for his passenger.
"Thank you Jeff!" said Sir Harold Reynolds.
Wearing a lightweight pin stripe suit and blue silk tie that matched his eyes, he stood taller than most. The suntan and grey hair gave his features a bright look for someone clearly in his sixties. He looked up at the gathering canopy of the sky, still dry for the moment.
"Rain?"
"I hope not Sir. Have a pleasant lunch Sir!"
Reynolds proceeded up the limestone steps of *The Reginald Gores*, a traditional Gentleman's Club now well subscribed by women in government service.
He surrendered his umbrella and briefcase to the attendant Maître D'.
John Wilkins had known Reynolds most of his life. He was a thin man with an obsequious manner who approached Reynolds with fun and familiarity. Even here distinctions were made.
"My dear man..." he said, clasping his hand. "So good of you to come. I know you're busy, and by

the sounds of things, you've had a hell of a time with governance..."

Reynolds took his hand, grinning like a schoolboy. "I'm grateful for the chance to have a drink!"

They roared.

"I know you're on a tight schedule, so we'll proceed right into the dining room shall we?..."

Wilkins led him through the club lounge, a cloister enclave clustered with leather armchairs, soft lighting and densely woven Persian carpets. The place was full.

Reynolds greeted all whom he met in procession. "Minister...Your Lordship...*Thomas* old boy!"

Wilkins finally got him seated in the dining room. "Ah...Here we are then!"

From the *Menu* Reynolds chose chicken pie, Duchess Potatoes and green beans. "Fare favored by Edward, Prince of Wales!" he remarked, lifting his Scotch off the sterling monogrammed tray.

The waiter bowed and disappeared.

Here, it was the reputation that food preparation traditionally began at dawn with fresh provisions from Covent Garden; the Scotch sent direct from Scotland, as it had for two centuries, compliments of the family that owned the distillery as members of the club.

They bantered.

"So, what've we got?" Reynolds said. Wilkins was to turn to the topic of investments.

"AIT...One of the longest and most venerated ventures in insurance. ...As you know, began with a rather quaint story then became the corporate giant considered 'Too Big to Fail' such that the US Treasury had to guarantee its liquidity."

"Umm" Reynolds nodded, his mouth full.

"Well, it divested rather nicely, jettisoned its toxic assets, and reinvented its insurance branches. The parent company has rehabilitated itself completely and continues to perform well. Some of its subsidiaries have reconsolidated under differing interests. Our investors abandoned the company as you know long ago. But it is one of our-own-insured that I bring before you now"

"Oh?"

Wilkins tucked into his grilled cod and mashed potatoes. Sir Reynolds was steadily eating.

Wilkins drank some water then continued.

"Shipping. Under a new name now, but the Carriers never lost a penny!"

Reynolds looked up and allowed the waiter to take away the plates as he reached for another scotch.

Wilkins waited.

"I'm only interested in half a million pounds at this time...Chiefly for small diversified options, John."

The table cleared, now was time for custard-rhubarb Celeste presented from a silver tray of assorted sweets. Coffee was served for Reynolds who turned it away and whispered to the waiter who appeared moments later with a Brazilian gateau glazed in raison rum.

Slowly lifting his elbows to the table, Wilkins gathered his hands to rest his chin on, and leaned inward.

Wilkins watched him, a silver spoon in hand, then leaned forward.

"Look. I'm all for diversifying. But there's a tremendous infusion of liquidity in the company, mostly coming from Sovereign investments. Quite frankly, I'd suggest put the lot in!"

"What?" Reynolds looked up. "The lot?"

"Yes!"

"Well that's a bit of a risk isn't it?"

"Not really. Word has it that there might be some trouble in one of the shipping lanes carrying oil. So they sold off any exposure to such an eventuality, and bought into the alternative ports as the default..."

"My God" said Reynolds, his mouth full "the government should be so well informed!"

Wilkins laughed. "Anyway. Let me know"

"I will..."

Just then the chauffeur approached the table "Its time sir."

"Right then!" He pulled down his napkin, looked up at Wilkins, smiled politely. "I've got to run...they're reconvening in the House..."

Wilkins was already standing "Of course!"

"I'll give you my decision soon. Next week I'm back at my post in Beirut. A spot of trouble there."

"A most thankless job, Ambassador in those parts, I should imagine ..."

"I appreciate the tip Wilkins, and there's a good chance I'll follow your advice...Thanks so much for lunch, I'm only sorry it had to be so rushed...My best to Kathleen and the children..."

"My pleasure Sir!"

* *

It was warm on the Mediterranean. Siesta hour occurred usually at the sun's zenith. Lizzie called at two o'clock.

"Amanda, you looked... like Ouch! Are you OK now?"

"Yes!"

She was in no mood for exposing her feelings. "I'm just a little tired. Besides...isn't there's a party to get dressed up for?"

"Right!"

Lizzie was easily distracted, Amanda wrapped it up.

Yet the sound of Lizzie's voice lingered. It nursed her through the motions of getting dressed for the party. From shower to dress selection to buttoning. Make-up and shoes next, all of it on auto-drive without much risk since little in Amanda's wardrobe was without charm.

A long mirror told her she looked fine. But as the memories of that dreadful moment came swarming in, she felt unsteady and judgment-impaired.

 She switched off the lights, pulled a shawl around her dress, and went downstairs to the Embassy Lobby.

They would pick her up, they said.

For the party at the American Embassy on the campus of the American University of Beirut, they said.

She waited, thirsty now, and chilly, her thoughts wandering ... Tall plants about, or were they? What? Yes. No. Thank you. Up the veranda...

Amanda's thoughts were unfocused, wandering. Her hand went to her head, flashes of fear left her shaky.

Still, the cocktail party provided the aid she needed as someone put a cocktail drink in her hand. She wandered about the crowd.

A few hors d'oevres here; a pretzel there; somewhere a celery stick...and she was muddling through the evening, smiling like a fool and nobody noticing a thing.

She went to the veranda rail.

Lights on the rooftop garden were just enough to elicit romance in the air, someone said. Paula presented an anniversary cake for the Simmons' Twenty-Fifth Wedding Anniversary, and eagerly everyone clapped. Gestures, said someone else, sustaining them through their tours of duty in a tenuous world of tropical reality.

Amanda turned to the railing and peered over the parapet, her head reeling. Below the steep hillside a dark sea lapped at the shores of Lebanon.

"Right then" bellowed Sam though a microphone. "We cut the cake..." The crowd crackled with cheers and fiendish sounds of food consumption. "We drink...and we P-A-R-T-Y!"

The crowd roared, lights flashed and a wicked amplifier exploded with "Jeremiah was a BULLFROG..."

Amanda extracted one more Champaign from a passing waiter and observed Lizzie gyrating to music on the dance floor, the boy not much older than herself.

Amanda looked about the crowd and she saw Trevor. He was on the upper terrace talking to an Italian girl.

Amanda approached casually and he turned.

"Your sister..." said Amanda over broaching noise, and pointing to the dance floor "She's having a wonderful time!"

Trevor laughed, his eyes rolling paternally.

To preclude any further conversation she tapped her watch and said "I'm leaving now!"

"Sure!" he said. "I'll keep an eye on her...You ok to get home?"

"Yes!" she said, and turned firmly to allay any further questioning.

The British Embassy was not far from the AUB on the Cornish.

MPs shuttled back and forth with some frequency. For Embassy staff, drivers and cars were used for routine operating procedures as a measure of security, not rank.

"Home Ma'am?" asked the driver as Amanda stepped into the bus.

"Yes please Tony, if you don't mind..."

She walked to the rear, and sat in the dark watching shiny night shadows caress waiting SUV as they pulled away. She spotted Yusuf leaning against his limo, a cigarette his only torch. Doubtless Trevor and Lizzie would be driven home. Amanda shut her eyes.

It was not that late when Amanda walked back into the font lobby and she waved at the Duty Security Guard. Inside the elevator she pressed the button for the top floors of the Embassy building.

The soft and decoratively edged hallway carpeting, flanked by bright whitewash walls, led her silently to her door.

Here lived certain personnel of the Embassy staff. Apartments, with access to the rooftop terraces were called heaven-by-the-sea said Jim, her neighbor, a junior Intelligence Analyst.

She did not switch on the lights, her front room a moonlit stage of silver. She just stood, her breathing shallow, disoriented. Without awareness she advanced slowly through the shadows shedding purse, shoes and shawl, then collapsed on the sofa. She curled up, clutched a satin pillow and closed her eyes. Trauma had given way to fatigue as it fingered its way into every muscle, and reached for her consciousness.

* *

Amanda opened her eyes.

Chiaroscuro ladders peeked through the wooden slats.

Sunrise on the Mediterranean had arrived, something the Greeks considered sacred enough to herald with song. Within minutes she was at her balcony, coffee in hand. It was Sunday. An early cedar mountain breeze carrying the night chill still prevailed. Today she wanted solitude.

 At some point, she would call Sam and Diane, and thank them for a wonderful party. Today she would mount her own Sunday ministry: She would drive south of the old city, stop at a quiet stretch of beach and go jogging.

She dressed.

If she were lucky, she would find a coin in the sand that spoke of Roman gods and Phonetician trade. If not, she would lose her mind. The day before yesterday, she thought she had lost her life.

Wearing shorts and sneakers, she put on a long Tee shirt, reached for her beach bag and found a brush to tie back her hair. She added a long skirt and full shirt to her gear. Then, wandering past the dining table, glanced at the parcel found in her bag. What was in its folds?

It was a horrible item, she thought, angry. Dark leather-bound and worn bare with age it lay there, its loose straps resembling some Holy relic pleading for attention. She did not want to touch it. Her fingers trailed the frayed edges, clearly accustomed to neglect. But it was those brittle leather ties, wiry thongs to the touch...*Ugh!*

She picked up her stuff and slammed the door behind her.

She jogged: Pace. Breath... and pace.

 What had happened?

One. Two. Pace. Breath.

Run.

Her heart was pounding like a drumbeat.

Water. Life. Her own. *Her own?*

From lemonade-to-death in one second?

Run.

Not exactly your average job description. Sure, hers was a field chosen by will, talent and training, they said. An accomplished linguist, tall, slender and athletic; she had picked the Foreign Service as a career because it was what her Academic councilor had suggested. "Why?"

She stopped running.

She had loved architecture, especially ancient structures, thinking that could be a choice for exposure to classical history. The *high road*, they said, a good career with field experience where she could solve "issues" and "values" of life.

Run.

Close on her heels was panic, ready to lunge at any moment. A career worth dying for on the shores of Beirut?

Run. Breathless.

Resign, she decided. That's what she'd do!

The sweat was pouring down her neck, her body glistening. She drank.

Worse was her awful response. Planted with a bomb and she was suddenly a public threat. *A public threat.* Yet at the time she had only one thought: How to reduce collateral damage. Regardless the cost to herself? *Who thought like that?*

Her toes slugged angrily into unyielding sand and her legs ached.

Somewhere in the distant past when she was normal, her friends would be there for her. Now? Was Evelyn chasing dragons in the law offices of McGowan, McGowan, and Stockman & Price? Was Ted? What of Peter, studying Mathematics at St. Andrews? And Susie, at Fleet Street, spending her evening hours with everyone else she knew clustered at a bar in London.

So what was Amanda Wells doing in Beirut?

She paused.

What was it about the damned Mediterranean that brought mighty men so easily to brinkmanship?

Sweat made a wad of her hair. She ploughed through the frothy remnant of a lingering wave and threw herself into the shallows, rolling like a beached whale.

She got up, stumbling in a sheen of dripping water and brought both wrists up to her face, staggering in a dry circle like a seagull. Where was she? *What* made such a fool of her on a new job? How could such a ridiculous error of judgment be made in such a *public* display?

Jesus!

How suited was she to peace if she screamed at the first sign of ...of...*what*? The entire staff would know about it and giggle in the halls of the office. The locals would mock the response of diplomatic staff on their soil. Hell, even the American MPs knew it for what it was, a false alarm! She even managed to scare Lizzie half to death. A report would doubtless be sent to Headquarters. Trevor said that...he said...He treated her like a child. How humiliating! How do you complete a tour of duty with no self-respect?

And for what? A stupid leather-jacketed pouch roughly dumped into her shopping bag by some *idiot*?

Bloody Hell. Who needed this job? She was done. *Finished.*

She stooped a little, her head still burning with fury, and stared.

A small green copper coin lay partially exposed by a fresh wave from the sea.

She sat down. Tossed centuries before by a Roman, perhaps a soldier, or a woman, or a trader, and it held her captive.

Self-pity washed in and washed out with the surf. She watched it, and waited, sitting in the sand, the tide now receding like a shy playmate.

She picked it up.

Her eyes closed, she held the little coin firmly in her grasp, complete with its story of humanity, corrosion, salt, bitterness and neglect.

She took a big breath. It belonged to someone now.

* *

Stuck to the front door of her apartment was a Yellow Post-it.

"Feed the beast next door. Pizza!"

Her neighbor Jim Calhoun, third tier staff IT specialist, lived three doors down, and was evidently bored.

Inside her sanctuary, she leaned back. Fatigued though she was, she felt she had accomplished something: She had regained her balance. She surveyed her surroundings, beige and neutral tones, tropical touches of color and intrigue. From a life well adjusted. Then she contemplated the article on the table.

The answering machine was blinking messages. She ignored it and went for the fridge. The freezer presented a cliff-face of frozen food begging to be thawed. She showered, picked a pizza (Thanks Jim, but no neighboring and movies tonight), and spent the evening on the veranda with a glass of Chianti.

She thought about it, fully expecting to find a treatise of some kind. Not unheard of in these parts. Relics and antiquities were traded as common commodities.

The sun had set.

Dinner, served and eaten, remained at one end of her oak dining table until late. She drained the last of her wine.

Slowly she approached, then sat very still.

At the other end of the table, behind the vase of white lilies, lay her *object d'art...* Yesterday's Object-of-Terror.

It was dark outside when she closed the veranda door. Indoors, the lighting was subdued, and she felt comfortable. She would stay calm.

The relic before her was old, she knew that. She picked it up.

Not a treatise. Not a codex. But a ledger of some sort.

Only it was illegible, or rather indecipherable. Plus it was strange.

The internal material had been rolled and then stitched at the spine with primitive fisherman's hook and twine. It had held remarkably well. The parchment, if it could be called that, was woven textile, like an Egyptian cloth of sail, once coated in a wax substance, some patches transparent, but mostly grimy and uneven...

The closest thing that Amanda would call it was...she wasn't sure. If she had to be historical, then she'd call it a... an ancient Account?

She put it down. It was old.

Her hand flew to her mouth at the thought of its uses: What events had occurred? What testimony did it witness, and what authority gave it meaning? It lay there. Mute.

The words, inked but badly carbonized, were half clear and half covered with other words.

Amanda knew enough to understand that the irregularity of it meant that it was a hand-drawn document of some kind. Some lettering was perhaps cuneiforms, maybe Hebrew or maybe Aramaic. Other letters and design were recognizably Holy depictions found in sacred works of Latin texts...

Her thoughts lapsed. The horror of its shape against her fingers...Those thongs, like wires...*What a fool she'd made of herself.*

She turned away.

* *

Two

The Nile flirted with ecology in various eras of recipro-locality. Depicted in the iconography of the ancient world, large wading birds contemplated locus leaves for eternity. In Exodus, it had hosted God's Children of Israel and then closed on pursuing Egyptians. Today it conveyed the burdens of fully laden industrial carriers that could roil both shorelines in one single ship's wake.

One such large commercial tanker, the *Zuberhold*, approached, pushing a surging wave off its bow in the confines of the Suez Canal with such force that it could leave any child, animal or boat that stood at shallows overturned and swamped.

The *Zuberhold* was full. Of older construction, its holds were carrying more oil than usual. Speculators had played the futures. It suited the buyers, knowing that the West would know no bounds for its re-purchase price.

Nor did the Canal authority notice its Plimsoll lines well submerged below carrying capacity.

A small fishing vessel pushed off the docks and steamed out to the center channel. David facing Goliath.

Onboard the fishing boat Azim stood in the cotton shrouds that passed for local clothing. The diver's wet-suite beneath his gabalayah clung to his skin like a girdle, and beads of strength-sapping sweat articulated the mantle of his broad face. At the tiller handle was a boy, perhaps nine years old, Indian.

He reached in to loosen his neckline for air, revealing instead, a keepsake chain that hung from his neck. It was linked by small black opals, white gold and diamonds. Even as he held his stop watch in his left hand he had to shake off streams of perspiration trickling down his fingers.

He looked up and eyed the grey ship. Its bow, at the waterline was lost to the lateral dimensionality of a ship coming head on, its girth hard. As an industrial Carrier, it filled the river. Perhaps it was the waterline itself, submerged by displacement that made the ship's beam advance wide like a steel wall.

Still. He counted.

One minute.

Two minutes.

Three minutes.

In the ship's wheelhouse radar screen the fishing vessel had been identified, and an earsplitting ship's blast rang out.

His ears ringing, Azim's gaze was unyielding as he watched the timepiece arch its way in seconds...He and the ship's bow would make contact for full impact, his dory bow loaded with sacks of explosives.

He looked back and lunged at the boy holding the helm of the fishing vessel, the roar of their outboard altering in pitch in echo off the oncoming wall of steel.

 The youth looked up too soon, and ducked before Azim landed his blow, rolling forward and kicking Azim in the knee. The stopwatch went flying, and the tiller handle swung to starboard, steering the vessel to port suddenly. In the struggle it became clear to Azim that nobody was going to be flung overboard in time to be saved.

He scrambled up, flew forward, and pulled away at the burlap sack that covered detonation wires. He made to press the switch, his weight perched against the gunwale. But the rail rope, jerked free from the tiller hold on the stern, ran through its threads around the deck and spun him off his purchase.

With no helm the keel slewed off its center and like a surfer, fell onto the portside chime, as it met the swelling bow wave of the ship. The fishing vessel was picked up, flipped into a capsize, and bounced off the passing steel hull, dislodging cargo sacks as it overturned, its wooden seams snapping and splintering into sharp projectiles before submerging.

Azim was overboard, as was the boy, dead... In that last look between them, he saw more injury in the expression of the youth than on his person. Whatever sense of justice prevailed in Azim's actions he couldn't ascertain. He had hesitated. Whether it was failure to throw the boy off the boat before impact, or unattained impact with the ship's bow as it steamed megatons of oil towards Port Said, Azim knew he had failed. His arms were heavy, and he saw himself swimming in water that was discoloring.

From below, a muffled explosion lifted like a bubble and erupted two meters behind him, perhaps caused by a drum hitting the bottom where water had not prevented the deadly combustibles from fusing for detonation. But it was a far cry from its intended function.

Wanting to save the boy's life, an unnecessary casualty, was his last thought before losing consciousness

* *

The phone by her bed awoke her. It was 5:45 AM. From between two silky blue sheets Amanda's arm emerged to pick up, a thin strap falling loose from her shoulder.

"Morning beautiful!" sang out Trevor. "I thought I'd warn you before you awoke that there's a malfunction in the building's air conditioning: Contractors zinged the wiring! Work for most personnel is cancelled"

She pushed back a cascading fall of shining hair.

"For everybody?" she asked sleepily.

"Essential Personnel only. For the day, maybe tomorrow. You have Emergency generators up there. But not in the offices. I'll let you know." He hung up.

Trevor was making the rounds. What he meant was that all non-essential Embassy personnel were to stay away. She yawned wide.

She was dry, a day on a beach could turn you into a dehydrated prune. She got up, rubbed swollen eyes and consulted the bathroom mirror. Definitely a sunburned pink face.

What a strange call from Trevor.

Cancelled? How do you cancel an Embassy exactly? Stop the world? Especially since they had been expected to work under less than ideal conditions during construction, "inconveniences" as the Ambassador called them – which meant stepping over workmen splayed on the deck, or working beneath open wires that sparked at will.

She paused, toothbrush in hand.

Her thoughts were racing. That could mean only one thing: There had been a breach of security! Did that mean a lockdown? If the security systems were compromised...

So What did that mean, her teeth frothy white already. True, her personal life was physically separate from her professional life. But she nevertheless lived in the same building!

Trevor did say Essential personnel only? Leave it alone stupid. Like you haven't displayed your ignorance already...

Besides, a day off suited her fine. Her limbs ached from stiffness.

She had called Paula and Sam Wickes. Ostensibly to thank them for a lovely party. With particular luck, Sam picked up the phone, and yes, he'd be available if she wanted to ask him about some ancient relic. He'd be in his office in an hour. Perfect.

Two hours later, she was jogging up the scrappy hillside of the American University of Beirut Compound, not far from the British Embassy.

Sam was a greybeard consultant, a term coined in Washington for those with expertise and intellectual specializations, released from government service with budget cuts in mind. It was an old political ploy.

He was inspecting a small clay oil lamp, turning it over for a good squint-eyed inspection beneath his blue smoking pipe. He retired both items to welcome her in, then sank into his swivel chair which squealed in protest. Clearly Beirut was his idea of field sabbatical. The pipe was soon out again and being pressed for fresh action.

Making light of her souvenir "find" Amanda told Sam of a relic she and Lizzie wanted to get all excited about, something they might send home...

"Relics of the sort you describe live largely in legend..." He poured himself a cup of coffee. "There are of course some authentic pieces here and there, but they're hard to identify, much less verify."

"What about manuscripts?"

"Umm. Manuscripts of the medieval era were mainly written in Latin. The old ones were often translations into Latin from older tongues of Coptic, Hebrew, Greek or Aramaic."

"So, err...how did they made the transition from the East to the West, in dating artifacts?" she asked softly.

"Oh, now that's a good question! Especially for dating or identifying any source of origin. Most answers are baloney. But it is known that legible Treatises, written by Romans, did exist. Many, it is said were brought back by Crusaders. What is commonly found" he said tactfully "is a Crusader Relic. Like a codex perhaps?" He raised his eyes in an ached question.

"Perhaps fake?"

He laughed softly. "Oh, almost certainly!" He sat back for enjoyment, sipping his coffee, his grey bushy eyebrows squinting with amusement.

She sat back and asked slowly "But how... did ...records like, parchments survive?"

"You'd be surprised how much was given to patents; knowledge and technological understanding back then! We know, for instance, of the earliest patents and trades through various means. One particular patent was for the making of ink. Other alchemical compounds, known to early pagan Gnostics, were recorded in Papyri, like the Papyrus of Ani - by early Egyptian scribes."

He paused thoughtfully, his fingers pressing at his pipe. "There is much yet to be said for the Ottoman occupation of Europe during the Middle Ages". He nodded to his Portuguese stone table which held a primitive dog. "The Arabs, for example, were the quintessential collectors of all things sacred and worthy, among them great works done by artisans of the Jewish faith: It is said that with the fall of the Byzantine Empire and the removal of its intellectual content to the West, the European Renaissance was born."

"What happened to it all?"

"Burned. Bomb fires!" Sam drew on his pipe "Arabs had a deep respect for learning, for societal living like sanitation, cleanliness. Trade. Law. Fiduciary accounting, architecture among other things...To say nothing of their own creative art, literature and religion: If much of the ancient world survived, it is thanks to them!"

"Wow!" mused Amanda "What a world!"

"You said it, kiddo. And by the time the Jews were exiled from the Spanish Holy Roman Empires, it's a wonder the Western Civilization ever survived!" He sipped at his coffee. "Anyway you have to remember that those were times of Conquest...for lands, treasure, heart, soul and mind..."

His pipe was not cooperating "So what exactly do you think you have?"

"I'm not sure. Perhaps nothing more than a tour book! I'll let you know more...err...when I know what I'm doing" she grinned.

"Well let me know if there's any research you'd like to do: You can access my academic data banks anytime you want Amanda. Just come in and I'll set you up with some passwords on the AUB computer web system..."

"Thank you! Probably what I need most is some basic understanding of the fundamental time line that informs the contexts of early writings? Especially how we date the markings they leave behind?"

"Sure! That's a very interesting topic. There is more to examine if you ask me. I'll see what I can find. For anything more, just come in and Jack my TA will set you up...Oh and you are coming to our Lecture here Tuesday night. Right? It's called *Women of the Ancient World in Three Cultures* by a local historian and eminent professor. Come! You'll enjoy it."

Amanda knew that they had reached the limit of their discussion. To push further was inappropriate. Sam Wickes worked in a volatile world of cultural sensitivity and military hostility. But oh, how she'd like three hours of research in his library collection of ancient texts!

* *

She had barely returned when her phone buzzed from nowhere.
"Yes?"
It was Trevor, confirming that all personnel were to stay away.
"Oh and Lizzie says hi...hang on...*Here, you talk to her* -Hey, Amanda... Can we go out and chill together?"
"Sure!"
"What are we doing tomorrow?"
"Ok.. Let's see. You have a tennis lesson at 10. Then lunch at the AUB clubhouse pool. Golf with your brother later in the day..."
"Cool!" she hung up.
That, Amanda smiled, was a distracted young adult.
Relaxed, she turned to the dining table and picked up her leather bound portfolio. Carefully, she opened the parchment. She examined the writing and its persistent scrawls.
Whatever fear the offending package once held now gave way to something between forgiveness and curiosity.
Before the day ended Amanda picked up the phone decisively.

The gentle voice that answered was unmistakably French

"Allo, Lycee Françoise?"

"Yes. Sister Margaret of the Grammar School please..."

"*Un moment* ...si'il vous plait"

"Hello Sister Margaret. How are you? Would you mind if I came over to speak with you?"

* *

Amanda waited. The great entrance hall was large, marked by marble floor tiles, checkered, that could suitably host a court jester.

The *Lycee Francaise* was a formidable fortress built of dark wood and granite. Within its palisade walls a Roman Villa stood in full bloom. The central courtyard harbored an oasis of tropical vegetation. Much of it was harvested for the mission, the rest delivered to market as fruit for the seasons. Behind it stood trees, fountains and statuary, all hidden behind its stone walls.

Over the years it had sheltered many children, both local and diplomatic. Those whose presence in Beirut were caught up in military turbulence sent their family to safety behind its walls. Beirut was a crucible that drew political malcontents and gun fire like a heavy star.

Sister Margaret came forward, white frock flowing and hands extended. She was smiling, her green eyes enhanced by the veil of her Holy Order.

There was sincerity to every word she uttered, chiefly from an intense interest in others.

She embraced Amanda then led the way into a vaulted white conference room. A dark stained wood table and oak chairs lay swathed in sunlight from a high window.

Sister Margaret waited.

"There is something I want to show you..." began Amanda. "It was posited in my handbag in the market place...not from an antiques dealer" She hesitated and found Sister Margaret listening intently.

She pulled out the parcel.

"I don't know if *I* was the intended recipient... Or if was just an accident. But at any rate, it alarmed me"

Actually it scared me half to death is what she wanted to say. Amanda looked down to hide her thoughts.

 "I don't know if it's...*what* it is... though I believe it valuable and old. Could you research it for me? Tell me what it is?"

Sister Margaret leaned forward, and peered closely into Amanda's face, sensing that it had come at some emotional cost. Mutely she put her hand on Amanda's clenched fingers.

 The walls were thick and cool, the shadows still. There was safety in the quietness that followed.

"Et bien. Lets `ave a look, que ce`qu`il y a ici?" She bantered and unraveled the scroll.

"Oh Mon Dieu" she uttered clamping her hand over her mouth.

It was a long time before she opened it again.

"Coptic!" she said softly, absorbed. "Non. Pas de tout! Aramaic...Si?" Her voice softened with an inner resonance "C'est un manuscript de meilleurs feuilles..."
She looked up. "But...err, where exactly did you get this?"
"It's a long story Sister Margaret, and I'd rather not go into it, if you don't mind..."
"I see" Again the close inspection. Then out came a pencil used as a wand to separate the folios.
Finally Amanda cleared her throat "The lettering is like... running into each other...can you recognize anything?"
Sister Margaret was muttering "There is one.... I have once looked at..."she began but her voice trailed.
"These are some Latin inscriptions...Yes? But, added much later it would seem...perhaps... No... Mais j 'ne le crois pas. A codex!"
Amanda drew a long breath as if inhaling for the first time in days, relieved that someone was taking her seriously.
Sister Margaret placed it carefully on the table and was so closely examining the codex that her starched veil tented the whole procedure as if it were a holy relic.
"It is a record of some fashion, like a testament, or treatise. A Legend perhaps. A list? Non? The Latin text is barely discernible. These words...Perhaps some kind of rubric...to what must follow."
Sister Margaret was a nun by calling. But she was also a Medievalist scholar. Her papers were the property of the Vatican research library.

"It is perhaps a translation from the days of the Crusades. They are - how shall I explain the Crusades, Saratian Knights, like Romans, from the conquests of the Arthurian tales. It was their mission to redeem Jerusalem from the heathen, as see here in the iconography point in picturesque language and parables of...le Bonheur du fruit... fruitfulness flowing from cornucopia baskets of bread of life. As to show great wealth and prosperity; fish of Christianity to suggest productivity and fertility." She looked up, her eyes bright with excitement.

"This, here, is the sacred symbol of the geometry... oui? Of early Greek acronym *Ichthys* (fish) for *Iesous Christos Theou Yios Soter,* or Jesus Christ." Amanda looked at her.

"This may explain the lettering. What you see is two signs of writing. One ancient language. The other Latin during the Church and Crusader years...But at a later date?"

 She stood upright and folded her hands, pondering.

"One thing you are right. It is very old. Very *very* old. I look into 'eet" she said in her French accent.

"I tell you the full histoire. Do you come next week, yes?" Her bright eyes looked up.

"You're on!"

"Tant bien! I see you in a week!" and with that she closed it neatly and placed it within the folds of her large frock. Seeing Amanda's concern she added "Yes, I keep eet safe. How shall I reach you?"

"No need. Next week... How many kids this time?"

"Oh, only a dozen or so" her eyes betraying a little disappointment at the inevitable: The Lycee had long run its course and the tradition of the mountain trips would soon come to an end. As it soon would for the school and the Sisters' Holy Order.

"Don't worry" she said gently patting her folds, "I keep 'eet safe in my office where it will remain security..." she smiled. "It if has survived all this time, we should ensure that its survival is an obligation to posterity..."

Sister Margaret gave Amanda kiss on the forehead. Either as a sign of affection or means of benediction... Either way, Amanda didn't mind.

Sister Margaret had just relieved her of her burden.

* *

Three

Trevor was in the Cipher Room at 7.45am. The room was a vault situated within a greater office secured by counter and bars. Admission for authorized personnel came only by electronic pass at the counter barn-door.

"We're still on EPO status" he called out, meaning Essential Personnel Only.

Amanda stood waiting at the bars. Her security pass failed to gain her entry. She paused.

"Oh that's alright" she yelled back, examining her dysfunctional security key card. "I thought I'd come into the office and do some extra work and clean up if necessary..."

Amanda expected him to open the gate from the inside. She waited. But the bars never budged.

Trevor popped his head around the vault door "Actually Amanda...I'm barred in" He wiped his forehead with the back of hand holding papers. He stepped out and looked at her apologetically. "And..." he paused "...under specific instructions to work alone! Please understand we're in a shut-down mode..." As an afterthought he added "damned air conditioning plant!"

As superior officers went, Trevor was amongst the most congenial and non-confrontational. But even as she glowered, he was clearly not going to budge. Amanda moved in closer and grabbed the security bars with both hands.

"Trevor. What's going on?" She noticed boxes in the communications room.

He moved back a step. "I err...I can't say just for now" He was perspiring and his blue eyes looked anxious.

"Are you *alright*?" she asked

"Yes. Yes. I'm fine... Heat!" he laughed.

He took a deep breath. "I didn't expect you to come in this morning that's all. You took me by surprise. Tell you what. I'll call you tonight. We have a party to go to right?"

"Right" said Amanda, vaguely remembering the date for some Cultural Attaché event at the French Embassy. "Lizzie too right?"

"Are you kidding? She's driving me nuts! I'll be glad to ship her back to New York. *She* won't miss this party for the world."

"I'll call later on from the pool" said Amanda backing off graciously.

She took the stairs down and knew she had the security clearance to enter all confidential spaces. That she was denied access by her boss was highly irregular. Lockdown!

She took the elevator down to the underground garage, which was operational. So that meant restricted areas only.

She climbed into her VW and made her way out of the parking lot, knowing that all movements were being monitored by electronic eyes. She demonstrated no alarm.

It wasn't usual to find her appearing at the AUB gate in her car, it was too close to drive to. She showed her ID anyway.

"You're in Miss Amanda!" said a snappy MP. Also her Softball team coach.

Amanda noticed he was heavily armed. Behind him was an Army truck and two Unit Combat Hummers making ready to leave the premises.

Something was terribly wrong she decided. No appreciable difference in the environment, but a distinct charge in the tension level. Then it hit her with sudden clarity. Trevor was shredding! The papers in his hand were arranged to be fed into the shredding machine: Judging from the number of boxes, he was buying himself two days of shredding time. Only one condition induced that kind of response.

There had been a terror alert.

"I've come to access the university research library" said Amanda to Jack, the TA of the Anthropology Department at AUB

It didn't take her long to find some general source material on the web.

Tour Guide through the Holy Land. She printed the brochures.

* *

The Auditorium of the AUB was filled to capacity; seating was arranged in theater style above the lecturer's platform. The speaker was a woman.

"Good Evening: I have come to talk to you about the role of women in my culture and religion. I speak not as an activist, for I am not. But as a Muslim scholar with the purpose to show you our place in the ancient texts... So call this your orientation course to our beautiful Lebanon!" she began.

"Now we go to the Hebron Shrine in the city of Hebron - the traditional burial site of the biblical Abraham, Isaac and Jacob and three of their wives, a place revered by both Jews and Muslims, and source of much tension between them.
"In this slide, the Biblical Archaeological Society finds scholarship on whether or not Abraham would really have killed his son.

"But if we examine the recent work of Delany printed by the Princeton University Press, we see how the sacrifice rather than the protection of children became the focus of faith; how the story of Abraham legitimates a hierarchical structure of authority, a specific form of family, definitions of gender, and the value of obedience that have become the bedrock of society.

"If we look at the concept of the word princess, emanating from the Muslim tradition you will find that in the ancient story of Hagar, she is referred to as an estranged "wife" to Abraham, a handmaid to Sarah (Midrash Agade, Bereishit 16:10).
In the Old Testament, we read "Sarah, Abraham's wife, took Hagar the Egyptian, her handmaid" (Genesis 16:3). She took her with words, saying: "Fortunate are you to be united with this holy man!" (Bereishit Rabbah 45:3).

In other texts we read "When Hagar parted from Abraham, she worshipped the idols of her father's house. Later she repented fully and bound herself to good deeds, for which her name was changed to Keturah. After this Abraham sent for and remarried her (Zohar 1:133b)."

The complexity of the narrative of Hagar, the Egyptian, and her resultant place in Biblical history cannot be overstated. If Ishmael would become a wanderer - pushed away from his father Abraham and his Israelite inheritance by the jealous Sarah - he came by it naturally, for Hagar, a daughter of Pharaoh, and Sarah's maidservant, endured great suffering and heartbreak in her association with the father and mother of the Jewish people.

So how did women, all coming from earlier pagan cultures, have a role in their various cultures?

In the texts of antiquity, we see that ancient women were used to make a contribution to the telling of the human story."

* *

As an orphanage it had limited staff. Amanda had her favorite Community Service Project: She drove the bus. It was her responsibility to drive the bus full of kids up to the mountains for their field day.

The excursion to the mountains of Lebanon was an old tradition for the Lycee, a memory that had been carried into adulthood by many.

Amanda had performed her service half a dozen times already, and the event was always stunning. The cedar trees of Lebanon- countenanced by

King Solomon, towered like pillars over crisp beds of pine needles and rock boulders fringed with purple cyclamen.

Such a mountainside presented the children with a veritable wonderland, as it did for Amanda. It was a day she relished. Even if at some points the mountain roads were treacherous.

"Qui est vous?" once asked a child at her elbow, clutching bluebells. Surprised, Amanda took her eyes off the wheel, just as she was negotiating a hairpin bend carved out of rock-face.

"*Mais quesceque'tu fait la' Nicole*?" admonished a Sister seizing the child and herding her back to her place on the bus. There, the stray child was firmly buckled in, her shiny shoes barely reaching over the edge of the seat.

Amanda waived in the rear view mirror. The child grinned, no fear, bluebells wilting.

Today the sun's rays filtered the forest. Beds of fallen tree bark entertained birds pecking for worms, and the smell of cedar perfumed the air of the legendary mountains.

"What exactly is it?" asked Amanda, now settled at the picnic site with Sister Margaret.

"A text of some Antiquity" She glanced up "Louis! Decendez, *immediatement*!" The boy arrested his ascent on a large boulder.

"Could you...err...understand what it said?"

"Well. Yes. Et Non!" said Sister Margaret in typical *Franglo* fashion as she called it.

She leaned back against the large bolder and turned her face up to the sun, sacred veil or no. "The lettering is merged, mixed in two languages" she said, eyes still closed.

Finally she sat up. "Voyez: In ancient times, words were written upon a scroll wound around a stuck, an *umbilicus,* and you read between the opened scrolls. Today, a scholar might attach small foam pads with retractor wires to the ends of the umbilicus with each wire anchored to the edge of la table, nec'est ce pas? Like so. That is alight beneath it, and secured with ...comment c'll dit? Les *Pinces*?"

"wratchets?"

"Si. Wratchets!"

"That is how the Greeks and the Romans read them, the classical period. And sometimes, wax or resin was appliqué on them to remain...err...*souple*? "

"pliable!" admonished Amanda.

"C'est ca!'" She paused. "It has voyaged through history, and you can find the answers... in its journey, so to speak."

"And was it translated?"

"Trans-*literated*...Because many of the early writers like Pliny the Elder, they write of other things...no? Like teachings of geography, nature etc...But mainly... by medieval monks. It was the Romans, a l`hors, conquering the East, Judea, and the writings they are all about all their conquests...like Britain, that we have records!"

They paused, both of thinking of the enormity of this item.

Sister Margaret took a big breath, looked up, then proceeded in carefully measured words.

"The Holy Roman Catholic Church. Ahh... How shall I say these things...In the 12th and 13th century, when the supremacy of the papal church was challenged, it had appropriated the faith of Christianity by calling it their *own* exclusive doctrine, resting on the *Four pillars of faith...*"

"Like a corporate ...infrastructure?"

"Yes. Not only... But also wealth and trade was at the core of social organization for the medieval world - all in the name of Christianity. Thus everything was heretic. And open to conquest!"

 Sister Margaret looked down, perhaps wondering if she had strayed beyond the bounds of what the Catholic Church would have liked.

Both she and Amanda knew of the breadth and depth of the Holy Roman Empire throughout the ages. Repositories today, were full of ancient texts and collections that were well beyond what the secular world held in knowledge, content or understanding of the medieval world. But in her case, there was more. A moral dilemma.

There was a tacit fiduciary responsibility amongst the faithful--an understanding that even if moral judgments had been horribly corrupted in the interests of administration, the Church had, for better or for worst, brought civilization through the Dark Ages. This, all the faithful knew. And must accept with grace. And silence.

Sister Margaret fell silent. Yet Amanda had come to her for help.

"My God!" muttered Amanda. "Then you're implying its real? Genuine?"

The blue eyes nodded up and down. "Quite possible!"

Then to help Amanda through her muddle she added gently "We have accounts of the Herod

Agrippa, grandson of Herod the Great, who knew Jesus Christ..."

"This..." she went on "This appears to be a patent for the making of oil from the pressed olives. She had an olive orchard, something very valuable, and other items for the trade, like wool from the lambs for weaving, and a city of the workers, like a seal for the sovereign legacy of a crown to a place. How you say, *suivant les titles du bonds de terroire*, yes?"

"A survey of the boundaries?"

"Yes, gave it, as a gift..." Sister Margaret paused, read, then looked up

"It says that is also have the secrets of the alchemy, and for the Ink...It had brought wealth to the woman. Here...she owned fruit trees of date figs in an oasis, and with lands of trees, timbers and for and the reeds, for the papyrus to make..."

She examined more closely a few words. "Forever as long as there is the need for ..err, ink" She stumbled "...To make markings or the *writing* and *finishing of markings* on tablets with the mallots..."

"Chiseling, carvings?"

"For to continue...with the seal of the markings..,"

"In other words, forever!" interrupted Amanda with some excitement

"Figuratively, c'est la, if you like...And, I think it was lost, or allegedly lost...Perhaps, like many other documents hidden during the invasions of the Romans, in the caves of the desert. Or by The Knights Templar. Or found by the Knights Templar as a treasure that the Church..." Her voice dropped off.

Then she handed it back to Amanda. "That is all I can tell..."

Amanda understood.

"But there is a problem" she said suddenly, as if in her thoughts.

"Two things. You see, the lettering appears to be a mixture...but it is not! "

"Meaning?"

"The parchment is written in two...err...two...*eras*! C'est pas?" her face was aggrieved "The one account is written in Coptic, or earlier: The other, written much later, is in Latin. That I can tell you all. This suggests that it was considered a sacred text added much later. Perhaps by scribes or knights...It has the lettering that has the unique calligraphy of medieval penmanship"

"Some Crusader!" said Amanda half joking.

"From Noyou in Picardy"

"The Crusader?"

"The Cistercian Monastery that did that Latin inscription" Sister Margaret said simply. "Like a modern Christian fundamentalism...if you will"

"My God" said Amanda

"Decendez!" yelled Sister Margaret to Jean-Paul standing over Louis, now atop a boulder, arms wide.

"Can you tell...how old it might be?"

"It depends which one! One is old. And the other is...is..." her brow furrowed in puzzlement "older!" She waved her hand backwards in time. Then she dove into a canvas tote at her feet filled with sweaters, scarves, first aid kit, little shoes, water, bananas, blanket and book

"Comment c'il dit...There is a book about the Crusaders. The Templar Knights. It is written by a respected historian Becker."

"Ici" she said, turning to the pages of his book.

"C'est peut'etre plus une legende de literoir. In grammar and character of another manuscript it is similar to *Perlesvaus*, a sequel to Robert de Boron's story about ze Holy Grail, a popular romance et continuation of des original legends of Christien de Troyes."

"This Becker, 'ee explain that Perlesvaus is a continuation of the story of the Grail" she looked up. It was commissionee' by ze Lord of Cambrin for Jean de Nesle, castellan of Bruges – and his town was central to the commerce-trade of Flanders. You know, wool and the cloth, it was very much a big trade and much gold. ..." she laughed at Amanda's unblinking eyes.

"Please continue!"

"Jean de Nesle, he started a Cistercian monastery at Noyou in Picardy. Then he go to Crusade, from Marseilles in 1204."

"Yes?"

"It was...how you say, a big thing for the kings and great men of the Church. But in reality, c'etait pour l'or de L'Orient et l'enrichment?"

"The riches of the orient, the silk trades?"

"Precisement!"

"So, 'ee go with the *Thierry of Flanders* a son of Count Philip –the great kings of Spain, they are king over the Lowlands, the Netherlands, non?"

Amanda nodded.

"And *Gautier de Montbeliard*, a patron of Robert de Boron, author of the *Grail stories*...?"

"Yes" said Amanda. "What happened?"

"Et bien. They want to come `ere! The Holy Land. They build their medieval castles in the desert!"

Amanda waited, giving Sister Margaret a chance to look over her charges.

"A 'l'ors.The first crusaders...They take ships from Venice, trading ships. But they cannot pay their passage! Oui? You understand? So the ships, the trader, they keep them passengers for their sea-venturing "

"Like pirates?" shot Amanda, her hand quickly to her mouth in mirth

"Mais oui!"

Amanda had to laugh. Raiders from the bosom of the Church was too funny to contemplate. Mercantilist commerce - downright plunder and territorial seizure exercised by the Holy Roman Empire! A far cry from questing knights and minstrels of the medieval courts of kings.

"Then they go Constantinople and sack Zadar, for the traders from Venice... to get rich!"

"Prize of war" added Amanda, helpfully, fully appreciating the complexity of the world at hand.

"But the second group, the man from Flanders, they have sufficient money to pay for ships, and they go straight to Syria, which was a Frankish kingdom, like France, and they stay three years!"

"Really?"

"Becker, he says they, the King of Jerusalem - not have enough Knights to do battle"

"Unbelievable!" said Amanda "Sounds like a novel"

"En tout cas, we do know from history that the *Jean de Nesle*, when he finally go home, he fought much later in a war on the side of the French, Bouvines, in 1214. Then he went again on the Crusade against the Albogensians in 1226".

"Well what does all this m mean, exactly? I mean, why all this crusading?"

"The manuscript you have may well be from that time, if it is authentic!" She was about to open her mouth when a child screamed.

A girl stood on the boulder, staring in disbelief at a mud-cake splattered on her dress. She pointed.

"Jean Paul!" admonished Sister Margaret.

Three boys flanking him ran for cover, leaving him standing with the evidence.

"Frogs" he said, relinquishing his next handful of dirt to Sister Margaret. She led them both off and wiped them clean.

With Sister Margaret preoccupied, Amanda understood the tension that had grown in the dark ages of Europe.

She read:

"*Crusading, depicted with the fruits of profit and trade, had spiritual overtones. The romances of the Holy Grail gave cultural and moral meaning to princes and knights who should go venturing to better the world for Christ. To redeem themselves from heretics, or European pagan worship and unruly civil order. They become important, rewarded with fame, land, and title for the administration of the early Catholic Church.*"

Sister Margaret returned. "So, it is in this context...that you must read the Latin inscriptions by the Crusaders on their mission for Christ."

"Thank you Sister Margaret. I do appreciate this very much - Please do not let me distract you from your charges here!" said Amanda

"Mais, pas du tout, Amanda. Je suis a votre service"

Children emerged when the bell for food was rung. Sandwiches of ham and cheese wrapped in wax paper were devoured. Some had egg salad. Some cucumber. A boy held an apple in one hand, a pine twig in another.

Sister Margaret was not so easily distracted. "But it is for this period of *l'histoire* that I am specialized. So, I tell you more, non?"

Amanda was only to pleased to hear it, both of them now relaxing on the grass after lunch "...and I 'ave a surprise for us, purquoi non?" she said, pulling out from her bag a small straw laced flagon of red wine "For the spirit, c'a vas?"

"c'a vas!" repeated Amanda.

"But whose story is this? ...What does it say, exactly?"

"I don't know. I can make out only a few words here and there!". She dipped into the folds of her dark robe, procured a white lace trimmed handkerchief and wiped the perspiration off her brow.

"It could be a forgery... a fake parchment designed to fetch a good price on the black market" said Amanda

"Maybe" she shrugged

"And why the inscriptions on top of the iconography?"

"I will treat it with care. It depends on the chorological dates, on the content... I will consult with my references, and make tests, then I tell you *exactement*?"

"... the authenticity of the parchment?"

"Si!"

"and olive oil..." ventured Amanda.

"And olive oil!" They laughed.

They sat there together on a rock. Pensive.

Sister Margaret patted her on the knee.

"Do not let this consume your soul, Amanda. I keep it with care and take responsibility of it for you, then I give it to you back, yes? You are able to do that?"

"Yes" said Amanda. At the end of the day, the responsibility of the disposition of this relic, was her burden, and her burden only. She sighed. *What a nightmare it had been!*

Amanda surveyed the views, they were endless from these mountains.

Sister Margaret was smiling.

"What's so funny?"

"It speaks also of love..." she said softly "of living and dying for one love...As an aphrodisiac, how is that?"

After a while she turned to face Amanda

"I have chosen the love of my life!"

Amanda knew that as a Holy Nun, she had taken the vows to be The Bride of Christ.

She added "Do you have a love in your life?"

Amanda smiled.

"Well...there've been a few boyfriends here and there... but no. Not what you would call real *down-in-your-heart* love; *love-for-ever* love"

"I shall pray for you Amanda" she said simply.
"There is a man sent by God for you!"
"Oh right!"
Sister Margaret turned to her. "I 'ave a codex, from this period, exact, I have 'eet from before I take my studies...It speak of love Amanda, like the Songs of Soloman! I give it you, a gift, for your happiness - to find the love of your life!"
They laughed and returned to the children.
Sister Margaret, decided Amanda, was one of the true romantics left in the world.

* *

She entered her apartment and closed the door, satisfied that the housekeeping maids had fully cleaned the place today.
They had washed down the windows with astringent cleaning solutions, including her desk, computer and system unit. They had laundered her white gauze drapes and table-mats. Wet-dusted her louvered shutters. Polished, vacuumed under her sofa, armchairs and entrance. The bathroom was disinfected and mildew free.
She looked at the floors. The apartment's marble flooring was mopped. In her bedroom the bedding, throw rugs and pillows had been changed. The air smelled clean.
Moreover, yesterday, all the filters were changed on the air-conditioning units. They hummed nicely to produce cool ambient air, free of humidity.

She stood looking at her Martha Stewart Cook book on the kitchen counter, and made her decision.

She swiveled and walked into her bedroom, opened a black hard case and disgorged a large battery and charger which she plugged into her wall converter. The light went red.

Amanda marched out her apartment, down the hall to Jim's apartment and knocked.

The disorganized bachelor, Jim was, but with the lucid mind of an IT specialist with dots, dashed and imagination wired into his thinking.

"Hia Geek!" she grinned at the door.

Clearly surprised to see her, he just stood there.

"I'm determined to make Baklava for Lizzie. Can I borrow your Betty Crocker?"

"Of Course! If Betty permits ...."

Jim was in his pink office shirt, underpants and socks and she was half way to his kitchen.

"Do come in!" he said following her.

All apartments being the same, furnished by the Ministry of Works, there was little Amanda didn't know about.

"Might I become the beneficiary of any such culinary creative works?" he asked in his sing song Welsh accent.

"Of course!" she cleared the counter and repositioned a few items.

"Along with Lizzie in company?"

"That's the trouble with the Welsh" she said looking at him squarely and waving a long wooden spoon "Singers and Dreamers!" She picked up the heavy cookbook, cradle and all.

"We didn't build our Castles for nothing!" he said trailing her out the door. "I for one would be happy to entertain the maiden ..."
Amanda turned.
"Thanks, Thomas boyo, but Trevor might object to your making advances to his maiden sister. See you later..."
"The English!" he was muttering "always cavorting with the Scottish!"

Amanda hated to be surreptitious, but she was on a roll right now, and Jim could be included later!
Amanda flung Betty Crocker out of the cradle and laid out a clean towel on her counter.
She sank the Plexiglas book holder into a sink full of warm soapy water and vinegar, stroking off residual staining with a soft wash cloth. The evidence of Jim's efforts at sauce-making was abundant.
Twice she drained off the water and repeated the process.
Satisfied, she picked up the Plexiglas cradle and wiped it evenly with chamois, then set on the veranda to air dry.
She closed the drapes. Pulled back chairs and dragged her dining table to meet her desk to create a workspace. She swiped the desk clear of clock, stapler, papers and pencil holders. Then she bent to her knees to examine the surface carefully. It must be a lab surface. Free of any latent dust for an optimum controlled environment.

With two large photographer's lamps flanking the plexi-glass holder, the light reflection was carefully balanced out with wax paper over each bulb.

She went into the bedroom and found the battery charger, its light now green. She inserted it back into her Nikon D80, changed the lens and set it to auto focus with a flash option.

Above the desk she rigged her photographer's tripod.

She settled in, waited for the bulbs to cool down, then turned on her laptop to open a spread sheet program.

Wearing white archivist cloth gloves, she gently lifted the manuscript, prying open the pages with a pair of tweezers. She placed each open page inside the Plexiglas container. Beneath it, she nudged a flat ruler, inches and centimeters clearly marked as reference, and it lay open evenly against the glass for imaging.

Amanda looked up, perspiration seeping down her shirt. She reached for a drink of water and continued her gaze on the splay of documents illuminated.

She switched on the flank lights and enabled the Nikon for high resolution imaging. Exposure was necessary. But bright lighting might do damage.

With the delicacy of a master magician examining vanishing words, she worked at each unbent pages. Arranged to rest within the cradle, the manuscript allowed even, odd and full text pages to press up flat against the Plexiglas.

At each presentation, she raised her hand to the mounted camera, focused and clicked.

The front. The back. The top of each page, the corners. Twice each, careful to record each image on the laptop spreadsheet to synchronize photographic digital sequence of date and time, like an electronic stamp.

Amanda worked in the dark room, an occasional fresh night breeze gently wafting through the curtains of her open window.

She worked methodically. Beads of sweat glistening her brow. Long Shots. Close-ups. Wide angle. Vertical. Horizontal.

Satisfied, she removed the codex from the Plexiglas and arranged them for images of its texture. Adjusting lamps for close work. Next, she captured weave, wear, coloring of the cover. The corners. Tops. Backs. Folds.

She made notations. There would be no doubt as to its parameters, numbers, sequence, timing and exposure.

Repeatedly, Amanda checked the focus of her lens; distance from the subject. The light; numeric order of shots. Each indexed, cited and described.

Amanda stood back to stretch her back, but her hand was steady and her resolve unwavering.

One by one the images filled the screen of her laptop. She felt as if the world of the Mediterranean sea, outside glittering with diamonds in the night, was about to reveal the theater of its history.

The night had advanced into the early hours of the morning. With all images saved she converted a copy into reduced deliverable *Jpeg* files.

By dawn, with damp hair clutched behind her moistened neck, she pressed the key:

"SEND"

Four

Clusters of guests wearing sparkle and evening gowns filled the ballroom.

The French Ambassador's Residence was the site of a Gala event.

Waiters, presenting food and drinks held up on silver platters, moved amongst guests as a Quartet played chamber music from the Romantic era. Tonight, it was clear, the French would have their night.

"For my favorite women in the world!" announced Trevor holding aloft two glasses of sparkling wine. He beamed triumphantly, his blue eyes accentuated by hair tamed for a white dinner jacket and silk cravat. He seemed quite at ease.

Amanda and Lizzie looked at each other with query

"...and may I say that I am staggered by their beauty, brains and Beirut sunburn!" he went on.

"Now Trevor, lets not wax lyrical here..." said Amanda taking her glass with thanks.

"Ladies, I have an Announcement to make: For my sister's benefit and to advance her learning, I have made arrangements for a road trip across some of the Holy Land's most historic places..."

"Really?" yelled Lizzie in glee "Like a Safari trip...?"

"Yes. Only no hunting guns!" he laughed.

Lizzie planted a lip-glossy kiss on his cheek.

"Oh...and Amanda comes as the family house guest?" he added, looking at her hopefully.

"Thank you. I'd be delighted" she smiled. "I need to take a few days off with my boss's permission!"

"That you shall have!" he bowed willingly

The details, dates and logistics would come later, Amanda knew. Probably close to the end of Lizzie's stay. But for now, there was too much going on.

"Emerson!" waved Trevor to a passing colleague.

"The place is some *soiree au salon*" said Lizzie admiring the haute décor. "Wow!"

"Quite!" said Trevor. "Follow me ladies!"

Trevor carved a way through the crowd and found a place on the veranda. Below, gardens alit with fountains, pond lilies, arbors and perambulating guests filled the night air with scent of blossom.

"Trevor, I want to have a chat with you..."

"I was afraid you'd say that...stunning as you look tonight!" he added seductively.

She noticed that he avoided her eyes and, sipping his drink observing a round faced girl who was dawdling close by

"Une dance Mademoiselle?" he said to the girl as she slid away.

"Trevor!" admonished his sister.

"Ah, err...Nothing to explain darling"

The music mellowed. All guests had arrived and the party was in full swing.

"No...I mean. Actually, I wanted to talk to you about antiquities, something that might be quite interesting" said Amanda

"What kind of antiquity?" he asked, sipping his campaign.

"A manuscript actually"
"Oh how boring Amanda! Couldn't it be a Holy Grail or something. You know these parts. Consider everything..."
"...has the earmarks of a possible Crusader relic..." said Amanda on her toes over the beating music.
Trevor was fixed on the gyrating girl, his mind elsewhere.
Amanda laughed at him. She sipped her drink, having enjoyed an earlier conversation on the drive to the party with Lizzie in the car.
 "Do you know anything about Vestal Virgins?" she had asked.
"Virgins? No" he chuckled "Nothing at all!"
"I do" chirped Lizzie "Something about this ancient Briton: What happened in Britain at about the time of Christ?"
What a question from Lizzie! He looked accusingly at Amanda. This time it was her turn to chuckle.
 A call to history was a call to duty for Trevor MacDonnell - of the Scottish clan - as he adroitly pointed out on one occasion.
"Well, it's been known we've had a goddess or two...We've found a few wine amphorae, *Sheepen* I think they're called. Grave relics of a Celtic noble warrior most probably, if you ask me, of good Scottish lineage. But historically speaking, we've found evidence of the English goddess *Andraste*."
"*And..?*"

"Well, she had those qualities...what do you call them...You know. Sibylline qualities of worship and prophesy, or so I was told by my colleagues at Cambridge..."

Trevor was lost.

But they enjoyed it. It made for much hubris before the party, and they had laughed.

Only now, at the party, over the Champaign Amanda decided to tell him. She would do so in a nonchalant way, as if making small-talk to minimize the impact. And she would pick her moment. That moment was now.

 "Trevor" she said lightly "I have a...relic of some significance!"

"Pardon...?" he gestured

"A relic!" she shouted, lifting up on her toes. Useless. The music was too loud.

"A relic?" said the high tones of a Frenchman behind her.

"Jacques!" said Trevor spinning suddenly to the bowing head of dark curls.

"What a splendid event this is! May I introduce my associate, err... Amanda Wells; Jacques de Torraine"

"Enchantee`" he said taking her hand and bestowing it with a kiss

"Merci" curtseyed Amanda, ignoring Trevor.

"I'll leave you two together. Amanda, the man is in your hands, and if he talks about Napoleon - Arrest him!"

Amanda smiled graciously, and, glimmering in her silver lame dress said "Please excuse our

Trevor, he does serve his purpose on the staff by keeping us all happy"

"Pas du tout!" the man expostulated with a grand gesture. "I wish I were in his shoes!"

"So" he added, his gaze steady "`e is your err...relic?"

She laughed, again aglitter, and sipped her wine, assuming the moment would pass without further comment.

"Please tell me...And what relics would that be?" he asked again.

She was either getting annoyed, overly sensitive or just plain drunk, she couldn't decide. Either way, she didn't like his intrusiveness.

"Oh, just some wild-ass guess about some stuff we found" she said defensively, laying on the American jargon to shut him down.

Clearly reduced by the cultural difference, he smiled politely.

"Perhaps I can help. As the Assistant to the Cultural Attaché, I 'ave some expertise in antiquities"

She didn't fall for his appeal to her professional standing, but she couldn't play the ditz for much longer. She changed the subject.

"What a lovely place the French have here" she said

"Yes" and without taking his eyes off her, added "The French 'ave been at the heart of this culture for a long time..."

"Since the turn of the century?" she said politely

"That depends on which century..."

Touché she thought.

"Shall we enter for the dinner? Please?" He offered his arm as escort.

Together they were seated at a table surrounded by Roses.

To great effect the Quartet played musical variations of soft rock and classic jazz in the Renaissance styles. Above them a vast and warm mid-Eastern sky twinkled.

The service was impeccable, the food of Five-star quality. The evening was sweeping by as a successful event by diplomatic standards.

 Amanda never drank at parties, but here with boeuf-au-jus served with a deep claret burgundy which she did not refuse, she felt the swirl of wine soften the sharp edges of her thoughts.

"You found something, then, that you like here?"

"Actually, it was nothing really. And old book, I think. I gave it to Lizzie with the idea that she'd enjoy the feel of historic ambiance in the Holy Land. But you know teenagers!"

"Of course" he laughed "It's probably and old ledger book!"

"No doubt of interest only to some historians" she added in a voice of ennui.

"Or to someone...interested in the human story of people. Perhaps even someone who cares about the region, non? Someone...such as yourself...perhaps?"

Dinner removed, the dance floor was once again open.

Amanda looked about for Lizzie. She found her talking to the sons of two American staffers, one of them clearly drunk, the other getting sloppily belligerent.

Amanda shortly she made it her business to approach Trevor with the unmistakable body language of making their exit.

Outside she asked him "What did you say his full name   was?"

"Alexander Jacques de Torraine, son of a *famille gallante*"

"Oh, I thought he said he was Secretary Chadenet's Assistant."

"Perhaps in some other capacity. He's their house guest!"

At their garden gate he said "I would invite you in, my dear...But for my official charge here."

"Geeze Hey... Guys. I'm OK with everything!"

Trevor looked at Amanda. "Send her to College and she's in charge of the world!"

"Yes, well. That's America for you!"

He chortled.

"Anyway, I must - as the responsible adult - bid you good night My Fair Lady. Thank you for your companionship. And your chaperoning service! You've been most kind" he gave a curt bow.

 "And most lovely..." he added softly with a look down her bare shoulders.

"My pleasure, Sir!"

* *

In the dark, the computer screen evoked a solitude that embraced the reader. Soft breezes swung through gauze curtains at the open veranda door, and Amanda was alone with her research and access codes:

As to women with agency, the pagan world was ruled by ritual ancient sayings, and cultural deities, many pronounced by priests and priestesses:

The first words of a woman priestess are identified two millennium before Christ in pagan cultures, through the age of early Judaic history when Abraham traveled from Mesopotamia to Palestine in 1877 BC.

By the time the Biblical cannon was closed, women still held the trust of the simpleminded in spiritual things, but also in things of trade, even as men were the warriors. This was what early Christianity had to subdue.

As to your context:

"Your original language has been identified: Time line still undetermined. But pre- Urartian, Assyrian cuneiform script derivations. Writings are several, ranges from scribal hieratic script to cursive demotic, also seen at votice statues and stelae of Twelfth Dynasty shrine, possible Senusret III. Also checking tomb paintings of Deir el Medina. Evidence of later Coptic additions, but original is Hebrew. Avram is cited.

As to the Crusades? Chiefly efforts to capture the trades and wealth of the orient ...The Templars are supposed to have amassed great wealth, secrets and knowledge...until that too was stamped out by the Holy Roman Catholic Church obliterating competition...

Next Item: If you are shown the written literature of the medieval era, you are likely to have gone past

the original deities and theologies that prevailed as competing polytheism - often rooted in sympathetic matriarchal beliefs that were contrary to the Roman belief of monotheistic control and social suppression.
Hope this helps...
Best, "H".

Amanda stared. "Several?" what did he mean by "several languages. And who was Avram?
She wrote *"Did women had Rights?"*

<SEND>
* *

Five

Amanda had risen early as if for no other reason than to stand with coffee in hand on her veranda and watch the sunrise.

It appeared over the ocean, filling the horizon with a discernible curvature of the earth.

A quick shower, some apartment rearranging and a few notes to set up for the day on her day planner sent her early to work wearing a black cotton top and white skirt with soft leather shoes. There she settled into her office routine with little fixing: In the tropics, order mattered over appearances. Not that her office environment was distant, but it was sharply different from the safety of living quarters of the same building.

Aside from some inbox paperwork which was clearly dated, there was little in Trevor's office that resembled disorder. Rather, Amanda knew it had just serviced as a small warehouse operation in the recent past. Plants, lights, wall decorations were slightly off center.

And gone were the boxes.

"Storage!" he had said when she gestured with some vagueness, both of them keen to avoid the tentative nature of their encounter there.

JoAnne walked in to deliver incoming paperwork, arms clinched in a silk battique chemise over a long linen skirt and thong sandals. Even a bronze medallion, the size of a discus, dangled from her neck as décor-de- theatre. Suitable, thought Amanda, for an outfitter of desert caravans. "Good morning!" she said cheerily. "Trevor is...?"

"Back by... mid-morning I should think"

"Well...alright." She let down her flourish and surveyed Amanda's plain look. "Just tell him as certain gentleman called and asked for him personally."

"Personally?"

"Yes. I tried to find out what he wanted..." she flounced out the door, the air still jingling.

* *

Trevor assembled his office group together for his Morning Coffee Briefing.

Ever the Executive, he acknowledged the work of his staff and enumerated the day's priorities.

JoAnne was present, though she did not technically work in their group. What mattered was that she sat facing him with long legs crossed and the buttons of her khaki skirt gaping.

Finally Trevor closed. "We received a terrorist threat. You know the usual... Something that might possibly target our staff. We are restricting some access points. But we should be fine. So, heads up. Keep smiling. And let's have a good day!"

Amanda got to work. The communiqués of the morning needed serious editing and redistribution to members of the Embassy staff. Some were Immigration issues, others Political in nature. Most were pending the new Trade Agreements Accord and should go to the Secretary of Commerce's office.

That was the office where JoAnne worked. She thought about calling JoAnne down to collect. But that would set them all back an hour. So she delivered the stack herself.

That's when she saw him.

Trevor stumbled out of his office and leaned against the doorway, his face pale.

"Lizzie has gone!"

"What..?"

"Fatima called. She thought she was sleeping in. Lizzie was not in her bedroom."

"That's ridiculous. She came home with us last night..."

The terrifying thought started to surface: Lizzie a *targeted* hostage?

They climbed into Trevor's car and drove to the house. The might get a clearer understanding. They found Fatima, who had served Embassy personnel for a long time, in a state of tears. She squealed in waves of wailing anxiety.

"Let's split up and check out her haunts just in case" said Amanda "Trevor, you go the AU Clubhouse, pool and ask around. I'll check out at my place. She may have crashed on the roof to sun herself"

"Right! Keep your cell phone on"

"Definitely!"

"Damn it to hell. Life's a joke for her. Should never have let come to the Middle East" he thundered Amanda could hear the rise of panic in his voice. There was something reminiscent about the moment that stung the air between them. Or was it something else lying just beneath the surface that bothered her.

Amanda's flat was empty. She returned to her own thinking about what possibilities might be. If Lizzie had been taken as a hostage, the response would be drastic and immediate - an official press pronouncement. A statement. No. This was not quite there yet. It was incumbent upon them not to make foolish assumptions.

Besides, who would want Lizzie? She checked the kitchen for signs of fridge snacking. She tore out the contents of the bedside table where Lizzie had spent the night two nights ago. The bathroom. Towels? A make-up bag, anything to indicate she'd been around, or dressed up to go out....

Her lips went suddenly dry at the thought of something that surfaced. Something Jacques said.

The "what" was a little sense of interest piqued in the mention of Lizzie's name. It was the last thing she remembered telling Jacques about her "relic"

"On my God. No way! Lizzie"

She took a deep breath. Her training kicked in. Examine the evidence first. Could there be some other explanation? Lizzie with those blue eyes and purple lipstick and tight jeans and constant talking...

The cell phone jingled. "Anything yet" asked Trevor.

"No. Not yet. She's not here. Look. There is something I've wanted to tell you about. Something I have... or rather – discovered. Perhaps related...I don't know!"

"What?"

Amanda suddenly stopped. She spotted the old shopping bag from the market souk, still sitting in the front room.

"Never mind! I'll call you back"

"Amanda, wait..."

She tore out the underground parking garage in the Morris and headed south.

The souk was no different today. Calmer perhaps for a mid-week morning. She re-traced their steps and walked quickly. She reached the jewelry kiosk that has so fascinated Lizzie and saw two of the girls.

"My friend...?"

They looked at her and gesticulated. Yes?

"My friend, the blonde hair..?"

"Aiwa. Aiwa." They nodded.

Amanda started running down the sidewalk towards the café. She dialed Trevor and suddenly stopped, breathless.

"Trevor! You're not going to believe this" she managed, her voice constricted

"God dammit" he exploded "I'm about to report her missing!"

"She's having...err... late Breakfast by the beach!"

That night Amanda sat at her dinning table. Why the feelings of apprehension mixed with annoyance?

She went to the fridge and reached for some cold orange juice. And it wasn't JoAnne and her stupid flirting...as if Trevor gave a damn. She slammed the fridge door shut.

After all, Lizzie did nothing unnatural for a visiting house guest... She just slipped out for the morning, and the maid panicked.

Amanda cleared away the dinner table and secured some provisions.

These things happen.

Trevor's invective did surprise her though. Clearly, the fear of Lizzie being in danger struck a fear deep within him.

Amanda sank onto a her retro-sofa held by chrome feet and surveyed the soft lights and familiar surroundings of her apartment.

But she felt a cold chill creep up her arms, perhaps reminiscent of the fear she felt on the day of her great book-bag gaffe - as she now called it.

She turned back to her computer and opened her mail.

Subject Re: Women, Rights:

First there is the assumption of pagan woman's agency, then the transition to patriarchal authority, and that authority serving to define what powers priests and priestesses had.
Here, as you can see, a scholarly article by John Gee cites ancient Egyptian documents in an effort to

establish the historicity of the Book of Abraham. The first An Ancient Window, published by the Ancient Research & Mormon Studies (FARMS), the second was Abraham in Egyptian literature

    "Gee concentrated on the Magical Papyrus of London and Leiden 8.8 (fig. 5). He claims to recognize the name of Abraham identified as the 'pupil [and iris] of the wedjat-eye', appealing to the Book of the Dead.

"If a parchment showing ownership is seen in the hands of a woman, then it is undoubtedly a woman of hierarchy, like a high priestess sheltering knowledge as part of her wisdom. Perhaps offering known ingredients for remedial effects. Or, protecting of codex under siege, perhaps invaders from the north, sea peoples or warriors in haste. She may have been brought wealth to manage, to own, or to process, like a resource if she was to own a date oasis – with deeds!
Such codex, writings and finishing of manuscripts and paintings, allegedly lost and hidden in the caves of the desert by The Knights Templar are said to have existed. One such manuscript appeared in a museum in Europe pointing directly to the group, Latin. The knights were said to have searched for it during their crusade. None was found. Except for a tapestry that advanced that theory and speculation..."

It wasn't until dawn that Amanda assembled her thoughts.
Too awake for any sleep, she decided to get up, make coffee, go out on her balcony.

The notion that Lizzie had walked off innocently without anyone noticing was naïve.

No.

 Someone was watching her!

 Why inform Trevor of Lizzie's absence, necessarily?

...Unless to alarm him. And with predictable response?

 Lizzie's episode was deliberately being exploited. The kid was doing nothing wrong.

It was ...what, a *message*?

She turned suddenly to her desk and glared at the computer.

* *

Six

Gibraltar.

It was a lavish affair. Billeted as *"Reception for Executives of Shipping,"* the staff served drinks to investors.

In the heat of the Mediterranean sun, the garden party was lavish. Bird song and peacock blended with nautical tunes of jazz emanating from a small band beneath a white canopy. Waiters passed with silver trays of drinks; everywhere guests clustered in spots of shade from trees; flowing trellis or lawn umbrellas, the air filled with the scent of bougainvillea.

"...Yes, they will be pleased with the returns..."

"That leaves the important port of Haifa, a Jewish port, with strong corporate ties ..."

The crowd was getting large as guests continued to arrive, apparently, from all corners of the globe. Dressed in hats with plumage and blossoms, or starched turbans, the ladies congregated in colorful folds of pastels and bright prints.

 Among them, wife of a senior official from the British Foreign Office. Another, a woman holding a permanent seat on the Board of Directors as Founder. Also present at the Annual Meeting was the wife to the American Ambassador to Lebanon. The guests mingled in animated conversation at Government House, as it was called.

"Government House" at Gibraltar had its history here, and was at its most splendid in the warm summer air at this vantage point. From the top of the ragged cliffs, in sight of the Atlantic ocean barely parting the continent of Africa from Spain, its commanding view of the portal to the Mediterranean Sea was undeniable.

The British had dominated that Rock of Gibraltar for centuries. First as a colonial outpost during its expansion, then in its unrivalled sea power and military dominance it held an official post for the British.

The structure, once central to the Admiralty, crafted walkways around formal gardens and still evoked the presence of garrisoned Admirals at anchor, their company of officers and retinues ashore; or midshipmen taking examinations for advancement of rank; or Pursers delivering accounts of Ships Store for His Majesties Royal Navy.

Now privately owned, the courtyard and lawns of the whitewashed colonial outpost was alive with verdant juniper, Astor, rosebud, mulberry plantings and ivy. Overhead, modern construction erected 24 ft. groined, vaulted ceiling beams that extruded from the large clerestory windows down to black Spanish limestone floors. Deep within the porch loggia of shell stone, tall bearing columns, with a fresh sensitivity for comfort, loomed like legends.

From here today, the new CEO of the one of Europe's largest shipping insurers would remind

the assembled stockholders, of their carriers' longstanding reputation in the maritime trades.
He welcomed London's stock brokers. He welcomed bankers and venture capital market fund managers. He hoped all were comfortable...
He waited as the house lights dimmed, and soon the cool air conditioning hummed like a dark sea breeze across the audience now settling in.

The room was filled to capacity. Damask covered tables along the perimeter and gilded seating was now hosting representatives from five continents and seven seas. This, it proudly showed on its Logo.
"Ladies and Gentlemen of Seaguild Enterprises..."
Giles Servoordt held a deliberative pause of appreciation for the ladies in the seated audience.
He opened with
"Ladies...you all look stunning!"
They chuckled and nodded, the last of the crowd settling down.
 "Please allow me please to thank our host for the event - Mr. Sergio Pullani, for his usual generosity and hospitality as we gather for our Annual Meeting. Err...Sergio? Stand!"
Applause.
A man in a brightly floral bush-shirt sitting to the rear of the Assembly Hall stood up partially, and waved back modestly at the applause.

"Today I am proud to introduce our new CEO as the latest member of our group: He is an innovator and spokesmen for the industry. He remains close to the heart of the financial community, and ...if I may say so...*far* from global corporate losses!"

Giles paused, his long hair pulled back from a poet's brow of dotcom virility. Then he smiled, leaning over microphone. "*How did he do it?*"

The audience looked up, theater at its height.

"Very simple. He kept to his creed...Yes, I said creed, not greed!"

They laughed, tension dissolving.

"No. I'm serious. When most companies turned their services into a means to an end for financials, *he* stood fast to the prow of his ship: Just shipping!"

.."When scrap metal sent ships to Gdansk for stripping down, *he* furbished them and turned them into cruise liners!"

.."When insurers tallied the balance sheets of empty vessels delivered of their cargo, *he* filled their holds with returning commodities..."

.."When carriers suffered losses due to weather or union demands, *he* hired the youngest and brightest merchant seamen from strong academies using new technologies and safer risk management....In sum, the fundamentals of an enterprise that showed increasing returns on the balance sheets every quarter!"

Applause

"Please give a warm welcome to Alex Gouldermeer, our new CEO of Seaguild Enterprises.."

The room roared with greeting.

Alex Gouldermeer made his way to the podium, looking easily under his age of 48 years, his calm eyes set wide apart. He had an embarrassed stiff-necked smile as he approached; his demeanor modest. His Armani jacket, jeans and a hand painted silk tie gave him the perfect touch of drama.

Silence finally settled in.

He held them in his gaze, unblinking, calculating that if they knew the industry, they would also know one bane to large ships on the high seas. He leaned forward to whisper.

"I own... a *sailboat!*"

The room erupted with laughter, eyes rolling and heads nodding, then drew silent again.

It was not the expected opening.

"And... it's a *big* sailboat...?"

Again the room filled with laughter and chuckle.

Behind the podium, a screen had materialized.

He took to the charts with a pointer.

"...If we look at the trans-traffic of our various shipping industries, you will see an interconnection between the ports.

If we look at the balance sheets of the last the past four years. You see reflected in those numbers corresponding flow charts of systemic cargo tonnage for fuel, containerized shipping and food in these northern ports of the Mediterranean sea. Below us is the flow of car transports shifting from eastward to westward. Haifa is a solidly well managed facility for dry goods and hardware. Brindizi, Marseilles and Malta solid ports for public transport and recreational shipping. Beirut a show port for military presence, and the Suez demonstrating remarkable resilience with the infusion of Chinese investments into Africa.

"Yes. We live in an uncertain world. Shut down any one of these ports, due to any number of natural disasters, socio-political or military intervention, and we see massive inland restructuring taking place...

If, for any reason, any of these ports are incapacitated, and the ports on the Mediterranean Sea are closed, great limits are presented to the world's gateways for traffic.

 I believe in competition, of course. But it behooves us to consider the strengths of these ports: He, who owns the port, owns the gateways of commerce. Eliminate a competitor, and you have diverted one eighth of the world's traffic.

Why do I say this? you ask. We are, after all, carriers and insurers...." He paused

"We are in a vertically integrated and centrally managed changing world. It's time to engage in port management before anyone out there gets creative!"

The room grew silent.

"It will be in our interests to anticipate such flows of trade and commerce with careful vigilance - and care at sea, certainly. But with planning for contingencies that capitalize on alternatives...

"Ladies and Gentlemen, these ports have been around since the Phoenicians, they have survived many civilizations, and their longevity is assured for the long term, yes?"

Laughter.

"...With more than ship cargo and traffic across the seas, we carry the legacy of an ancient tradition of seafaring trade. The Mediterranean has eight critical ports, and we service 50% of the market share using those ports. ..

I intend to make it 75%..."

Applause.

"In fact, I will go so far as to clean up the portside usages with better communications, upgrades safety standards, cargo shipping security for each and every sea port that we use... as if they too were part of our team..."

A soft, hushed wonder filled the room.

"...Because, you see, I believe that if you raise the standards of everyone else's facility, they are all the more dependent on you as their providers...like a community, one growing, the other profiting..."

Applause.

"Ambitious? Global? Yes! And why not?" he asserted with growing crescendo.

"Each of these port facilities holds specialized and critical functions: We will support their further refinement and multiple uses as critical pipelines to inland economies!

... And the more customized their regional requirements are, the more specialized we will be as their Service providers; Carriers; Clearing-houses and Technical experts. Such that their development... is ours! Their expansion...is ours! And their success...."

The audience drowned him "*is ours!*"

"Clearly, we are in the right business!" he concluded.

His easy American jargon and technical expertise, delivered in calm and measured ways, sealed his discipleship. He was their man!

The lights came up and relief showed on faces adjusting to the change as they left for the rest rooms and cocktail bars. Those standing against the rear wall glad to move off and mingle.

The cell phone that vibrated in the Hawaiian bush shirt of the man standing closest to the rear entrance had been going off relentless for at least five minutes. He was about to turn the thing off altogether when the lights went up, and he strolled towards the loggia to take his call.

Once he heard the voice on the other end, he offered to call back, and made his way out the room, beads of sweat filming his scalp.

He walked towards his parked BMW, palm fronds waving in the breeze and he leaned against the parapet to open his encrypted message. His turned his back to the crowd now spilling from the loggia and faced a sandstone parapet overlooking a vast sea below.

He put the cell to his ear. "Is there any news?"

What was a dark fleshy face with blue accommodating eyes turned into an expression of hard steel with sneering contempt. He cast an eye behind him towards the broaching noise.

"The boy?"

He moved closer to the edge of the cliff, he gaze fixed on the horizon.

"Azim?"

Wind tussled at his shirt with little effect as he stood, stone like, for several minutes. Then he shut his cell.

He turned to his car, and opened the door, leaning heavily on the frame as he got in. He started the

engine and drove through the gate with a gripped smile across his face, waving at the guard who recognized the BMW with the tags labeled "ATZAR"
He turned on the radio for news and disappeared down the mountain, sunlight glinting off a large girasols signet ring made from opal.

* *

Seven

Dawn presented a cerulean sky over a majestic Mediterranean sea at calm. She turned away.
 Before dressing for the office, Amanda went online to check her email. There was a reply to something she had sent before visiting Sister Margaret.

"Two scholars in particular explain about women. Savina J. Teubal, in Sarah the Priestess, and Tikva Frymer-Kensky, in Reading the Women of the Bible, both draw on historical evidence from the ancient Near East in order to address the role and authority of a woman. They both come to different opinions about Sarah, wife of Abraham.
"Teubal says that Sarah was once a high priestess herself before she left with Abraham. Once Sarah arrives in Canaan, argues Teubal, she struggles to preserve the matriarchal traditions of her homeland against the patriarchal society in Canaan. The Genesis narratives in the Bible thus form a bridge between the matriarchal pre-historic world and the patriarchal historic world.
"Teubal says that, drawing on historical evidence from the ancient Near East, Sarah asserts her traditional role as priestess. Teubal cites Paragraph 146 of Frymer-Kensky, on the other hand explains Sarah's behavior in a different light

when she argues that written records from the beginning of writing in ancient Sumer show that patriarchy was well-entrenched in the ancient Near East over 1500 years before the Bible; the Genesis narratives are not a bridge between some matriarchal pre-history and patriarchal history"

Amanda wondered about the freedom Sister Margaret enjoyed as an academic, and imagined her smiling through her findings...

"So this text is a woman's agency?" Amanda emailed back.

Within two hours she opened her response.

" Not only is it about a woman's right, but a right of ownership, which assumes human ownership, like slaves as well as land ownership, or land and territorial boundaries - something that only the patriarchs would assimilate as their own over time, space, and belief."

Amanda got up and poured herself a cup of coffee. It was bitter to swallow, and she plugged in for a fresh grind. On a quick impulse she popped two pieces of toast into the toaster and walked back to the computer.

"Further, there are certain scribal annotations of textual gender, suggesting the story being told about ....well... a woman. Talking about a family legend that has been given to the author as a sort of legacy...

Most significantly, this document appears to be written - less about gender of ownership, as if by legacy and ownership, but by the hand of a woman as priestess!"

That's hardly a favorite Holy Roman position thought Amanda. What could she say in response? Nor was it the Islamic tradition necessarily. In fact, as far as she knew, and she knew very little, Islamic women whose ownership of possessions was traditional could find it forfeited to the husband upon marriage... With only one exception: If ownership established that the title of ownership was handed down by special dispensation from a *Priestess?*
She paused.
She wrote "So, when in Rome...?" she typed it. Then hit SEND.
Her cell phone purred, it was time to get dressed, clearly.
But the answer came quickly.
"Drink only bottled water. And share with nobody!"

Amanda recoiled from the computer.
What did just say?
Sister Margaret had given her a warning?

Be cautious!

The next morning was no clearer. It took her all day to make up her mind. Should she share the information, should she not? What harm was there, after all? But to whom, exactly?
"Did you get my message?" yelled Jo Anne going up as the elevators closed"
"Err..Yes.." nodded Amanda, not having a clue.

Eight

"Good Morning All... I trust you've had a restful weekend and a happy week!"

Just returned from London, the speaker was wearing his blue and white striped shirt, purple bow tie and salamander trousers. Ambassador Sir Harold Reynolds looked flamboyant.

It was the Ambassador's habit to call a monthly meeting of all Embassy personnel. He found it an effective way to stay in touch, he said.

Ambassadors, like much of the traditional diplomatic corps, were political appointees.

If Sir Reynolds was singular in his approach to diplomacy it was because of his own firebrand of politics. He was an economist.

An American educated economist with notions of commercial enterprise being the solution to political conflict.

Much to the consternation of the Central Office, he was frequently unpredictable.

"There is word of local unrest. Be careful! We've had a few close brushes..."

Amanda thought the room fairly bristled with thoughts pointing at her. *How often does a junior staffer get you into the newspaper within weeks of arriving on post?*

"...also, some upcoming political events that might affect the air, such as the elections in Iraq, and a few local religious holidays, as you well know."

"Tourists are flooding the area over the holidays. And Syrians who continue to pour in Lebanon. Finally, I just want to touch on some public disputes arising over commercial interchange and intellectual proprietary materials. Mainly, propaganda I should imagine. But the newspapers are increasing their interest in the Embassy activities.

So, again. Please stay close and keep travel to a minimum...and be vigilant with our affairs of state. Oh, and I almost forgot: Please welcome the visiting Royal Navy personnel coming in "shortly" And also other commercial Air flight personnel."

Trevor jumped up to add a page to his list. He nodded   only.

"Again. There's a lot of traffic, tourists and events going on this month ...so stay alert at all times... And as always, I can't thank you enough for your diligence, and your personal efforts. It makes our experiences here that much more secure. And our mission a little smoother. Thank you."

It was a good briefing, thought Amanda, if a little distracted and tenuous. She wondered at the item he ignored.

Perhaps a reference to happenings at the AUB. Or *Hostage-taking Central* as the American MPs called it.

Reynolds shook hands with a few people, chatted casually, then his cell phone went off. He snapped shut his cell and marched out the room.

"Hello Amanda!" said Julia Reynolds touching her elbow unexpectedly. "How are you?"

"Very well thank you, Lady Reynolds!"

"Trevor tells us you've been entertaining his sister?"

"Yes, we've all come to enjoy her very much. She has a particular fondness for the fine arts of the souks" Amanda laughed

"Oh what fun!" She had a wide smile in her very slim face of brown eyes and short curly hair. For a woman of her age she looked like she belonged in a magazine.

"I was wondering Amanda if you would be kind enough to assist me in the hosting of a cocktail party at the Residence on the 23rd. I'm entertaining some flight personnel from British Air, their security staff and other representatives of the travel industry. There's to be a fashion show if you can arrange it for me...?"

"Ooo!"

"Yes. Isn't that wonderful?"

"Of course ma'am, I'd be happy to help."

"I'll make sure Trevor doesn't wear you out with work before I get you!"

"Not at all. I'd consider it a treat to be there! Thank you."

"I'll have Susan send you some details, then..."

Lady Julia turned away "lovely girl!" and melted into the Ambassador's entourage. A security detail was already waiting to escort them to an engagement.

* *

Little new correspondence was happening in the incoming traffic, other than a possible visit by a Royal, which required special arrangements. Security, she noticed, was taking up large measures of time for high exposure diplomats.

What she hadn't counted on was Trevor's workload of unattended backlog. He was neglecting it all.

"Non-critical material" he said sheepishly.

"Playing?"

"Me? A Scotsman?"

"When does anything become critical for you Trevor?"

She informed the Security Front Desk of the Embassy that she would be working late, and it took most of the night to deplete his Inbox correspondence with timely answers and polite acknowledgements.

"I've left a few essentials pieces on your desk" she emailed him. Just sign and add a few personal words."

Officially, Trevor was temporarily serving the staff of the Naval Attaché headed by Admiral Adams of the Royal Navy. Little else was known.

But it was beginning to annoy her that much of the Incoming messages were left unattended by other Embassy personnel. These, she addressed with direct responses of an appropriate nature, affixing the title of Trevor's office.

Finally, she switched off the office lights and left.

By Thursday she felt as if she was the only staffer in the building answering mail. She was even rerouting traffic to other legations coming through Beirut.

By Friday, with the Royal visit to the Middle East cancelled, she was cleaning out work spaces; polishing desktops and rearranging furniture like a woman reformed.

"It's not that people are saying anything *about* you, Amanda" Sam told her in the cafeteria, "It's that..."

"I made a bloody fool of myself with a package that made me a suicide bomber!" she said.

"False Alarm" he said with a palliative smile.

"Loose cannon" she said "--without a shred of professional credibility left!"

"But you are very good at administrative paperwork ..."

"So everyone leaves me to it. Is that it?"

"Well..." he began "they do like their golf..."

To hell with it.

She was going to have a wonderful weekend, she decided.

There was a scheduled party that night.

Amanda didn't realize how exhausted she felt until she stepped into her apartment. Telephone messages were endless, she listened, extinguishing each one as noted, or completed.

She would go to the party, she decided, and take a brief rest first.

It was 10 pm at night when she woke up.

She had missed the party.

* *

Amanda stared at the clock, then at the phone messages. There were none!

Ten thirty, and Trevor had not called even to ask about her absence.

Not that she regretted missing the party. But she had planned to say something to Trevor. Could he perhaps understand and investigate the local source of the foreign object placed upon her?

Could Lizzie even have noticed something, if she were asked...?

It was not for her to investigate: Lizzie was her charge, not her cohort.

It was time she revealed all to Trevor.

Why had she hung her hopes on him? Was it appropriate? Or was there something else occurring here?

She stood up and walked to window, undecided.

Did his dismissive ways annoy her? Or was she suspecting something deeper in his offhand remarks?

She needed him because she had to trust him.

This post was an environment highly sensitized to local struggle. There had been after all, a number of abductions and international incidents over the years. Beirut was an Embassy in a hot spot - one of the most dangerous regions of conflict.

She had already overreacted.

She needed help, she decided.

She looked again at the clock. Was it too late to visit? She had waited all week. Today was Friday. And this was important. She hesitated... her appearance?

On impulse, she got dressed, checked out at the Front Security Desk.

"Everything okay Ms. Wells?" asked the security officer, glancing at the time.

"Yes!"

"Would you prefer I sent for a driver ma...am?"

"No thank you Mr. Thomas. That's not necessary. I'm going to Trevor MacDonnell's house. That's all. I won't be long!"

He smiled, assured, looking away.

"But thank you Harry...for asking" she sang and disappearing through the elevator to the garage.

She drove to Trevor's house. No one was home and she waited in her car, one block away from the bougainvillea wall that surrounded his swimming pool.

She must have dozed off because it was 12.30 when headlights aroused her. Clearly, this was Trevor returning and she reached thankfully for her bag to exit the car. But she halted suddenly.

Trevor had moved around his car and was opening the door to the passenger's seat. Amanda sat frozen.

The long bare legs that emerged preceded a woman who took Trevor's hand to step out. She was tall, coiffed loosely, and judging from the diamond glitter, dressed easily for an Embassy function. Italian, perhaps...She lingered. Close to his face, as if having him drink in the scent of her perfume, she moved around the car door, and it was clear she was unsteady.

Neither was Trevor steady. Amanda watched as both weaved towards the front door, laughing, leaning, she, clutching her high heels in her hand, he, spreading his fingers down her bare back...

Somehow Amanda wasn't prepared for this. She switched on the engine and went back to the Embassy garage.

How stupid could she be, she decided.

* *

Azim opened his eyes. Sunlight diffused through the grated openings above him lit upon a decorative carving from Kashmir.
A soft smell of burning rosewood permeated the air. And an occasional tinkle of jeweled sequins told him where he was. The home of Saphira's mother.
"Azim!" she said, holding a brass tray with a pitcher of water and sweet figs "You're awake!"
He could hardly move.
"Your arm..." she put down the tray. "We saved it! But you must stay in cloth bindings for burns on the shoulder." She spoke Egyptian. He nodded.
"Saphira?"
"She'll be home from classes any minute now. We did not want to cast any suspicion on the household, you understand...Now, eat a little..."
He smiled at her.
"Welcome! Welcome! " she hushed him, examining his dressing with some gravity.
 "..It was the boy who came to tell us...before they found you, those murderous sons of dogs! You were floating face down on the other side." She put her waving hand to her mouth.
He groaned with pain.
"No more weeping. You are alive. We heal now. Yes? Truthfully. Nobody knows you're here."
She got up and poured the water in a glass. Then unfolded a muslin doily embroidered with stones

and covered the drink. "They have taken you for dead!" she said. "But live you shall. I swear it ...on your mother's grave!"

She left the room.

It was three days before he could talk clearly, and Saphira spent most of the time tending to his burn dressing while keeping up the appearances of a normal undisturbed household. She went to school daily, and sat there, smiling, giggling and lingering...

Infection was not a life threat, though clearly it was entertained. They bathed him, added emollients, fed him and kept him hydrated. As painful as it was, what hurt more was the inter turmoil that roiled him. He shrieked out at a sense of betrayal in his sleep, they told him. They sedated him.

Sometimes they let him talk.

"They care little for human life anymore.." he said. "They are fundamentalists with nothing to live for other than to express their anger..."

Saphira helped. Her voice assuaged his frustration.

Before long he was up, bathing, strengthening and rehabilitating his arm.

He anticipated her return, and started to look at her playfully.

But he was taking a chance. Every day at her home put his cousin's household in jeopardy.

Finally, he was saying good bye, only because the truth was crystallizing.

"Tell them nothing! They think I'm a good brother...Even if they discover my stay here... You say only that I needed medical help. You knew nothing of what happened or why...Understand? I was found by a boyhood friend. Like good family you cared but discovered nothing! That's all you say."

He threaded his way through the Souk. There was one more stop to make before he left.

The home of the Indian was secure, chiefly because of his known hospitality. And even if there was little in the city that he did not know about, he was a community fixture. Nobody asked any more.

The pipe, coffee and food was a habit he had acquired over the decades of living in Egypt. Even if, at heart, he viewed himself less as Indian for doing so.

"They ...are searching..." he said, his floor cushion set against the wall. "A smart one, that Englishman! They know something went wrong...they have identified three of the group."

"That's what terrifies me..." said Azim "The ship was one assignment. But I was supposed to be a *casualty*."

The Indian leaned over to dip into the food on the tray. "Well, you were certainly not supposed to scuttle their plans!" he said deliberately

Azim winced, arm pain tearing slightly at his strained neck muscles.

"No!" he shook his head. "There's more. I know it."

"Certainly, there's more. A reason perhaps. You were not chosen by accident" He inhaled. "And it helps little that you worried about saving that boy's life, as well! They were testing your loyalty. Better to have let him die."

Azim cursed.

" He was a nobody! But he talked, and he saw everything"
"Do you think they suspect my allegiance?"
"Possibly. When you are rigged to damage a carrier with a boat full of explosives you are not supposed to survive, let alone save yourself and your driver. Then avoid the collision!"
Azim's eyes searched the Indian's carapace face.
"But that's not... Who wants me dead?"
The Indian's face was suited to many masks.
Azim urged. "And you, now what? What will you tell them about me?" he tested.
"That a friend of the Library returned my books before leaving the country...They know I read. Why should I know anything they plotted?"
"So...What do you think?"
"Since when do I say anything?"
"Salim, please. I ask you!"
"I think the one who is your greatest threat is your uncle: He it was who managed the affair for the purpose of causing an incident.
"But ...?"
The man shrugged, knowing dangerously well the meaning of questioning. He popped a date in his mouth, and casually looked around the room.
"Remember, you were chosen by him. Yet it is your family legacy, not his, that has the controlling interests of the commerce in the port!"

"Me and my sister Sophie!"
"Only if she is without a legal guardian!"
"Or if the deed of the inheritance is lost..."
The Indian inclined his head, and removed his glasses. "And this deed...it is in a safe place?

Perhaps with your mother's people? Remember, with you dead...your Uncle has a clear chance at managing her... She is the incumbent of this ancient err...tradition. Bequest?

"It is safe. You know a lot, Salim! "

"Too much, sadly, for an old fool like me. What do I know? I know nothing! Now go back to Beirut, before they see you eating in my house...May we Trust in God. Azim. And do not approach the Englishman! *They* are watching him...As honey"

* *

Trevor pulled his hand away from the silky mass of hair on the pillow besides him and eased himself off the bed to the shower. It was 4.00 am. He left word for Leona his housekeeper to lay out a breakfast for "his houseguest" on the veranda. There, she would doubtless find his Note, and help herself to a swim in the pool before leaving the grounds of his house.

Leona too, was to keep an eye on Lizzie when she returned. He would be back soon.

From his BMW at 5.45 AM he checked his overnight calls, and noticed one message from Amanda. He would have like to dial back, but here was another incoming from Sir Reynolds.

"You're good to go and will be joined by Sergeant Seavant for dinner when you get there. Have a good trip!"

"Yes sir!"

With unsecure lines it was the Ambassadors voice telling him his border crossings was cleared in advance, and his operations to commence immediately.

In Cairo he would be joined by a colleague, probably Special Forces flying in from London.

Trevor MacDonnell had been trained as a cadet at Sandhurst, like his father and grandfather before him. Gunnery history was what he grew up with in Scotland.

New Arms & Tactical Maneuvers was what he had been trained for before joining the Foreign Service. It was partly why he'd been posted to Beirut.

Cairo, however, was altogether another beast. Little else did he know about this destination that had intruded itself with unabashed urgency into his dalliance with the Italian girl for the night.

It was dark when he arrived at the Ambassador's residence. They were briefing dressed variously in pajamas; dressing gowns and dinner jackets. Coffee was on the buffet. Two ministers were present, one the head of Security. This little party was for real.

"The communiqué we received a few hours ago suggests he was at Shepherds...

The terrorist is a young red head, last seen in Beirut, and believed to have relatives here. He is at the center of much attention by fundamentalists and he is of Caucasian extraction as this image shows...

We do know a strike is imminent. Probably in Cairo within the next 24 to 48 hours....

"If all you do is identify him, we'd be happy" said Phillip Beckins the Charge' D'Affairs in evening attire. "But reconnoiter all you can. And if you do make contact and are able to throw his timing somehow, that might have some derailment value..."

"But no harm to yourself..." insisted Sir Reynolds

Trevor checked his watch. It was 4 am. It would be a long drive south down the coastline, his supplies already pre-stowed in a car of special manufacture. Within minutes he would be driving out of communication.

He had not logged in to check his security cameras. He had no idea Amanda had been at his gate earlier that night.

* *

Nine

Cairo, Egypt.

Trevor ordered tea and scones.
He could have been sitting with the literary figure of Amelia Peabody at Shepherds for mid-afternoon refreshment. The scotch, he decided, could come later.
His white jacket and baseball hat blended well with the ladies, waiters, cane chairs and potted plants that overlooked the highway.
Little had changed in two generations. Other than iPods and laptops and Internet access.
He gazed about with the gestures of a grinning tourist.
It was barely noticeable, the rhythm and flow of movement below him. Nothing unusual in the dusty road of traffic and pedestrian motion.
From the intersection of one boulevard another debouched into a stretch of road before him. On the Veranda of Shepherds he had a front row seat of Cairo. From this position, Trevor was nicely ignored. So he waited. And he observed.
Distantly the wailing call to prayers came from a minaret, the day passing calmly.

Then the street saw some activity.

On either side of the street, boys peddled baskets of flowers; fruit, sodas and lemonade for the crowd. Behind were their provisions in a truck.

To the left, two women selected lemons by hand, receiving them in a brown paper bag.

Across the street to the right was a truck of T-shirt paraphernalia, manned, it seemed by an oriental man.

The two women hidden under full burqa dress were talking with the careful grace of limited peripheral visibility within their clothing.

The short woman pressed a wad of money into the hands of the other, for paying the vendor. But so much shorter was she than the other, that she had to tap her companion at the midriff to have the money noticed. Once paid, they wandered off, leaving the vendor to rearrange his fruit into a new stack, the taller to carry the basket on his head.

Shortly, a new supplier appeared with fresh provisions. What amazed Trevor was the strength of the man's neck. On his head was a large basket loaded with kilos of oranges and limes..

Trevor ordered more tea, and watched. Beside him at the rail of the wide veranda was a man of Indian origin, reading.

Politely, he smiled at Trevor. He was elderly.

"Ideal spot for reading" said Trevor

"Indeed it is" he responded with clear English articulation. "It is the Koran!"

"Ah!" nodded Trevor

"Do you read such religious texts?"

Trevor laughed. "I'm afraid that religion has fled the English lexicon"

The Indian smiled "the Bible is well versed in Islam" he added

"Well you have me there...since I'm rather illiterate. But yes, I do believe Abraham's descendants are described in the Bible."

The Indian removed his glasses as a gesture to listen politely.

 Trevor continued "Unfortunately, I'm unqualified to presume much understanding on these matters. But if I were, I would say there have been too many misunderstandings of religious history already ..."

"A very wise man, I see" said the Indian. He replaced his reading glasses.

The flutter in the crowd began with two boys running up to a gathering of men. Two stood at the tourist van parked in an area for visitors shaded by landscaped shrubs and palm trees. One man leaned down to speak to the other.

Trevor recognized them both from the gestures of the shortest. He looked back at the fruit vendor where they had previously stood together. These were not women, he realized.

The tall one, his working clothes changed, turned now to the driver of the tourist van. He was gesticulating wildly and speaking savagely, evidently believing himself sheltered by the shaded privacy of perimeter bushes.

They separated. One hailed a black taxi, the other crossing the street.

Trevor pressed the dial button on his cell, taking images as he did so. Within two seconds a message returned.

"Confirmed"

Trevor got up, his task done, and went inside for dinner.

By dawn he'd be on a flight back to Beirut with a full dossier on his laptop. His car, he knew, had been checked into the Embassy compound in Cairo. It would be driven north for him after an appropriate lapse of time.

* *

The Indian walked into the café.

There he would consort with men. They joined him, one, a tall man and three others. Tea and sweet dates were procured by the waiter, and they talked.

They discussed the means of transport; the means of sale and the kind of banking required for a commodity soon to arrive.

Finally, it was time to discuss the port. The disaster that failed to occur on Egyptian soil had caused little disturbance, it was noted. The port was undamaged, they said. That was of concern to many in the hierarchy of these operations. The port that was of concern to them was another. Further up the coast, and fraught with political overtones. Too dangerous even to discuss in the open café.

They drank tea, tossed money to the kids sitting by, laughed happily, nodding to the passers by. Then resumed in earnest.

Another port was to be identified as a possible target, however. *That* would come soon enough. A decision would be given from the superiors and down through the cells.

The Indian nodded.

Truth be told, he disliked these Islamists. He was Indian. Of Hindu tradition. For that they all hated him. But they tolerated him. He had his purposes here. As long as he caused no trouble, the Arabs said, they included him!

Fine. That suited him. He had bigger fish to fry.

He hated the idea of *cells*. That meant that what made for good commerce had now become a *cause celebre* for those, frankly, who had been left out of the wealth circuit. A circuit now nicely capitalized by Asians investing in the continent of Africa, and Russians seeking to enhance their commercial visibility: Jihadism was a lazy excuse to steal business away from his own business, he decided.

His eyes were brown, his skin olive, and they smiled easily for those at the table around him, his head nodding in acquiescence. But a thought flickered across his mind, and he looked down, afraid that such a haunting prospect might be visible.

Something more than your garden variety of Arms was coming across the transom. Something far more insidious and dangerous. The question was, *what?*

He looked up.

As far as he was concerned, he could care little who did what with which commodity. Money was money. Trade was trade. As it had been for years in these parts. But he was Ghandi-like, right?...And a reader of books.

Meantime, the cargo had to be delivered. There was no getting around this. So, he would sit here and press the flesh, if necessary. There were *other* reasons, even more important that prevailed on them for the moment, they said.

 The route of delivery was to reach its final destination only when it was received by the right hands. And the port, as Allah and his divine wisdom had intended, would be the one to be damaged. But first, it must serve its purpose.

A simple nod indicated which port it was, although a second was quickly assessed by each of them. A nod that hinted at being geographically further north along the Mediterranean sea, up from Egypt. A port was a port. As it had been for centuries before. Phoenician ports, or now commercial Lebanese ports; Israeli ports. All of them good for business, and even better as investments.

The cargo, they said, had to be picked up then delivered by truck the longer way around the Holy Land to reach its destination.

What did that mean?

Casually, they sat there, their legs protruding from their long robes and jackets. Some wore trousers. Some a hat. They had jokes to share. They talked, casually, until they heard the call of the faithful from the mosque.

As was the routine, they went to the shelf and took down a rolled sajada, which they unrolled, and each of them facing Qibla on a brick patio, stood erect.

Humbled before Allah, a peace settled upon them, as upon the faithful of all who contemplated God. Through the sallat prayers, they whispered the

Iqama. Finally, as the angels would note their good behavior, they ended with the salawat.
They parted company: The Englishman shall be watched, they agreed.

* *

The Indian was pleased. He tapped the pocket where his notepad lay, and continued to peddle his bicycle.
Yes, the order pleased the Indian. Twelve crates of AK-47s. Five cases of grenades. Twenty four boxes of M84 flash-bangs, to note that they should be sheathed in plastic and able to deliver a sunburst and noise that could announce the arrival of Allah himself. Two crates of PVS-17 night vision goggles, and ten SAW Squad Automatic Weapons.
Everyone knew that no M4 carbines were available. The Americans made sure of that, for now. Perhaps one day soon. Perhaps.
Not bad, in all. Not large. But the hint of a larger prize left him eager. Something big. Something new technologically. And something that flies. Not only flies, but flies in high altitudes.
That told him that the end user was neither Iran nor even Pakistan. But Afghanistan.
Now we are talking, he thought. New parties meant new wars. And new wars meant new markets. Yes, thought the Indian. Now we are talking!
He wrote it all down in a small spiral notepad, the order. The entire order, in pencil, written in light lead, and the pencil short, green, with no eraser.

No 2 yellow pencil made of sweet scented cedar from Lebanon and manufactured in Israel that could be noticed two blocks away.

Yes. Now we are talking, he thought, patting the notepad into his shirt pocket.

It was hot. He took out a handkerchief and wiped clean his eye glasses, dark, round and a little unclean around the rims.

He would go back to his books. The Library. He hobbled across the street, between the taxis which roused up dirt in the Egyptian capital city. He would cross over to the Library where the innocent and the learned could learn, a hundred eyes watching him carefully.

He was a little man, in the general order of things. A man who read books and stayed amongst the hedges of humanity. The stupidest things could amuse him. Like giants who ignored gnats. Or Islamic Fundamentalists who evolved from rag heads to terror.

But more than anything, he knew this. Whereas the Americans and her Allies liked to cut off the head of a snake, these people concentrated their effectiveness through other mechanisms, multiple approaches, using perhaps lesser functioning parts of the body, to achieve their goal. And most dangerous of all, they were getting focused on one goal. A goal he happened to disagree with himself, but had learned not to concern himself with. Exploitation, after all, was nothing new. Hell, Wall Street had even engineered a franchise out of exploitation!

The ship that left the Baltimore dock was a decommissioned Hospital Ship that had served during the Vietnam War and cycled many onboard for treatment; convalescence and retreat operations. On two occasions it has served as a strategic conference center for Generals and Flight Commands.

The Vietnam War had not gone well for Americans. Yet here it sat with its large Red Cross Insignia across its bow, USS Sanctuary. It had international passage as a rescue and medical ship.

Nestled within her bow thrusters and down along the keel below the engine rooms were her ballast weights of heavy lead ingots, each weighing close to 70 lbs.

Amongst them two bombs were lodged to work off an electronic timer. Each Bomb was almost nine pounds – four kilograms of PETN and RDX plastic explosive, Semtex.

There would three legs to this journey. From the United States to Greece where it would put on cargo, then to another port to be arranged at a later leg of the journey.

* *

The local debriefing at the Embassy went smoothly enough for Trevor, and his flight into Lod Airport safely uneventful. A briefing in Jerusalem was required of him before returning to post. Intelligence, useful to the Israeli government.

He was driven by a courier in a dark Lincoln, he opened the rear window slightly, even as it quickly compromised the air-controlled ambient comfort of the rear cab. He couldn't help it. This was unmistakably a world by itself, perched on a progressive economy, yet harking to an age of the ancient, the sacred, the Holy.

He was drawn hazily along the highways, passing the well fertilized fields of orange groves irrigated by acres of overarching spray systems, all of it inducing a soft water hissing and blossom scent that swirled in middle eastern air.

* *

The civil war made headlines in today's Arab newspapers. Syrian uprisings, an ongoing armed battled between the Ba'ath Party of government and those seeking to replace it, was the central issue, clearly a matter with far more sweeping consequences for the Arab world, now swelling with refugees and dissidents in their streets. It was news.

 Everywhere in the Middle East, from café houses to institutional offices, hope for the Arab Spring budded in sprigs and branches upon the hearts of all thinking Arabs. Youth and aspiring communities had hoped to the join the new millennium with vibrant economies; working governments and happy homes. Most said that religion - if only the West would realize - had very little to do with anything! But like the middle Ages, the language of religion was closely entwined with the language of society: It implied ethics; professional conduct; hierarchical allegiances if not political absolutism. None could fully embrace it in one swoop, and none could fully stop it as it drew people inexorably into its vortex.

It was, as the Indian thought, always the same: A matter of socio-economic prosperity which, because of poor leadership, had bypassed the Arabs by the turn of the millennium, and advanced to pick up all other nations of the world. Even allowing for pockets of development deficiencies, this he knew only too well.

The West of course, understood this. And Israel, always. But globalism had advanced many nations, swooping up commerce to shape changing democracies and emerging economies. If not by Persian Oil, then by China's technological rise. Now for Russia, Turkey, India, even those war zones occupied by the Americans – where democracy, if tenuous, had arrived, some economic prosperity had entered the mainstream. Industries had roared forward, like software; hardware; transport, global shipping, commodities, resources, finance, and education. Damaging to the old perhaps, but moving at light speeds with programmatic efficiencies and fast-paced trading.

This outpaced local populations, like the elderly, the dislocated, the undercapitalized, the debt-encumbered – all of them outside the franchising network; all of them victims to clever business paradigms produced in Business schools like Harvard.

The Indian read the news, knowing that even centralization had its downsides. The Chinese discovered the groundswell power of networking. The Arab revolution was captured on Face book.

The Indian turned the newspaper page, and took a big breath, knowing that at the end day, for all the centralized efficiencies, it came to one net result. No jobs.

The Syrian civil war was one nation in a global wave of change. Sure, the West did what it could to lodge its vote of protest against the Syrian Army deployment of troops against civilians. As did the Arab League. Even s China and Russia objected on the grounds of commercial advantages given to the West - advantages that might damage their own commercial ties with Syria!

Humanitarianism, they said, was inherently political. Observers had been sent in with proposals for a peaceful resolution. The International Committee of the Red Cross had declared the Syrian conflict as being a civil war, therefore applying international humanitarian law under the Geneva Conventions to Syria. Still, it was a deadly game with thousands still involved, and a living hell.

Still, the Arabs were no fools, this the Indian knew. Given half a chance, they would re-organize, re-tool, and re-energize themselves as a vibrant people. Many of them were locals from a European colonial era of migration! All that had bound them could be reshaped to serve them in intelligent and sensible ways, surely. Including religion, which they would find a way to pocket in dignified ways... Only a matter of time, he concluded.

Except that Syria had its own dangers. And these were in *his* lifetime: Arms dealing, trading and transport. *Where would it end?*

The train station was filling up with travelers.

Egypt was a center for offices, headquarters, servicing and processing industries. Those more educated from neighboring nations came to work, then returned home with their paychecks. Some travelled south, mostly international traders and brokers where they had affluence and villas. Others to major cities on the continent of Africa. One party of three, disembarking a taxi, were clearly locals - she, a woman with a baby and her brothers, the facial features all alike. The baby too, if it ever stopped wailing! They were paying the taxi, and the woman and her baby were escorted to the ticketing booths. She got a big hug from both brothers, the baby mollified, and they dispersed.

He saw the man from a distance, just a head in a cloth wrapped head covering, really. An Islamist, like everyone else. Well, that is, his stature blended, only his deportment gave him away. And besides, he was wearing Brooks Brother's shoes as the saying went in spy circles.

He was an Israeli. Plus the source of information about the Indian's next target, shipment and destination of arms deals. Not that he was very tall, just a gate, if you will, something that emanates from being an ill-local, if there was such a word, out of place psychologically. Still, nobody was really watching. And he was alone. Or so the Indian thought.

He had his instructions. He was to buy his ticket to Alexandria at the Ticket Window number 6, and then sit at the East end of the station. He was to wait until he saw a bouquet of flowers appearing for a welcoming party at the Arrivals gate, just beyond the ticket window turnstiles.

Anyway, he was early. He stood in line to get his ticket, peering down at his newspaper.

He read his English crossword puzzle. The station was teeming with people, noise, whistles, fans, music and traffic. He shuffled forward. He listened, his eyes down. There must have been half a dozen different languages he recognized. None that sounded unusual to him. He was not looking up when the commotion occurred at Ticket-Window 8. (Ticket- Window 7 was shuttered). An argument, doubtless.

Someone had fallen and needed attention. Two guards were hailed over. Mobs had a tendency to trample the fallen, and the guards held off a few onlookers, then the crowd dissipated as the police waved them off.

The Indian was surprised. It wasn't an old woman who collapsed, or an angry ticket buyer. A senior police officer came striding over. The first guard moved sideways and opened her burka to reveal her face to his superior, and that's when the Indian saw it. The mark on her forehead, that of a small close- quartered entry wound from a 9 millimeter hand gun. It had popped in her face at close range and dropped her like a rag doll. The woman with the baby! Neither did her two brothers appear, nor was the baby anywhere in sight: No paraphernalia related to infants was near the body.

His ticket queue advanced. To the left of his line, not far from the ticket window was a large trash bin. Inside was a bouquet of flowers, upside down, evidently trashed?

As was his intended meeting.

He moved away, certain that the incident was an interdiction made by agents whose interests were threatened by the woman. This, even the police knew as they showed little sign of alarm, preferring instead not to incite a crowd in volatile public areas.

Two nurses appeared with a stretcher. Heat exhaustion, they said.

Who was she? What was she doing there, arriving with two men and a baby, like the movie...then dead with a bullet and *no* infant? Clearly, she was there to execute a plan, or a person. Obviously, she had had the means beneath all that covering to do so, observed the Indian.

 The Israeli contact had spotted her and shut off. As an Indian, he hated the loss of life. At any rate, that meant only one thing: The Arms deal *was* of major significance to someone.

He moved on, eyes to the door, commotion behind him. Outside the station he hailed a taxi.

He would wait for word. He crossed the street, demonstrating impatient protest at the ineptitudes and buggers of life, like any good local would do, swatting a fly from his face.

He walked off. For now, he would not show that he could afford to pay for any taxi.

The raid then, was cancelled.
Intelligence.

Ten

At the AUB Clubhouse, Amanda saw Lizzie outdoors by the pool. She was sitting under a green canvas umbrella with Paula Wickes, both of them in watersport chatter as children splashed and tossed balls around them.

"Over here!" she waved, her tanned body in a bright colored life vest, if over a thong bikini; a whistle on a necklace, and her nose a white ski jump heavily caked with emollients - their plan for emulation by the children around them: *Water safety. Whistles. Sun protection!* Amanda got it, and laughed.

Lizzie, who delighted most people, had fallen easily into Paula's entourage of Embassy wives. When Amanda joined them, Paula gave her a big hug.

"Pull up a chair" she said, pouring three large lemonades. She added a paper plate of chips, pickle and a hotdog on a bun hot off the barbeque grill plate. "Ketchup...mustard?"

"I'm famished!" nodded Amanda.

Lizzie munched down her hotdog, stuffed her mouth with potato chips and made for the pool with a splash bomb with the kids.

"She's having a blast!" said Paula, stretching out.

"She's right at home. Thanks for your kind entertainment!"
Paula's feckless dedication to righting the wrongs of the world seemed a natural fit for herself and her husband Steve.
That they should find themselves in Beirut, she said – she, working at the American Embassy and he, on the Faculty of American University of Beirut - seemed ideally suited to their sense of societal contribution.
As an anthropologist Steve had worked for the World Bank in Washington DC. His specialty was economic organizations, and his mission was to find areas of cultural common ground to build global trade bridges – even while teaching.
Paula on the other hand, who could not balance her own check book, was happy to offer their careers for the betterment of humanity. Even it if placed them both in harm's way.
And harm's way it was. Steve Wickes' predecessor walked into a street gun battle on his way the home one night.

People like the Wickes were rare. It was the common perception about most personnel in diplomatic missions that somehow, in doing duty overseas, they were sacrificing the fundamentals at home and not taking care of business.
Nor were neighbors, when they returned home, interested in seeing pictures of exotic postings overseas, let alone considering the disadvantages of serving overseas. For Paula and Sam, it was considered a privilege to serve their government.

"Oh, I almost forgot. I have something for you Amanda. Sam asked me to give it to Lizzie for you. He wants you to read his notes on something you asked about. Here!"

She pulled out a folder of notes, papers, and citations, something only a college professor might value over all else.

Amanda wanted to sit and read immediately, and she looked apologetically at Paula who understood.

"Please go ahead!"

Amanda looked up.

"Any chance of going back to the French quarter tomorrow to see how my dresses are coming along?" asked Lizzie standing over her dripping wet.

"What?" It took a few seconds to register Lizzie's request.

"Oh, that's right. Of course."

Since Amanda had failed to produce the finished garments on her own sewing machine as promised, getting them fitted and made locally was the least she could do. Especially since Lizzie wanted to wear one that night.

"You're on!" said Amanda, folding away the notes and thanking Paula profusely.

"Ladies..." said Paula "Don't forget our Seminar tonight in the Auditorium. The second of our series about ancient women. It's supposed to be a light show. Steve is over there now setting it up. He'll want us there, I'm sure. And a party for the speaker, after the event...yes?"

"You're on!" said Lizzie and Amanda, together.

    * *

The open air auditorium was full to capacity, and Steve Wickes introduced the Speaker with as much respect as he had for her first Orientation presentation offered on the campus of the AUB for the staff and families of the diplomatic colony in Beirut.

The Son et Lumiere show would not disappoint.

Above them the stars of Lebanon spoke to the audience rapt in the magic.

The houselights went down, and the soft sounds of an ancient land trickled...

"In 1926, Henry Chevrier made a remarkable discovery" began the Professor. "He found this in the sands of Egypt..."

The audience gasped as the colors of stone and sand colors emerged upon a large theater screen. It reflected an eerie display from the past.

"It weighed 120 tons - a pure-cut, precision engineered monument, an ornate red granite obelisks to celebrate the thirtieth year of the Pharoah, inscribed with some of the most refined reliefs ever seen on the life of Senusret I at Karnak...And it was intact after four millennium."

"...In a world where men received holy messages in their dreams about fruit of the land, or the womb, God was smiling upon a people when a girl called Neferet gave birth to Amenemhat I."

The sounds of an prehistoric lute cast soft blues and deep hues upon the stone.

"The story of this Pharoah bears telling. For it has been described in many ways and for many cultures. It has even found its way into the greater storytelling of the Bible."

The dark strong features of a profile materialized, those of a virile young man found in texts and records of the ancient world.

"The birth of Amenemhat was significant. Mentuhotep IV, his father, had wives; women and concubines. Plus two notable daughters in the kingdom. Yet, even as he was celebrated as the greatest of the Old Kingdom Pharaohs of Egypt, he had no son. Thus, when Amenemhat was delivered to him as his only bloodline, the infant was considered the godsend of titular descendants; waterfall to a drought-prone people; hope to a dying dynasty. His sisters did not count, because only now was the kingdom and it regency rulers to be protected, even if his mother was not a royal-born herself."

"In ancient Egypt, immediately, we know that in this royal household, they worshiped the single god *Re*, and the infant was given the Prenomen as the one *Who satisfies the heart of Re* as ruler.

"...And Wehemmesut, it was recorded, was his Horus name; Amenemhat his Pharoahic title. Even if he had to overthrow the kingdom of his father to become the legitimate Golden Horus in 1991 BC: His rule would start the great period of the Twelfth Dynasty of the Egyptian Pharaohs...

"...At puberty, he was given Neferitatjenen as consort. She was beautiful.

"He produced Sunusret I; Neferu III who would rule for the ancient record and siblings Neferusherit, Kayet all in the royal lineage of succession.

"Age 10, Sunusret ruled as co-Regency with his father in Amenemhat's 20th regnal year - assurance of royal lineage and continued inerrant.

"The Sebayt ethical teachings disseminated by Egyptian monarchs could now allude to Old Kingdom conventions, whose cultural icons and models were emulated by the new Twelfth Dynasty stabilized a centralized government in Egypt.

"Treasurers were Ipi, and Intefiger to oversee the royal expenses and developments of reign. Stewards called Meketre and Sobeknakht to establish the popular perpetuity.

Both leave accounts of merchant exchanges.

Senusret I led a campaign in Libya, chronicled in the famous Story of Sinuhe when an account came out, in story-telling tradition told from the dead, about his father's assassination"

Another voice of distant places spoke of the dream:

"It was after supper, when night had fallen, and I had spent an hour of happiness (with a woman). I was asleep upon my bed, having become weary, and my heart had begun to follow sleep. When weapons of my counsel were wielded, I had become like a snake of the necropolis...

"As I came to, I awoke to fighting, and found that it was an attack of the bodyguard. If I had quickly taken weapons in my hand, I would have made the wretches retreat with a charge! But there is none mighty in the night, none who can fight alone; no success will come without a helper. Look, my injury happened while I was without you, when the

entourage had not yet heard that I would hand over to you (my legacy) when I had not yet sat with you, that I might make counsels for you; for I did not plan it, I did not foresee it, and my heart had not taken thought of the negligence of servants..."

The narrator picked up the account to explain that the assignation had occurred in his thirtieth year, dawn, *"whilst the Residence was hushed, now hearts ...in mourning, the Great Gates ...closed, the courtiers crouched, head on lap, and the nobles grieved"*

The account went on to explain *"Now His Majesty had sent an army to the land of the Tjemeh (Libyans), his eldest son as the captain thereof, the goodly god Senusret. He had been sent to smite the foreign countries, and to take prisoner the dwellers in the Tjehnu-land, and now indeed he was returning ..carried off all living prisoners of the Tjehnu and all kinds of cattle limitless.*

It happened as *"the Companions of the Palace went to the western side to acquaint the king's son concerning the position that had arisen in the Royal Apartments, and the messengers found him upon the road, they (had) reached him at time of night"*

Then,

"Not a moment did (the son) linger, the falcon flew off with (him and) his followers, not letting his army know."

Even as *"the king's children who accompanied him in this army had been sent for as the one of them had been summoned."*

"The narrative, a poem that enjoins his son to trust no-one, delivers an apologia of the deeds of the old king's reign, and ends with an exhortation to Senusret to ascend the throne and rule wisely in Amenemhat's stead. Note: This implies a source of new wealth for the dynasty that would have domestic consequences. "

Maps of the ancient world filled the screen.

"This, he would do" continued the speaker "as the records would later show. But of one incident that might have begun on the reign of his father, even God was to notice, according to the historical records of the time..."

The houselights came up for a short recess.

Both Amanda and Lizzie left their seats to stretch their legs. Many did not leave the auditorium, choosing rather to remain in their seats, their attention fixed on the stone wall behind the speaker, now a silver waterfall representing the passage of time.

Others strolled about - the ladies in summer evening shawls slack about their shoulders; and everywhere the scent of the sea permeated the night air, bewitching, beckoning to Mediterranean legend.

"I sure wish Trevor were here to see this with me..." said Lizzie

Amanda looked at her, and gently smiled.

The Intermission ended with a small gong. The house lights dimmed, like magic. The speaker's voice had command.

"We are about to witness a turn in the history of civilization in the ancient world...Once marked by barbarian rites, tribal survival, conquest for food and culture undefined, we now find something recognizable occurring."

A gong.

"...As the second pharaoh of the Twelfth Dynasty of Egypt Senusret Ist would continue the building program begun under his father, he become one of the most powerful kings of the Dynasty: He would marry his wife and distant sister Neferu in a priestess/wife narrative. Together, they produced the next successor to the throne of Egypt Amenemhat II, or Kheperkare, meaning, *the Ka of Re is created*.

"The reign of that Pharoah was marked by more than monuments and architectural structure, if unparalleled in the ancient world...

"It should be considered a new *Reform*, with a new economy and new commerce of trade; exchange and documentation.   Upon   his   father's instructions he proceeded aggressively with expansionist policies against Nubia with two strategic expeditions of conquest, (ten and eight years later,) each expanding Egypt's territorial southern border near the second cataract of the Nile, where he placed a garrison. A reverential victory stele of writings there was erected to records the conquests and boundary. From these we get our records of what happened...

"He managed resources, and stockpiled wealth for his kingdom in an organized fashion. He cultivated amethyst mines, and gold, silver, cedar wood for furnishings; he encouraged a silk trade route for trade fashion and food spices. Further, he established diplomacy with rulers of towns in

Syria and Canaan - places where it was said that some of the most prizes beauties, princesses and priestesses dwelled.

"He cultivated communities, artisans, skilled workers, builders and transport-carriers to enlarge the Egyptian kingdom. It remained the hallmark of Amenhentep.

"To those loyal to him and his building program, he rewarded as smaller monarchs; proprietary princes who, by royal Pharoahic title, were an extension to his kingdom.

"One such Prince was called Abimblebec, a shipright."

"Their goal was fantastic. They continued the quarrying expeditions of the fathers into the Sinai and Wadi Hammamat. They built shrines and temples thoughout Egypt, Nubia, the Sinai and coastal lands.

They built the temple of Re-Atum in Heliopolis, and Alexandria; completed the temples of Min at Kptos, the Satet. Temples on Elephantine, Armant and El-Tod whereupon were writ the longest inscription of his life and that of his father were inscribed.

Finally, Senusret remodeled the Temple of Khenti-Amentiu Osiris at Karnak, something his father erected and named the White Chapel of Senusret I.

"Today, what we see is the work of his chief architect Sobktotep, who had worked for his father and grandfather before him. Here is building of the large tomb of the Amun Temple pyramid at Karnak..."

The party that followed the talk was attended by almost everyone in the Auditorium. It had been a stunning success.

* *

The French Quarter Boutique of prints and dressmakers was buzzing. But not to the extent that Amanda and Lizzie were left unattended.
"A fashion show.." the salesperson said. "A wedding fitting for a celebrated event in a month!" she said.
Lizzie was given her dress which she was to try on. Only when they reached the Inner chambers of runways and fitting rooms did Amanda recognize the woman for whom the show was being performed.
"Professor!" she exclaimed, extending her hand.
The Lebanese woman instantly recognized her and jumped up. "Of course! How nice to see you!"
"We so enjoyed your talk at the AUB" said Amanda.
"It was me who enjoyed it!" she laughed.
The girl was a bride standing in a muddle of white gauze cascade of satin; sequins and pink rosebuds beneath a heart shaped bodice. She looked like she had been in a battle with the gauze, the hair bobbins or the rosebuds, all. And she had been weeping, her eye makeup blotched down her face.

"My niece, Sophia" declared the professor, hardly noticing.

"She is getting married in a month to Saoud Malmook of the Beirut business community!"

The name was lost on Amanda. But Lizzie was openmouthed. "Hey" she said to the girl. Instant recognition dawned on them both, and they both retreated to the fitting rooms under clouds of white rustling and Lizzie's pink paisley cocktail dress.

"You must be very excited about this moment" said Amanda in polite conversation.

"We are indeed. There is so much to do. A trousseau for one thing. Papers. Affairs. Transactions. You know..."

"Our weddings are today less covenants than carnivals, I'm afraid" laughed Amanda.

The woman looked down.

"My sister, the girl's mother...died, I mean... was buried a Christian. And the *one* concession we got was that the wedding be sanctified in a Church!"

"How lovely!"

The woman looked up, her eyes glazed with pain, as if to say *–For which she will pay dearly once married...*

Amanda could have been imagining.

A burst of laughter from the fitting room brought out both girls in a flustering wave of fun. Sophia was wearing Lizzie's pink paisley, Lizzie the gown. They fitted neither.

The woman lifted both hands to her face. They all froze. It was too comical. They all laughed like Merry men.

"You knew her?" said Amanda, outside.
"Sure. She was one of the girls from the souk. We're friends!"

* *

Amanda got a call from the front desk. It was the weekend, after all.
The package had already passed the prescribed security scanning device.
"The Convent at the Lycee Francais called to inform us that they were delivering a parcel for you, Ms Amanda. A book" said the Security officer as he handed it to her with a big smile.
"Thanks! Can't a woman have any secrets any more?" she said. "Please tell Mr. Thomas that I'm expecting company at 7 pm. Mr. Jacques de Torraine, He is tall, dark ..."
"and handsome?"
"And French!" she laughed.
"Right you are, Miss Amanda. I'll tell our chief of security and give you a ring."
"We shall be going out!"
"Yes Ma'am"
Taking the package upstairs, she knew that Sister Margaret would be returning her relic. She tore open the outer box container, and found it inside, wrapped in a further layer soft tissue paper and pretty white ribbon, its clear, square outline beautifully contained as if it were newly store bought! She looked at it, and smiled. At the top corned was tied red velvet ribbon of the Convent itself, embossed in gold and red "Croce" of the Holy Roman Catholic Order.

The note from Sister Margaret was written with exquisite calligraphy.

"I have found more resources which will be sent to you by mail. Please send an example of the text to the University of America. They are experts in medieval manuscripts and the conservators of the Arts Gallery are most kind about these things. They are informed. And would like to share..."

Sister Margaret had made a palatable item out of the scary relic. Time had passed, and Amanda was now fully recovered from the early shock and distress in had provoked. It was now a work of historical integrity. Period.
She should be able to cope, fine. Even if placed as it was, on the sideboard, unwrapped for now.

* *

Eleven

The newly commissioned *USS California* was a Guided Missile Cruiser surface combatant.

Below the purring decks and topside configuration lay an arsenal of nuclear capabilities. As a ship of the line she was rarely visible, always in a state of Preparedness and supported in Washington by a phalanx of technical contractors and support staff.

On this occasion she made herself highly visible and was engaging in what Roosevelt termed *"Big-stick diplomacy."* With a potential reach several thousand miles in range, her presence in Beirut was an event.

She was docked at harbor, and counting...

In the purple dusk of the port, she lay at anchor peacefully, the picture of calm assurance and seafaring romance, her profile outlined with lights from stem to stern. At her aft section flagstaff, fluttering softly, was the proud American ensign.

Her crew, Amanda knew, would be a highly trained and disciplined contingent. They would move with respectful diligence in every direction. Tonight, their ship was hosting a party on board. In Beirut, the guest list of invitees was everywhere touted.

Only Amanda knew that the two other Naval Frigates – whose mission it was to protect the *USS California* – stood silently off shore.

* *

 Jacques de Torraine was to pick Amanda up. They would be admitted at the Security Gate on the docks before climbing the ramp lined with ship's sailors in full white dress uniform.
Dinner and Dancing, the invitation said.
Amanda was excited.

White tables and a ballroom floor would be set up on the Aft helo-deck with dignified décor, she imagined, such that they would dance under a full panoply of stars to the tunes of a naval musical ensemble.
They would be introduced to several representatives from other missions...
There was something about ships that made the world go round, she thought. And while she knew enough about Naval Affairs not to get cozy about their technology and intent, she wondered about Christopher Columbus and his first voyage to the New World. What an exciting time of history that would have been!
By the time Amanda looked at herself in the mirror she was coiffed, dressed and ready to go. She approved of what she saw, having transformed herself into someone even Trevor would find surprising.
Her hair, softly pulled back from her forehead gathered to fall only down her bare back. A

lavender evening gown flowed freely to the ground, thin silk straps at her shoulders.

But why should she care what Trevor noticed?

She walked to the dresser and picked up a brush. Would *Jacques* approve she wondered? Perhaps she should wear a white shawl over her shoulders? Jacques - how did he style his mission here...on the staff of the French Cultural Attaché? A house guest... "Pour le moment" but only to review the position he was about the resume in Paris.

Whatever. Another day.

Amanda decided to take him at face value. She glanced at the time and saw that she was fifteen minutes ahead of schedule.

 The phone nearly shot her from her seat. It was the front desk asking for permission to admit her guest...Should he wait in the lobby?

"Send him up, thanks!"

The doorbell rang.

At 6ft 4" Jacques was not only filled the door frame standing in full white-tie formalwear, but with a cape; cane and top hat from which protruded a few poetic curls and an arch smile.

"Mademoiselle?" he said, suddenly producing two dozen white roses "pour vous!"

"Wow" said Amanda, her face caught in transfixed surprise.

"*Ravissant!*" he said, surveying her appearance. Lifting the hem off dainty silver sandals, she turned with a big swirl.

She took the flowers, now wondering whether she owned a decent vase.

He entered, and she offered a small silver tray of pre-event cocktail bites and a glass of Champaign from the sideboard decanter.

They bantered.

"Is the lady ready leave?" he said finally.

"The lady is!" she smiled "I'll put these up and fetch my shawl."

She returned to find him surveying the surroundings of her apartment – standard issue furnishing by the British Ministry of Works, she explained.   Then suddenly her own touches of bright cushions - some glistening with tiny mirrors and desert braids, and her medieval tapestry made her feel like a refugee gypsy. Or was it the haughty demeanor of Jacques?

His eyes had settled, she noticed, on the white package on the side-board, still unopened from Sister Margaret with its velvet ribbon unmistakably visible.

"I see you are the repository for the ancient manuscript of *questionable origin!*" he grinned, teasing.

"I'm the one who feels like the questionable origin, frankly. I wish it hadn't thrust itself upon me..." began Amanda.

He watched her carefully. "I heard!"

She turned away, wishing instead that what happened on that day rested still between her and Trevor. Perhaps that was expecting too much. Lizzie, perhaps, might have said something without intending any harm. She was there, after all. And it did leave its impression on her first few days of her visit. Talk about it was inevitable.

"You know" he said, lowering his glass in a grand gesture "There are some very wonderful old legacies that still surface as surprises!"

"Oh?"

"Take, for example, the recent find of a Roman shipwreck in the Red Sea, with cargo of gold bullion in transit to India. Something described in the *Periplus of the Erythraean Sea*: A Roman merchant's guide to the Red and Indian Ocean, written in Greek in Egypt."

"Wow!"

"Yes, it is considered on the most remarkable ancient texts on seafaring and maritime exploration in trade to survive!"

He got up, and moved to the sideboard for another hors d'euvres, just a few feet away from the package and pouch, still there in its red Croche ribbon from the Convent.

He lingered, perhaps he would have liked to be invited to inspect it. Amanda did not invite him to do so, and he returned to the settee.

"You have heard of the Heidelberg Codex?"

She looked at him.

"*Codex Palatines Graecus 398* is a compilation of copies - ancient texts on geography and exploration created in the tenth century made in a monastery of the Byzantine East. It was, how shall we put it, the latest technology of the time?"

He paused, for effect, adding "He who sailed on the trades from sea to sea with navigational success could bring much wealth and power to the feet of his king!"

Amanda commended his knowledge and interest.

Yet somehow she felt frustrated. Here was a man fully savoring the endless possibilities of her acquisition, while Trevor could not be found to show interest if she wrote a report on it!

Her eyes dropped. Jacques drained his cocktail, and leapt to his feet.

"Shall we go?" he prompted, offering his arm gallantly.

"But of course!" she said politely.

Jacques, it was clear, intended to spare no cost for transportation to the ship. His was a dark, chauffeur-driven Mercedes, the door held open at the entrance of the Embassy. The sun had just set, and dusk, its afterglow, refused to cede to the night sky. A sea breeze swept over them as they stepped in the car, and it was for an evening full of promise.

Only as they accelerated down the long stretch did Amanda stop her conversation and look forward, wondering what it was that caused some swerving.

The driver, it seemed, was uncomfortable and trying to hold his shoulders up to mask his disquiet. He kept peering into his rearview mirror. The answer came soon enough as a headlight swept the inner cab so brightly that the driver accelerated. Twice he responded to the vehicle behind him until their speed was noticeably alarming.

"Estc'qui'l y as de problem?" asked Jacques leaning forward.

"Pardon Monsieur...c'est l'auto derriere nous...Je ne sais pas leurs intentions..Mais je pense qui'lles...

Amanda looked back to see the SUV recoil, then rev-up for full impact.

"Jacques!" she screamed

The burst that came upon them shattered the windows. It filled the black Mercedes with white bags; lifted the car up to scrape along the side of the boulevard, then flipping over the concrete bulkhead where it propelled forward on its roof, still spinning towards oncoming traffic.

By the time they were released from the Emergency Room at the AUB hospital, it was clear they had been the object of a hostile attack.

She had received phone calls from the Chief of Security and the Ambassador, and she assured them both that she had escaped unharmed.

She was to be escorted by an MP from the hospital back to the Embassy.

"You're good as new!" announced Dr. Yani, the physician in the Emergency room

"Thank you!"

"Other than a shock, and few bruises, I recommend a common aspirin for a day or two. Then you'll be fine." he said

She smiled. She looked at his Assistant.

"Oh, I'm sorry. May I introduce my Intern, Emmanuel."

"How do you do" he said shyly taking her hand.

"Actually, he's my son!" said Dr. Yani. "...If he ever makes it through medical school!" he said playfully.

"You must be very proud of him" she said.
He smiled. "I am. His heart is in the right place!"
Amanda got up to leave.
"I'm sorry for the accident Ms. Wells. It happens too often in this part of the world. But the good news is you are unhurt and will enjoy a full and complete recovery. Just take it easy for a few days…If you find anything new, or need to call, please don't hesitate, will you?"
"Thank   you."
She asked about Jacques.
He was safe, they said. He was being held overnight for more tests only.
Finally, as she walked out of the hospital, she was thinking how glad she was that her first incident had been kept off the record by Trevor.
Now this.
Outside she was met by a member of the AUB personnel patrol staff.
"The driver? She asked the MP walking beside her, an African-American with a square, proud face.
"Yes Ma'am?"
"How is the taxi-driver?"
"The driver was killed Ma'am."
"God! I'm so sorry…" She stopped.
Tears fell and she didn't care how she looked any more. What she was not prepared for was what he added.
"He was found with a bullet wound to the head"
She leaned against the wall. Lightheaded, nausea was threatening to buckle her knees.
The MP took her arm and gently led her forward.
"No need to blame yourself Ma'am: I can assure you that if you were a target, it is because you

represent a government disliked by the enemy. And you are not alone!"

He opened the Exit doors for her and then ushered her into the Embassy car.

She looked at him.

"Here....we are *All* targets!" he said demurely.

Less than five hours later, the ship that had entertained her guests so lavishly at the docks of Beirut slipped her moorings and was already out to sea, her presence in Beirut yesterday highly visible and now vacated.

* *

Abimlebac was frustrated.

The building and expansion program for the Pharaohs had been going on for two decades, he knew. But as the scribe explained to him, increasingly the outlet for timbers was threatened by the enemy. Not because of the Port site itself, but because important supply commodities coming from the North into the Southern middle kingdom of Egypt was failing due to troubles up there. The Egyptians were looking elsewhere for import sources.

Abimlebac had a vast force of laborers in attendance, waiting for their work. Certainly, he could pay them. Gold came easily from the mines to pay for his mariners, tradesmen, builders, carpenters, sculptors, stone masons, artistry painters, scribes, craftsmen and rope-makers. Plus a community of workers from quarries, his pottery mill makers, paint and dye mixers, tool smiths, ironworks and bookkeepers.

There was no question that the quest of the Pharaohs to expand their markets by sea travel and trade had been of the highest importance to the Twelfth Dynasty.

He was the shipwright, he would know.

For those with higher skills, or trade, contracts and covenants, they would make for lucrative exchange and development - as long as he was faithful to feed his infrastructure into the court of the Pharaoh.

It was expected of him: A contract devised between the Pharaoh and a Prince was a covenant agreement. Something sealed as sacred from the God. He must be above reproach, and meet the highest standards of morality and ethics to serve... His was the exclusive right and ownerships of docks and ports of the Egyptian Empire, in perpetuity. As a Prince favored by the Pharaoh, he might easily have all management, shipbuilding, and delivery of materials and shipping wealth into the Pharaoh's kingdoms. In particular, the vaunted cedar woods from Lebanon, delivered by ships...

"So far" the scribe explained, Byblos was the port amongst "those who are on his waters."

True, since First Dynasty times, it had been virtually an Egyptian colony, having provided the timbers found in tombs built for the Pharaoh. Indeed, the "Byblos ship," as it had been known, had served them well. Certainly, women had sent enough gifts to the shrine of the "Mistress of

Byblos," many of them fine specimens of artifacts and treasure.

"But look here!" said the scribe "some 60 letters from Rib-Hadda and his successor Ili-Rapih, Rulers of Bylos petition the Egyptian government for military assistance from Akhenaten, and on down...? How do you solve this?"

"Like the Romans!" argued the Prince.

"If what they do - conquer, then leave their generals to defend, making them resident regents - then the state does have to pay for the Conqueror's expenses to defend his territory! He must capitalize for his own defense, with a hefty tax, which he also pays to the state!"

"Clever!" said the scribe. "You should advise the Pharaoh!"

"But he does..." said one of his lieutenants, stepping forward.

"Only troublesome territories require full support of military garrisons. *You have no troubles!*" persisted the scribe. "Otherwise, the outlying regions are by proxy owned by the state, or by title to the Prince Regent. Someone upon whom the favor of Pharaoh is bestowed as a Prince..."

The scribe got up. "I have here a gift for you. In the absence of gold, I am authorized to give you title." He unrolled his papyrus. "Affix your Seal, here. It is for your to own!"

"I have enough!"

"For you, my friend, you have done much to earn the trust of the Pharaoh. How many ships have you built, and how many timbers have you brought for the construction of this kingdom over the years, you and your father's household?"

Twelve

There was only one person who called at 6.45 in the morning.

She groaned.

"Morning Beautiful. This the Day the Lord Hath Made!"

"Really?"

"Precisely! We leave at 8.30 on the dot. Get my sister up! Bring passports"

"Don't you keep normal hours Trevor?" she looked out the door and could see Lizzie's foot "like your sister?"

Amanda staggered out of the bedroom and found Lizzie sprawled over her couch in something of a coma. No *on the dot* chance, she thought. Lizzie would need serious coaxing with serious coffee.

Last night, what began as a downtown Bistro dinner outing with the Wickes intended to commemorate Lizzie's "last week in town" turned out to be a Ritzy pub-crawl comprising of local Arak tasting.

Amanda did recall Trevor saying something about the long weekend excursion.

She had made a determination to mention nothing to him. Especially about her showing up at his place...in the middle of the night!
Besides, Amanda had been thinking, with all the mounting information, she was a little irked that she and Trevor had become more distant from the original threat. Forget it, she decided.
Forget the whole damned thing every happened.
Have a little fun!
And fun they had, all night.
Trevor and his sister had been talking.
"The Holy Land" interrupted his sister "Is it..like, *real?*"
"Absolutely. So be ready at dawn!" he finished.
"Yes Moses! Into which wilderness might you be taking us?" she asked.
"You'll see!" he offered with a look.

Lizzie collapsed on Amanda's sofa.
Late as it was when they got back, Amanda still held that there was something peaceful about consulting your computer when the house slumbered.
She had opened her email and found a message: She read it again, and printed it up for the morning. She would read it all ...on the way for enjoyment. Who knows what they would find in the deserts of the Holy Land, she wondered.
But as she pulled out the beach bag last used by the Pool with Paula and Lizzie, she found Bill's material that he had so kindly prepared for her. The sheets were welded together - no doubt from Lizzie's wetness and dog-shaking. The rest had been left unread.

They too should go
 Wow, she thought. What a way to prepare for a
trip through the Holy Land!

* *

Abimlebec held a thunderous scowl across his
face.
The sea voyage north out of Egypt was long
enough to allow for some serious calculations and
accounting.
Things had changed since the tremors in the
valley of Siddim. The towns there, while fortified,
had gathered their forces for an assault against the
border skirmishes. But the region had yielded
little and suffered from neglect following
extraordinary damage. The construction was not
good - the structures should have held.
Plus the economics of the region had changed, as
had most certainly the demographics.
Labor was a problem. Where to find adequate
workers with the kind of strength and skill needed
for timber dressing; haulage and transport?
Carvers, he already had in abundance. They had
long ago been shipped to Egypt for their work on
Temples, and on residences of the elite, and on
refinements of the Palaces and Pharaoh Tombs.
His own commissions for the delivery of cargo by
sea as supplies of materials were well known.

Now, his titular deeds to the ports served to keep
the Egyptian colonies from falling into the hands
of the enemy, and that was gratifying. But the task
of keeping them intact; well managed, and able to

continue functioning in the midst of such turmoil was the challenge. Especially in this region now.

He unfurled the charts in the Red Sea.

The harbor of Mersa Gawasis had been shipping their goods into the Egyptian capitals - through Punt -ever since the reign of the Pharaoh Sahure of the previous century!

Even using his vessels to export Egyptian culture far and wide across the Atlantic of wide berth, manned by at least two dozen oarsmen per flank. Of that he was eminently proud. They carried grain as cargo, protected by tall double-ended prow and stern drafts that survived well in big swells of the sea, and made speed in far waters. He knew of their spread of canvas sail, made of strong Egyptian cloth. It was remarkable, requiring booms as long as the ship itself, carrying crewmen aloft to man the twenty four stays per sail as it worked with the wind to traverse the great ocean beyond the Atlantis Gates. From the coast of Africa southward, around the lands, east, west, north and south.

All for the glory of Egypt, a culture that would spread - building cities like temple pyramids; using flint tools and blades, invoking the gods for the children of the land to labor and toil.

If ever there was a port to turn to, if all markets failed to produce, it was Mersa Gawasis, once much used, now little used. It was a little secret gem, he decided. It should be not forgotten.

Navigation was something for those who knew, and the repository of navigation was ancient. This

port would serve well for spices, tobacco, embalming oils, and even wheat in exchange for gold from the Western lands to the south, and to the north...Ships from Tarshish, even.
That would be the harbor that he cherished the most.
Now, if he was to receive the titular ownership to those ports as well, then indeed he would be well endowed.

* *

The journey into Syria over the Lebanese mountains was folly. If "early start" was the only way to make the journey an "educational Tour" for his sister, then Trevor was fiercely deceived.

Frequently, he stopped. Shortly after leaving the urban settings of the city he was producing one pamphlet after another from a seemingly bottomless glove compartment.
No planned sequence. No marked-up map. And no advance warning about what was upcoming.
That surprised Amanda.
Trevor was so determined to convert this journey into an adventure, that he was neglecting the basics. Like distance and time calculations, let alone pit stops and overnight plans. *So much for family security and safety!*

Still, if the road was tedious across a barren terrain, there was no shortage of Gas Depots and kiosk stops, suggesting a long tradition of voyagers making this pilgrimage.

Occasionally, the road seemed unassailable for anything but rugged terrain vehicles. Nor was it all flatland. Amanda more than once reached for the roof as the vehicle had to negotiate uneven roadbed or fallen rock. The Land Rover was fit for the job, Trevor announced more than once.

"I have a friend called Achmed, brother to my driver Yusef, whose family has invited us to spend the night at their home" he admitted mysteriously.

But that was early in the day, and not until dusty faces and parched throats begged for mercy did he stop and promise to reveal their final destination. *Later!*

Amanda was wondering what rationale prompted his tossing care to the wind. Especially after he had admonished her about visiting souks with bomb-makers. She knew better than to ask.

Besides, Lizzie was in the back seat enjoying a world of her own: Gaping out the window in wonder, taking pictures, following charts, reading tour guides, making drawings, and sending text messaging in rapid rotations, she seemed happy enough. Even plugged into her tunes.

For now Trevor was a tour guide – the unrelenting archaeologist rather, on a quest to take his "family" on an expedition. He even produced his pith helmet when the road stopped him, fallen rock blocking his way. This, to supervise his "road crew" as they cleared rock in feverish fashion under blistering heat. His sister gave him a few choice enjoinders.

"This too..." he added blithely "is part of the Adventures of Travel in the desert!"

Lizzie peeled with laughter and Amanda collapsed on the nearest boulder for a long chug of bottled water.

But Trevor had been busy. The car was loaded with extra gas tanks and emergency water and supplies. To the horror of his passengers, even sun-dried snacks that only a man could stomach. And there was something else that Amanda noticed. He was keeping notations of time and compass bearings at many lengths of the road. That, plus a certain edginess to his demeanor made her suspicious of his motives.

"This is *too* cool" squealed Lizzie from the rear seat as the car raised up on two wheels, lurching over a boulder to land hard on its axle with clear engine warning.

Trevor laughed.

Resisting fatigue, Amanda relished the company of brother and sister, it felt like good family-time, and his forbearance was unending.

Then abruptly Trevor stopped the car and would take dozens of pictures of long roads and mile-markers with his digital camera. He had an agenda, she decided.

A comment he had made lingered still. It was in reference to the police report they received about the traffic "accident" that she and Jacques de Torraine had sustained. The driver, he said, had been shot. A youth, he said, from Cairo. Believed to be a terrorist. His arm had been badly burned. It was perhaps the way Trevor said it that surprised her. Not just a report, evidently. It caused him some anguish.

But that was for another day to discuss thought Amanda, turning her gaze to the barren terrain out the window.

"The sights" Trevor was saying "...are magnificent!"

Lizzie just shrugged. As the day wore on, Lizzie was lapsing into bouts of ennui; excitement and fatigue.

Fortunately Amanda had reminded her to bring her iPod, CD player, battery charger and earplugs. They came in handy across the Anti-Lebanon stretch of mountains. Because neither Trevor nor Amanda had imagined them to be so rough and desolate.

Where she wanted to go was Haran, explained Amanda, the place where "Abraham and Sarah arrived after leaving their native land of Ur."

They were arguing, Amanda and Trevor, when he brought the car to a full stop and climbed out for a moving object that was crossing the road.

Lizzie picked it up, and though it resembled a stone, the creature retreated into his shell when she perched it precariously upon her hand. It was turtle which she placed on the rear seat above the picnic basket. Trevor and Amanda turned to study a map spread over the hood of the car.

"Here, amongst the Canaanites..." Amanda was saying

"So?" said Trevor, looked up to a distant open-top lorry full of workers. It was not a mirage on their highway.

"Get in!" he said abruptly, and started the engine before she could object.

"Quarry workers" he said, as they passed uneventfully.

They drove on, Amanda certain of his malaise.

Car travel has its lapses of silence, Amanda knew. Usually when thoughts and questions resolve themselves. But suddenly Trevor announced they could cover the distance intended, and that he had a plan in mind.

Amanda had her doubts, her face now shinning with perspiration. This was going to be a long trip. She consulted her guide book:

> *"Haran was a significant moment in the life of Sarah, Abraham's wife!"*

Trevor looked at Amanda. "Trust me, you're about to take in a few more millennia over the next couple days!" Then added "Ok. Next trip will be to Haran, I promise. Any err.. reason in particular?"

"Love" She grinned, her hair now a hopeless loss to humid curls and nose freckles.

Trevor wasn't listening. He was peering anxiously into the rear-view mirror, his own face moist with perspiration.

What does the official guide book says.

"Ancient history" said Trevor. Much of it needs updating. We've had a few wars since then." He paused, a sadness in his eyes.

He turned. "Our first stop Ladies, is going to have to be in Syria!"

"You're kidding!" chirped Lizzie.

Amanda looked up, surprised.

"Read on!" he admonished

> "Lattakia, Syria. Ancient Canaanite. After the fall of Alexander's Empire, it became a

major city and port named after the governor's mother Laodicea, mentioned in the book of Revelations and Paul's letter to the Colossians.

"After the fall of Rome, it was exposed to cultures of the Byzantines, Arab, Seljuk, Crusaders, Mamluks and Ottomans" ...

"And I am quoting from the guide book."

"We'll find some refreshments here, drive around for some viewing, take a short museum tour, and then proceed to Ugarit. OK ladies?" said Trevor.

Amanda was intrigued and took pictures.

By the time they reached Aleppo, even Lizzie was overwhelmed with the antiquity of the place.

"One of the oldest continuously inhabited cities in history. Abraham (pbuh) is said to have camped on the acropolis which, long before his time, served as the foundation of a fortress..."

"Wow" Lizzie sighed.

"Ladies...err..." began Trevor.

"And..." continued Amanda

"He milked his grey cow there, hence Aleppo's name "Halab Al-Shahba""

They were not paying attention to Trevor.

Trevor made it out of town and saw his way clear into a good stretch of road, up an incline, then where he picked up some speed.

It happened without warning and occurred just over the rise when the car had picked up some momentum and started its decent with no restraint.

"What the hell… !" exploded Trevor, his foot banging on the brake pedal "I've got a problem"

"What…?" they both yelled.

"No brakes!"

They jerked forward bracing, and tried to respond.

"The turtle…" he screamed. The engine started racing its rpm with menacing abandon "It's under the brake pedal …. I can't get any purchase! Hold on!"

The pass below looked treacherous, and Amanda knew that to avert disaster they had to act now.

She dove down to the steering column and reached under his legs to pull the carapace creature away from under the brake pedal, the heel of his boot searching for control and mangling her hand.

She screamed.

"Bloody Hell!" said Trevor stopping the car on its nose.

She pulled up, both of them dumbstruck at the prospects before them, dust and stone still settling.

Finally Trevor spoke.

"How badly did I hurt your hand?"

"I…err…" said Amanda, nursing her wrist. Her head moving blankly from side to side…

"*Poor baby!*" moaned Lizzie to the creature cupped in her hand like a rock.

Trevor turned abruptly to his sister, his beaded forehead and hair wet with spraying droplets of perspiration. He wiped them away to survey for any damage and opened his mouth to speak.

Instead he glowered at the object in her lap.

"You ok?" he said.

She nodded, holding up her turtle.

He looking over the precipice of the road that attended the left flank, and then facing Amanda, their eyes meeting in alarm and relief. "Let's take a break" volunteered Amanda, promising lemonade for parched throats.

There was no sight of traffic. Or life, thought Amanda grimly. But the break was well chosen. It gave everyone a chance to recover, and the car was inspected and repacked.

"On to Ebla!" announced Trevor, a new man.

> It was noted in the guidebook as being a *"commercial route since ancient times; the arched stones of Aleppo the link in trade between Mesopotamia; the Fertile Crescent and Egypt.*
>
> *"The Amorites made it their capital in the 18th century BC. And many invasions followed from Hittites, Egyptians, Assyrians, Persians, Greeks and Romans"*

It was a landscape of limestone, sand and sun bleached roads that passed them over the next few hours, all of it seemingly holding civilization's greatest secrets at bay. And they were caught in the wonder of it. Puzzled by the conflicts over the centuries. Drawn by the enigma that beckoned to time travelers.

"Wow!" said Lizzie at the 955 BC discovery of the basalt altar in the museum of Ebla.

Amanda was getting antsy. Not only did they seem to be drawn into the interior of some vast and alien territory, but further away from all that they held safe and structured. Somehow, they were losing their grip on the trip, she felt.

They had found a small café and gorged on coke, barbequed beef stripes found on a spit, and honey dripping baklavas.

"The Crusaders came half way across the world for this! And I thought they were in search of the Holy Grail...Wow!" said Lizzie again and again.

Amanda read on in the tourist pamphlet

> *"In the palace of this great kingdom; Ebla's real treasure; a library of the Royal Archives containing more than 17,000 clay tablets was uncovered. These tablets; recording an important period in Syria history; are the earliest written documents in Syria, among these was the world's earliest bilingual dictionary".*

Her thoughts went to the content of her email received a few days ago from a trusted scholar:

Worship of goddesses, like Sarah, did not lessen the actual social subordination of women. How then can we understand the active, independent role of Sarah and the other matriarchs in directing them and their family's lives?

Later, as the sun traveled its day's journey across the desert, the water wheels and gardens of Hama presented a refreshing stop. Trevor declared that their destination for the night was not far.

"Known in the book of Joshua, Hama is mentioned at the time when the land was divided up between the 12 tribes" said Amanda. "It is a splendid example of 18th century Ottoman architecture with its courtyards, fountains, mosaics, richly decorated wood ceilings and paneled walls, marble floors..."

She looked up. "The life of a Pasha suits you does it Trevor?" She pointed to the mosaics of maidenhood.

"Indeed it does!" he replied, flashing a smile at her.

"So where to bed, Pasha?" asked Amanda, her eyes twinkling with a tease.

"Damascus!" he declared. "Achmed and his family are waiting for us. "But first, a-crusading we shall go!"

"Damascus" they both echoed.

"And not far at all...:" he insisted.

Amanda's thoughts drifted as the landscape became flat and barren. Here was the world of the Coptic script written by the hand of a woman. Why was it so venerated?

The surroundings were dust and nothing but tones of terracotta, yet secretive and magically promising - as mile after mile marked subtle differences and hues of intensity, perhaps markings left by man. Or was it the call of the desert as some had said.

Nor did time change anything in the endless landscape of red sands caressing out deep truths. *If Sarah represented the children of Israel, what she was doing being barren, mused Amanda, now clearly fatigued.*

So, she wondered. It was on this soil upon which the early human condition had been writ, and she thought of her manuscript. Was *this* perhaps where it had originated?

Then she saw it. Or rather imagined it.

Trevor interrupted their thoughts.

> *"Crac des Chevaliers (Qal'at Al-Hosn in Arabic) was 65 km west of Homs and 75 km south-east of Tartus.*

It was the most formidable medieval crusaders castle in the world, built to control the so-called "Homs Gap", the gateway to Syria.

Lizzie could hardly believe her eyes *"Oh my God! ...you're kidding right? Only in monster movies and English literature. This! Never! Homs, once called Mesa in ancient times, was the third station on the Silk route after Dura Europos and Palmyra"* she pointed to her notes.

Trevor drove them passed the mosque of Khalid ibn Al-Walid, with its tall white-stone minarets preparing to bring the day to a close in prayer.

"Who built these things?" asked Lizzie in wonder "I mean to dream up such design so long ago with ancient technology only available...Wow!"

It was a mystical spell that wouldn't end, except for the dust and fatigue that was clearly visible on Amanda's face.

"I feel as if I'm on hallowed ground..."mused Amanda.

"You are!" said Trevor. "Here is where the great religions converged in great battle..."

"How come?" chirped Lizzie.

"Because each felt they had a mandate from God to be here, and to defend it as faithful and devoted servants"

"I can see it..." said Amanda suddenly.

Trevor smiled, the road bumpy.

"What do you mean?" asked Lizzie

"Well, it's where Abraham was born, father of the Jewish Religion. Then Christ, center of the Christian. And then Muhammad, the Muslim...I mean, it's easy to understand here why they felt drawn by this land, and by their calling."

"True. But at great cost" added Trevor.

"Look at what the Jewish tradition has given to the world from here...Ethics and laws of society that we still obey today handed down by Sarah and Abraham through her son Isaac?"

He nodded.

"And then Abraham's other son through Hagar. Some say the progenitor of the Muslim traditions, fought and defended though the ages, right here!"

"Gees!" said Lizzie, now listening.

Amanda turned to her "And the Christian faiths, inspired by Jesus Christ of Nazareth, from *this* region!"

"How come?"

"Because each offered hope, inspiration and a doctrine to uphold their beliefs...The Jewish promise of Abraham offers a cohesive belief in Righteousness and a promise of Salvation by God..."

Lizzie was listening.

"...and the Muslim Religion, based on the teachings of the prophet Muhammad with a set of admonitions for comfort and assurance...And Christianity with a gospel of hope and redemption..."

"So how come they could be so deadly?" quizzed Lizzie.

"Good question" added Trevor.

They all laughed.

Trevor found a gas station, and filled all his traveling tanks for the balance of the journey. He pressed on to the Qattina Lake, still rich in fish, with a rainwater dam used in the 2nd millennium BC.

Lizzie turned again to the tour book which she referred to as they passed by the archaeological hill called Tel Ennabi Mand (Qadesh) *where a historic battle took place between the Hittites and the Egyptians in the 13th century BC"*

It was blistering hot by the time they spotted Damascus, *"oldest city in the world"*

Trevor stopped abruptly, and turned off the engine. He got out, walked some 25 meters, and stood, almost listening, dust and echoes still swirling.

He took out his binoculars and scanned the distant hills.

As they approached the city Amanda could imagine the ancient soft wailing of minaret prayers across the ancient city...

All three religions held mention of this city. The Jewish, Christian and Muslim faiths. Yet here it stood, serving its intended purpose as a trade center and central post to the region.

* *

The home of Achmed and his wife was just outside Damascus.

Kids at the top of the street, playing in party clothes came roaring down to the car as their target. They evidently had been waiting at the top of the hill for the arrival of the Land Rover for several hours.

"Long dusty roads!" said Trevor apologetically as he unraveled his 6ft 3 frame from the car and gave the man a manly embrace.

"*Long* dusty roads. *Long*!" agreed Achmed, grinning and shaking his arm. "Thank God for cell phones! You were kind enough to text me where you were for half the day."

Trevor introduced Amanda and Lizzie his sister.

"Welcome" said Achmed's wife Sissi wearing a long embroidered and mirrored Afghan dress.

"Fahdhal" said the rest of household, inside, bowing respectfully and offering their hospitality"

"My parents, uncles, sisters and cousins!" said Achmed proudly

"Very nice to meet you" said Amanda, shaking hands with everyone. Two of the portly ladies, Lizzie later remarked, had several gold teeth.

"An old and venerated tradition" said Trevor in his patriarch's voice.

Amanda looked at him and realized he was having the time of his life. All this to show his sister parts of the world that would expand her horizons.

The house itself surrounded an internal courtyard with a fountain. Tiered levels of verandas, covered by lattice work, perched upon columns that exposed Moorish architecture and mosaic frescos.

It was a villa, exquisitely furnished with Eurasian art in quiet, unadorned spaces.

Amanda looked up at the vaulted roofing and arches. Timbers, carved and painted in ocher; indigo greens, gold and whitewash, depicted the heavenly journey of life. It was a serene setting for those whose constellation it defined.

Whereas hers was a world cluttered by conflicting ideals, voices and aimless without singularity, this was a place of calm.

She could understand why Muslim Fundamentalism arose in protest to Western clutter. Such clutter threatened their very existence. Even bereft of a gospel, it had relevance here, in isolation and in contemplation.

Their private rooms, aired with white muslin curtains and open to bougainvillea verandas, were cool and shaded, the overhead plastered vaulted ceilings supporting beams and simple fenestration.

Furnishing was sparse, chiefly rattan, cedar wood and cushions of soft desert hues. It refreshed.

Amanda walked out on the veranda. The day was already closing with the last of the blasting sunlight.

Further down Lizzie emerged from her room, as Trevor would be able to do from his room down the balcony.

For now, the instructions were to wash and make ready for a feast that would be served on the terrace.

Amanda was glad of the twenty minute reprieve in the coolness of her room.

Later, as the sun reclined to leave them a crystal golden evening, Achmed and his wife welcomed them on the rooftop veranda lit with copper torches. It was a garden, softly fed by the trickle of water from cistern wells.

At the center of the walled terrazzo, a central brazier held bay, luminescent in softly glowing embers.

A desert breeze husked softly to remind them of an outer vastness, still able to hold secrets under the searching sun. But closer, lest any doubts about relevance lingered, the din of industry and a modern held the background as the noise of tinkling traffic never ceased.

For now, the scent of orange blossom from irrigation groves permeated the air.

Ahmed and his wife had other guests, all of whom spoke English, invited for the pleasure of Trevor and his company.

Food arrived in a procession of platters rich in citrus and olive flavors. A rich rack of stacked lamb, fahool, hummus, roasted red peppers, stuffed grape leaves, feta cheese and pita bread.

Slowly, for Amanda, the tension of her world fell away.

Lizzie was in heaven, surrounded by admiring teenagers. Some of the boys opened up and tried to show off, but still having to compete with their excited sisters.

Trevor was in his element, listening to Yusef and his brother Achmed. They were storytelling, intermittently laughing and gesticulating with unabashed intensity, each offering an episode of harrowing encounters with the strange and the awful. Including twenty years as a Driver for the British Embassy in Beirut.

Trevor turned periodically to Amanda. But Mrs. Achmed and two professors kept her entertained as waiters topped her glass of anarak.

A short performance of belly dancing and music brought glitter and laughter all round, followed by sweets and coffee.

Amanda was relaxed against the gold satin cushions, her shawl drawn around her shoulders for the warm scented night, if touched only briefly with a cooler wind from the desert. She drew closer the muslin shawl given her by Lizzie in the souk. It suited the evening.

Later, as the party subdued and the children retired, adults sat around the glowing embers of the brass brazier, their only torchlight.

Above them the starlit sky of the desert rotated in gentle axis to display for them the full panoply of the galaxy.

Amanda saw Trevor watching her. It was a look she could not fathom, his eyes both hazy and wary. For one brief moment she thought he was intently focused on her alone, amidst the general chatter, not missing a thing.

He was a different man off duty, it seemed. She felt as if he had penetrated her soul suddenly.

* *

She awoke to a soft knocking on the door. A young housemaid left a brass tray of freshly brewed Coffee and Croissants on a side table. Amanda responded to the aroma of the coffee. She took it out to the veranda to sip.

Beneath a golden sunrise was an ancient city, now stirring with mournful minarets and early vendors to market.

Beyond, lay distant lands, peopled in legends and lore and conquests. The wilderness went far into the mountains. She breathed in the sight with awe.

Sunday was spent touring the city and viewing the olive grove that Achmed and his family had owned for generations. Then to the house farm where the smell of orange blossom, desert dirt and freshly manured fields mingled with charcoal fired cooking saneyahs.

It would go on forever this way, thought Amanda, with or without the wars and warriors that moved across the great stage of the world. Or would it, she wondered.

Perhaps every soul did make a difference.

Finally, it was time to leave. Achmed's wife presented Amanda with a gift - a small token of friendship. Amanda thanked her, promising to open it at home.

Trevor was anxious to reach Beirut before dark. The journey home would be different, and as they drove out of the city to the major highways, Amanda knew to relish the moments.

He stopped briefly, and as he and Lizzie were debating with a Jeweler, Amanda took the opportunity to reorganize the car for refreshments and a good supply of bottled water. Trevor had bought his sister a square amethyst set in a 22 carat gold ring. The beveled jewel flashed its multi-faceted hues of wine and lavender as if to capture every inflection and mystery of the orient. Lizzie was delighted.

"Magical" said Amanda.

"Your graduation gift!" said Trevor, putting away his wallet.

They grinned and hugged.

"We'd better get going!" said Trevor, suddenly aware of his surroundings and wanting to get the journey home underway.

There was little said as they passed the rugged terrain of desert wadis; rock falls and woods that marked the Anti-Lebanon Mountains. Only this time there was no sightseeing. A straight run home, he said.

And as the map suggested, the Lebanon mountains soon followed.

Only slowly did they evidence reminders of the present. Like official border checkpoints. Passport inspections. There was no room for laughter here, Amanda noticed.

Gas stations serviced trucks with armed guards. Jeep patrols passed frequently. Rusted relics and armor pierced defenses littered the roadside.

Only when the Mediterranean Sea met them on the horizon at dusk did they recognize the roads leading into the city. It was somber sight, yet welcome.

It had been a wonderful weekend, their quiet thoughts would attest, silent and exhausted.

That night, as she opened the gift that Achmed's wife gave her, she found a small carved alabaster box filled with sweet smelling pearl emollient.

Amanda lay in bed, recalling the ancient biblical parable of the woman who approached Jesus of Nazareth in this landscape with her alabaster box of perfumed oils. Much to the scorn of his Treasurer, it was broken over his feet for the Last Supper.

Thirteen

The Monday morning meeting was not unusual.
Ambassador Reynolds - who liked having every member of the Embassy in attendance, sent his regrets today. Trevor took the podium.
With the Naval contingent gone, his time was finally detached from his duties there, he said.
Amanda took notes, still smitten with the euphoria of travel.
As was Trevor, clearly.
When she entered a small cubicle behind the security bars for mail, she noticed a box of files delivered for "Senior Official of the Post, from the Home Office"
"By Special Delivery" said the courier, waiting for a signature.
She signed. Not for her to ask, she decided.
Or so she thought, until she saw Trevor coming through the doorway with a scowl on his face that could slay a horse.

"Now listen up!" he bellowed for everyone to hear and gather around.
His voice carried for two floors of the building.
"*Come On! Com'on!*" he shouted to beckon a gathering. Back into the meeting room.

One soul actually rushed up and saluted him which he took with a painful smile. Not for nothing did he run a department thought Amanda. Clearly he was in no mood for frivolity.

A gathering of Information Specialists, Analysts, Cryptologists and Security personnel came around. And of course, JoAnne called in to see if she should come down.

"Our monitors have picked up - a possible terrorist assailant *on the premises*!"

The room hushed suddenly.

"What...?" said one secretary under his dark glasses.

'I'm going to put it up on the monitor - if you would be so kind Gwen - with the lights out"

"We've been suspecting some unusual movements recently in a number of cells. And you know we're on a military Code 3 status"

Amanda knew this was not exactly unusual when ships of the line approached key foreign ports. But it surprised her nevertheless.

"Here is a person actually in *our* underground parking garage inspecting cars!"

"*Doing what*?" came the inevitable question

"Well, nothing really. Expect walking around. However, it's on the premises - and that's enough to alarm us."

"It's a woman in a burka! She could be looking for ...charity?"

"She just appears to be looking inside the cars. Never really touching or placing any attachments, as you can see from this monitor. But just walking about..."

"The face is obstructed by those confounded veils. But the intent is unclear" said Trevor.

Amanda couldn't believe what she was seeing.

"She is reconnoitering..." said one from the Intelligence section.

"Or trying to find something!" said another.

Mrs. Olson, one of the Executive secretaries said "honestly, it looks as if the woman *wanted* to be seen on our monitors!"

"This person is *looking* for someone. One of you is a possible target!" said Trevor bluntly.

Amanda wanted to vomit and pressed hard against her belt.

"How did they get on the premises, passed security?" Was it another question

"We can't exactly bar people at the street." It shows bad faith to the host country. Only if we go to a formal heightened security alert can we do so! However, we would have to explain ourselves to the local administration. So, we've decided to inform internal security and have an unofficial Alert, for our eyes only" said Trevor.

He was met with silence.

"So I want everyone to be super cautious. Don't take or leave your cars anywhere that is not securely monitored. Lock them. Inspect them. Report *anyone* who approaches you. And stick to the basics of life wills you? We need to minimize exposure. I'll hand out close ups on the monitors as imaged blowups. If you recognize *anything*, let us know ok? Class dismissed!"

 Trevor looked at Amanda.

She said in a normal voice "you're not telling us everything are you?"

He looked up and answered quietly.

"This person has been spotted before Amanda. Just sitting across the street. Or walking. The point is, we don't know. *But they know us!*"

Amanda fled the room. She felt lightheaded as she walked along the hallway.

Inside the Ladies Room Amanda she paused, then moved to the basin and washed her face.

It had a nice scent, clean. More importantly, it was usually silent - with infrequent visitors. From the window, rarely open, you could see the sea at an oblique angle. If the window frame were pushed outward on its full arm, a rush of wind could fill the room with a saline draught.

Not often did she find herself wanting solitude and some fresh air, but as the beads of sweat trickled down her neck and her blouse cloyed at her hairline, she knew she need to think. She splashed fresh water on her face and neck.

Slowly, her breathing returned to normal.

She could hardly believe how she managed to remain so unmoving, when the image they observed nearly reverted her to into a state of shock...

The image of the intruder was *familiar*!

The girl in the souk at the jewelry store! One of the three that had sold the necklace to Lizzie! How could she not recognize those green eyes...

She *must* talk to Trevor.

The girl was clearly looking for her car. Amanda was known to them!

She just saw her assailant!

After lunch Amanda settled to her desk. Perhaps Mrs. Olson was right. The *person of interest* perhaps *wanted* to be seen.

The same thought lingered in Amanda's mind. The intruder was being too obvious. She must have known she'd be captured on camera.

No. *She wanted to meet*.

She wanted Amanda!

The Close-up photos were passed around, and Amanda looked carefully. It was definitely the image of a woman in a shapeless burka. No one could possibly identify her from these photos.

But yes, there was something in the picture that Amanda knew. She put her desk magnifying glass against the face.

Even beneath the black veil, the sun had imperceptibly glinted off something on the face. It was the scarab jewel in her nose.

Amanda wanted to – *No* - *MUST* talk with Trevor...

The hours passed, and the building returned to calm, an inspection by security having swept the grounds and garage. No. The incident was over.

Trevor was out, the crisis over. But he would returned soon. Returning from his briefings with various Embassy personnel. Chiefly those in liaisons with specialists and analysts outlying at various posts with the rim of their geographic region, those reporting in.

Finally, he appeared, his face pale.

He looked anxiously for Amanda, and all she could do was wave a hand and affect a happy smile. The chances of approaching him were close to nil at the moment, the staff crowding him.

The opportunity came at the coffee pot, a routine pilgrimage made by all, but happily at random.

Their eyes met briefly, and it was clear he wanted to speak to her directly, even will all ears listening on deck.

"Lizzie having a good vacation?" asked Amanda.

"A wonderful time!" he said loudly.

People turned back to work. Then she whispered the inevitable, in view of the calendar.

"I'll take her to the airport if you like..."

He looked down, nodded, clearly chagrined to be parting with family when family was what he needed most right now, Amanda knew. He turned away and took a call.

Amanda was left standing with her coffee in hand, stirring aimlessly. She followed him into his office and shut the door.

"There is something I want to tell you about" she said softly.

He looked up. She wanted to say...

Or, was it that she wanted to *thank him* for a wonderful weekend? Or did she just want his attention. Was there something in his eyes, *expecting...*?

Her thoughts muddled. The girl; the picture; the Italian woman in the car that night; the turmoil of it all...*Where* to begin? She opened her mouth to speak.

"Amanda!" yelled JoAnne opening the door suddenly. "*There* you are!" She laughed gleefully. "I was just wondering what you wanted done with all that delivery out there?"

"I'm on it!" said Amanda, spinning on heels and leaving.

"Come in!" Trevor was saying.

* *

It was a Farewell Party.

Her dining room setting had been transformed from angular functionality to a candlelight supper table.

For balcony seating were fashioned bowers of soft gauze netting; vine-trellis blossoms and potted gardenias. Soft Greek music added to the warm Mediterranean air.

It could have been theater. The occasion was a casual evening at her apartment, for Lizzie.

"Oh my God" Jim repeated, unable to stay out of her apartment all day "this is going to look ...*gorgeous!*"

"Shoo...Shoo" she paddled, sending back to his own quarters like a duck.

She wore a silk shift dress of sea-blue. Later, she might add her muslin scarf as adornment. For Lizzie.

More than anything, Amanda loved to cook. Not often did her position in Beirut offer that opportunity. Today she had been to market early. She had baked, stewed, grilled and roasted with an assortment of ingredients that near maxed-out the capacity of her kitchenware to procure.

"Your cooking things yourself?" said Paula incredulously on the phone. "Goodness! That's a change. Let us know what we can bring, then..."

Amanda had a few moments to herself for the first time today. Actually, she was having fun. She grinned. Far from being a duty, Lizzie had brought joy to her life. How could you explain it? When the doorbell rang for the first guest, Amanda was excited. With this crowd, she knew it would be a success from the first foot over the threshold, and the party was quickly underway, everyone bearing gifts.

Seated at the center of a table filled with silverware; damask napkins, blue glassware, candles and flowers was Lizzie - Jim having positioned himself at her side.

They chatted up the Menu-Card:

> *Feast of wild Cornish hen in wine sauce over rice with Greek salad.*

"Oh Yes" said Trevor. "I can't wait to see what else!"

> *"Baklavas, pastries and Turkish coffee"*

Had he implied his appreciation, wondered Amanda. Or was he just a party animal of the superficial sort?

No matter. Everyone was enjoying themselves for the evening.

When it was discovered what was happening that night, the guest list had exploded. Even Ambassador Reynolds heard about the soiree, and sent over a case of Champaign - of course it would be shared with the Security Group downstairs. And Yusef, Trevor's driver.

Susan found out that it was Lizzie's last night, and said she, Beth, Marci and Walter would be popping in to say Farewell. The Wickes, naturally, were there.

So for a full house Amanda had Jim bring in more chairs from next door.

At the buffet Amanda piled on more rice; fresh pita bread, extra salad. Plus one Rum cake and thee additional cases of beer for some of the AUB MPs coming over to say goodbye to Lizzie...

If it got confusing at times, Lizzie loved it.

Jim, in a toast of longwinded sequiturs with his cheeks aflame said "So, in conclusion, we say farewell to our Dizzie Lizzie -- and may our gloomy lives find a way to recover!"

"*Here! Here!*" proclaimed the assembled bunch of inebriated guests.

Lizzie was showered with gifts and gadgets that only a teenager could want, or as Jim pointed out, all of it utterly useless stuff.

"Nonsense!" said Trevor, setting aside his unfinished glass of champagne. "None of it is wasted on Lizzie" He was leaning back on his chair, arms out for Susie and Beth.

Lizzie took the cue.

She stood up and addressed them all with a heartfelt thanks. "It's been a wonderful trip, really..."

"Damned *expensive* trip!" muttered Trevor without conviction. She giggled.

"No, I mean it, guys. I mean, I thought I'd be bored out of my mind visiting Trev on an official mission here. I thought you'd all be stodgy and old and I didn't think you were all so, well, fun and human!"

"Not really!" said Jim. Susan pushed at him with suggested contrition. They were laughing, clearly.

"No. Seriously. Ok Jim. I guess you're a smart techie but you are honestly a... a..."

"*Freak!*" said someone. Lizzie giggled.

"Ho! Alien!" added Marci placing her hands on her head and sprouting two pony bunches of hair, antennas.

Lizzie made a go of her speech with great charm.

"And you Susan are so cute with your skirts and all that stuff you carry around when you work with this lot..."

"Stuff? What stuff?"

"You know what stuff Susan. What do you carry around in your fortune-telling caravan?" added Paula with a beer in her hand.

"At least *my* beach bags are not carrying diapers and bottles..."

"Oh... for Steve you mean?" said Jim

"Bullshit!" growled Steve from the far end of the table, his reading classes loosely perched on his nose as they all roared.

"And then..." commandeered Lizzie, not yet finished "Here's to my all-time favorite *Coach*. If there's ever someone I want to be, it's her. Here's to you, Amanda!"

"Here! Here!" they all cheered, gleefully downing more duty-free alcohol on premises that was a world away from policed prohibition.

"To good friends!" said Amanda.

Lizzie looked at Trevor who was still looking at Amanda.

"Absolutely!"

Here, in a building by-the-sea, wrapped up in the events of an ancient world that held them captive in a mystical bond, they had gathered. The important thing was that Lizzie was surrounded by friends. That, and a memory that would last for a lifetime, thought Amanda.

Later that evening, Trevor found Amanda on the veranda talking. He leaned over the rail, and he tapped her elbow to lean with him overlooking the sea and the Cornish beneath them.

"Do you remember your first day, down there on the rocks, Amanda?"

"Oh God..." she said, for the first acknowledging her distress. She rolled her eyes. *"Don't* remind me..."

"No. That's alright! You did what you thought was right. Plus I want to thank you for what you've done for Lizzie, here..."

Amanda could hardly believe the words she was hearing, as if still resonating, they assured her in such a way as nobody else had done - affirming her place almost, recognizing her responsiveness, if only for a second...

"Hey Trevor! Over here..." He turned away.

Yes she decided. It had been a spending evening. And Lizzie finally crashed.

She lay on the couch fast asleep, her tiny charm bracelet hanging from her outstretched arm. Amanda raised the elbow to rest it gently on her chest, and then covered her with a lightweight traveling rug.

Evidence of a wonderful evening was cleared away, and with one last look at Lizzie, Amanda dimmed the lights for the night and turned into her bedroom where three red leather matching bags held the floor as Airport luggage.

Lizzie had packed and taken her stuff to Amanda's apartment. She was spending the night, a sleep-over before leaving directly for the airport the following morning. It was a decision the girls had made on Amanda's suggestion.

For a teenager with a backpack and suitcase, leaving her brother's place after a vacation was tantamount to a family breakup. This was simpler. Trevor agreed. Besides, most of Lizzie's make-up and paraphernalia were at Amanda's place anyway.

As for Trevor, after a harrowing day of terrorist scenarios, he was delighted to have her stay with Amanda, upstairs on the top floors of the Embassy building.

Yet Amanda was tossing and beating her pillow for comfort. She got up and walked to the kitchen for a glass of water, shut the windows and returned to bed.

Her thoughts were left somehow unsettled.

Trevor had been propelled out the door with the promise that he'd back first thing in the morning to pick up the "girls" for the airport.

Perhaps it was anticipation of the morning's flight departure. She fretted that he would not come!

He was distracted. Amanda thought it about. No. there was more.

It occurred to her that her that life at the office was becoming increasingly stressed. There was much going on. Added security, for example. The political situation was heating up across the borders of Syria; Iraq and Iran.

Trevor, clearly, was showing signs of duress.

Nor had she had a chance to disclose to Trevor the identity of the woman in the photograph!

Moreover, Sister Margaret was suggesting she remain quiet. *But where was she?*
Amanda would have liked to talk...
A cell phone buzzed. It was Lizzie's cell phone. Trevor was leaving a message. Evidently, he too was up, and pacing, and thinking of her. He wanted her to know how much he liked having her, how proud he was of his sister, and how she did well during her stay...He loved her, he said. Goodnight. Have a safe trip!
Amanda smiled.
First things first. Lizzie was off in the morning, Trevor was coming to collect his sister at 9.00 AM and accompany her to the Airport in the Embassy car for a 12 o'clock flight.
She closed her eyes, resolved

* *

From the quarterdeck on the prow, Abimlebec looked down as his vessel. Still rocking in aquamarine waters of the Mediterranean Sea, it approached the stone pier, broadside.
A ramp was extended to the ship's gunwale, and he crossed it with few lithe strides.
Fastened to terra firma at a latitude of 34 degrees N, 35 degrees 39' East, he stood at the Canaanite port city of Byblos.
His mission was to find the consignment that was to be shipped back to Egypt. And not just the consignment, but the craftsmen, carvers and saw-blades that would work the massive cargo. Timbers, for they had been hauled down from the

mountains of Lebanon to the port. Timbers - cedar timbers for the great tombs; pyramids, construction ramps of Egypt.

But he was under pressure. There had been some uprisings. And the Egyptians had stated their concern. Should they favor Tire and Sidon instead of Byblos?

Philo of Byblos, quoting Sanchuniathon of the Eusebius, said it was an ancient port.

Founded by Cronus of the 3rd millennium of the ancient calendar BC, Byblos held the reputation of being the oldest city of the world.

Known for its items of trade and manufacture like flint tools, it held items of sacred value that the population revered and placed in tombs as funerary artifacts for their journey into the afterlife. Items like pottery; sickle blades, figurines and small points made by a peoples who had settled in Jericho - a people who inhabited domiciles with plastered floors, and had naviform technology never before known.

Byblos wares were legendary, their advancements unique: They stored remarkable Chalcolithic and Beth Shean pottery; stone vessels, silos for storage for settlement-dwellers. They understood chamber tombs and seals for trade accounts in records.

And they had refined elements for the gods and kings, like jar burials; pierced and decorated flint, churn and violin figurines; carving glyphs with architecture and cylinder seal impressions. They had skilled men living in settlements in the surrounding Beqaa Valley - like Labweh and Ard Tlaili, where water flowed and irrigated farming...

Not that the area was very big, noted Abimlebec, approximately 1.2 hectares, but enough landing places for boats and perhaps about twenty houses surrounding. The dwellings themselves, he particularly noted, were rectangular with plastered floors, dark faced and burnished walls with decorative shell impressions for aesthetics, some even, Roman like, of larger variety with silica.

Abimlebec's retinue made their way to the Moyen building. There they manufactured Canaanean blades and fan scrapers. Used for armaments, this was something the Egyptians wanted in abundance for shipment. That, plus Adult burial jars -some lined with white plaster that was applied with a self-hardening technique after firing.

Next on his shopping list were copper hooks used for the catch of jars, like seafood in preservation of brines.

Artistry, like that of the Byblos combed ware, would one day be called *Eneoloithique Recent*, much of it decorative in nature. These, Abimlebec would order for Egyptians from this colony.

Not that these items were new to the Prince of the Pharaoh. Much of Egyptian culture had long imprinted itself upon this market. But with his trade accounts in order, he had other business.

Here he was, now that he was made titular owner of the port as he delivered the critical supplies needed for the pharaohs, and his ownership of these outposts was inconsequential to the Pharaoh.

"In perpetuity!" said the papyrus in his leather pouch. *In perpetuity...* This he could hardly believe.

In a world where life itself was owned by others, only the monarchs, the gods, were proprietors! That, and of course, those people known from Canaan who had their own ways, with their own God.

But *in perpetuity* was a gift of appreciation from the Pharaoh to him forever. For now. For the afterlife. For eternity. For as long *as his seed would remain*, said the scribe, handing him the scroll with the seal of the Pharaoh affixed upon it. For it was his ships going and coming to Byblos, travelling far and wide, that helped to make Egypt a great kingdom of trade, wealth and glory!

Abimlebec rushed through his days at this port. On the last day, he went to the scribe accounting house. He left his retinue outside, waiting.

Inside, he could rely on writings as being universally understood, accounts honored by all peoples of trade.

"You have news?" he asked the chief accounting magistrate of the house.

"No. Nothing! Not at all..." he sulked.

Abimlebec approached him and opened his hand. Seeing the silver it held, the scribe melted with smiling.

"May you rely on us until the sun ceases to ascend, and the waters are no more..." he said, reaching for his papyrus in a great room.

He shuffled around the myriad pigeon holes holding rolled scrolls. They were organized along the walls of his chamber: Known by event. By account. By ship. By traders. Conquests. An entire archive of parchments with accounts; expository readings; old writings; new records; narrative; chronologies; genealogies; barter and market exchanges. A warehouse of written record - articulated in a language recognized widely as Phoenician. A language script of twenty-two characters that defined, amongst its many markings, the story of the king Ahiram on his sarcophagus, as a Phoenician alphabetic script that belonged across the seas to North Africa, Europe; the ancient eastern and far away western continents – all carried by Phoenician ships of trade and merchants.

The scribe pulled from one hole a scrolled parchment. Abimlebec pressed the merchant at the thigh, furtively. "Can you hide your scripts in jars and hide them in the hills for safekeeping?" he wanted to know.

The merchant looked at him, and with his eyes, nodded.

This parchment then, would hold words tantamount to scriptural writings. Words that must be forever sheltered accounts from marauders; invading forces and competing cultures intent on demolition, erasure, de-territorialization and diviner advocacy of the most unsacred kind, like Resheph, a Canaanite war god.

Yes, those parchments would be hidden in the hills. Knowing of things that might come, Abimlebec remained silent.

Abimlebec had other ports to purvey, lands also given to his proprietorship which served the same purpose as Byblos. Like Jaffa, or Joppa as it was sometimes called...

The scribe wrote out the parchment.

"Bequest of a city-state?..."

"A gift..."said Abimlebec, pausing. "Now, change that symbol..."

The scribe stared at the pointing. *A woman?*

Abimlebec remained still.

"Your bloodline? *A possession?*" the scribe asked.

Abimlebec's eyes filled with pain.

"She is not mine to possess!"

The scribe took the money, and his eyes followed him out the door. Then he spat on the ground. *You and your gods...As if anyone will remember you!*

* *

Fourteen

The Building Fire Alarm went off. It was 8 AM.

If not fully dressed, Amanda and Lizzie had packed with suitcases at the door. The alarm startled them.

The phone rang.

Amanda was about to speak, she thought she felt a tremor. An earthquake?

The phone rang.

"Amanda..." Trevor's voice was calm.

"I'm in the Cypher Room. The building is going into Lockdown. Get Lizzie gone! There's a military flight for medical personnel waiting on the tarmac. Lizzie needs to get to Istanbul, then Frankfurt, London. Got it?"

"Wait ...Trevor?" gasped Amanda. He was gone.

It took Amanda half a second to understand. She knew what he was working on. He was shredding.

Get Lizzie gone?

"Lizzie?" she called, dialing the Front Desk for transport to the airport. Seeing the fear in Lizzie's eyes, she added "Trevor is coming later!"

"Let's go. The car is downstairs!"
Amanda grabbing the canvas tote, scarf, bottle of water and a small bag she had planned to give to Lizzie at the airport as a travelling giftbag.
Amanda walked out behind Lizzie and almost closed the door of the apartment. But she paused.
"Call up the elevator!" she yelled out
"No elevators!" cried Lizzie.
Amanda was back inside, a clown dangling bags, clothes, keys in her mouth. She raced to the dresser, pulled out the package with the red ribbon and jammed it deep into Lizzie's giftbag.
The trip to the airport was rough. Even with empty streets, the roads were buckling and heaving. The car navigating jagged tears in the street.
Trevor would be alright, she told Lizzie. There was change of flight plan. Apologies if he wasn't there to see her off. But just get on the plane, right?
 Another big hug, and Amanda fairly pushed Lizzie off into the boarding passage.
She saw him then.
Beyond the crowd, his head easily distinguishable, in the queue to board the flight she saw Jacques de Touraine. He too saw her waived and signaled his tickets that he was on his way to Istanbul.
He understood.
Amanda focused back to Lizzie, now well advanced through the security line, and Jacques joined her.

Perspiration soaking her shirt, Amanda swiveled and ran to the upper viewing deck. She saw the

plane, a private jet, now gathering speed through disintegrating runway. It roared, gaining acceleration to reach maximum speed.
 With a surge, the fuselage flexed as it pushed up on very short thrust with extraordinary incline. But the wheels were up..

Amanda stood there, clutching the rails as the Airport screeched with sirens and Emergency vehicles.
Amanda had managed to mask the realities for Lizzie, suggesting these quakes were not unusual. And yes, frankly, not too unlike a "routine fire drill" for Embassy personnel, even if untrue.
Amanda was about to turn away.

Chaos began to erupt in the street. At the airport a gas explosion by fuel depots filled the air with black smoke.
The driver was still waiting and held the door open. "I've instructions to leave drive you to the AUB Miss Wells, you have a room booked at the Inn there for tonight I believe, as do most of the Embassy live-ins. The Embassy is off limits for the present."

Amanda acquiesced, too fatigued to argue.
At the Hotel Inn she walked through the lobby.
 The earthquake had passed, but personnel had clustered into the Hotel as a routine precaution.
She saw staffers, friends, some at the bar, some in the main foyer, all congregating like anxious journalists waiting for word on something. She

found her way to her room. At least the Hotel was situated on the premises of the AUB.

It was almost too surreal.

How do you keep getting back on your feet in a world like this?

She put her face in her hands, sitting on the edge of the bed. It wasn't long before a message came through informing her that the Ambassador had arrived and wanted a word with everyone in the lounge.

And thank God!

Only he could articulate the sentiments that remained firmly tamped down by all.

 Ambassador Reynolds expressed his sympathy with the situation, and understood everyone's shock, displacement and disorientation. He gave them all the information he knew. The Embassy was safe, but needing to be fully inspected for damages. Everyone should stay here for at least 24 hours. Fortunately he said, there was no loss of life.

Amanda detected vulnerability. But like all courageous Ambassadors, he rallied his staff, thanked them for their patience and endurance, and promised to have them back on the job in "no time at all..."

It helped.

"At least we aren't under fire" said one disgruntled staffer heading for the bar.

Amanda breathed.

Each room now contained a care package. She opened hers.   Essential toiletries, prepaid cell phones, note pads, lists of network information and personnel. Water bottles, small wallet of money and emergency ID credentials.

She stood there, staring. She could well have been checking into a hotel in Paris or London.

She looked around. Everyone was exhausted.

It wasn't until she was organizing some toiletries that it struck her.

Lizzie had left with her packet from the dresser drawer still in her gift bag!

"Oh God!" she muttered, her memory begging for a full recall of what happened.

She sat, her thoughts in a reel.

The *package?*

Between pacifying Lizzie with a hasty farewell and then...instructions from Trevor...then sighting Jacques in the queue at the Airport for transit...

Amanda now realized that all thoughts of the package had fled in that moment.

"Oh God!" she muttered. Had she told Lizzie anything?

No!

So, if Lizzie was in possession of the valuable item how could she *know* it? She might just lose it!

It all just...happened so fast.

* *

Jacques de Touraine and his Associate stepped out of the rail station and walked across the campus of Oxford University to St. Giles. They checked in, made their calls, and proceeded to the Library.

A secure conference room was arranged for their meeting. Along the tables were laid out all the manuscripts under present analysis.

Waiting for them were Professors Hannivon and Luther Magellan each respectively from the faculties of Ioannou Centre for Classical and Byzantine Studies, and the Oxford Centre for Late Antiquity. Others included two resident scholars, and one visiting. The matter had been under some serious discussion.

But even Jacques was little surprised at the exposure, since his project was ostensibly secret and under the supervision of only one man in the room. *Who were all these others?*

Hannivon met him at the oak door, and instantly with one look, made it clear that the best way to hide an agenda in the academic world was to lay everything open, for cover.

Jacques got it. *Be discrete. Say nothing telling. Show interest.*

As an Antiquities dealer, Jacques wondered if they would like to feast on him for dinner. But he held his nerve and kept a steady face. His interest, he said, was in Archaeology, to which they all nodded dismissively –the least of all disciplines, and they returned their attention to the table.

But the question was tacit. How could someone such as *he* have a copy of such a relic?

Could it be possible that it was, after all, authentic? In which case, it would be binding.

He smiled.

* *

There was little chance for a quiet evening at the hotel, decided Amanda Wells.

Secure as it was on the campus premises of the American University of Beirut, the Hotel Inn was the center of everything. News of the Embassy Lockdown was a concern to them all.

Extra MPs had been posted at all quarters, and staffers from the American delegation showed up in the lobby for drinks, discussions and an informal gathering of what was happening.

Amanda added little to the discussion. But she had received a salutary phone call from Lady Reynolds. Everything would turn out alright and they could be "back in the swing of things in no time at all" No specifics, Amanda noticed.

She had an uneasy feeling about the event.

 At any rate, it was out of her control just now. So she decided for a drink at the bar with the rest.

Except, she hadn't heard from Trevor.

Amanda knew that under the protocols of hierarchy, it would *not* have been appropriate for her to ask for his whereabouts. Especially once the Ambassador had "made the rounds" and found his staff fully accounted for. Trevor after all, was in the realm of Essential Personnel.

She realized the real source of her anxiety was not Trevor. Nor the parcel on Lizzie, but something else. *Someone* else.

Jacques de Touraine.

On the same flight!

Why did it bother her?

She searched for an available computer. She wanted to send an email to Lizzie. She could send a simple welcoming message. Or she could ask directly about the package. Or ...

In any event, the thought was useless. Messages into a mission under siege were unauthorized. She knew the procedure, not until given the All Clear.
However, she decided she would confide all to Trevor. At the next possibly opportunity...

* *

The next day Amanda called in. The Chief of Staff had left a recorded message. All personnel could approach the Embassy after 5 pm today. All Clear.
She called Trevor.
Still no answer.
For now, she should use the day to her advantage.
She dressed and went out into the morning sun.
Best to keep a calm appearance.

The Great Door of the *Lycee Françoise* looked undamaged. It was a solid oak work of medieval reinforcement. Ostensibly a tourist attraction, the door was forbidding.
Amanda rang and someone opened the porthole.
"I am Amanda Wells, come to see Sister Margaret?" she said to the face behind the square.
"Un moment still vous plait?" said the nun and disappeared.
Amanda was let in and welcomed by Mother Superior Antonia. She was flanked by two other sisters who remained in the background.
Amanda began by asking if all was well after the earthquake. It was. With God's Grace.

Then she apologized for making her visit without an appointment. She did not need to explain the Embassy crisis here, it was beyond the scope.

"I am sorry. But Sister Margaret is no longer with us"

Amanda found the surprise somehow hard to absorb.

"No...no longer...?" She looked at the two sisters behind Mother Antonio and found one looking down at her fidgeting hands, the other looking resolutely forward. They would say nothing without being prompted, she knew.

"Oh...I'm so sorry. I'm a little disappointed... I had hoped to talk with her about...She is well?"

"Yes!" came a firm answer "She has occasion to be called to Rome for our Annual Convocation... And for her ...scholarship!" she added as an afterthought, her eyes unwavering. She pursed her lips together in admonition, thought Amanda, clearly wanting to bring closure to the exchange.

One of the sisters from behind moved forward, tiptoed in childlike manner and whispered something in her ear.

"It seems Sister Margaret has left ...something for you!" She turned to the girl and nodded briefly. Then they left.

Amanda waited in the hallway, its vaulted ceilings letting sunlight filter through the gothic shapes that was the world of Sister Margaret. A note was given her, and a small box. "A gift," it said, "not to be opened until you wedding day!"

Amanda's hand flew to her chest in delight, and she looked at the sister that presented her with the gift.

Here then, was the *original*?

* *

They gathered at the International Hotel of Beirut, a center for anyone seeking high end luxury in travel and space for professional meetings, as necessary. It was an easy jaunt in and out of Beirut for visitors.

Frequently, the conferences on Antiquities from the Holy Land were conducted here with scholars, experts and museum curators arriving from all over the world.

Jacques was with friends, mostly. Others were professional contacts in his world of commercial auction items.

 "Moreover, they get rather entrenched about the importance when they attach era and region; as if a territorial survey marker..."

Finally, this chart shows the *graphical* evolution of Phoenician letterforms into other alphabets. We can identify the initial creation and the new alphabets, even pronunciation changes of languages over time..."

"Like a DNA imprint?" asked Jacques.

"Yes! Very good..." they laughed.

After the conference, Jacques went back to the International Hotel.

Jacques left feeling elevated. This analysis was as good as it gets, coming from Europe. The real research was evolving elsewhere. In academic institutes in the Middle East, like the Bar Ilan University.

Understood, of course, was the he could get the article out of the country.

Legally.

Tonight, he would take dinner downstairs. at his Hotel. He consulted his watch, would shoot off a few emails from his room.

He got an email. Signed "H"

> *We are all of a like mind.*
> *Your copies of the manuscript show authenticity.*
> *Acquire the original.*

Jacques was pleased with himself. When asked how he would pull it off, he said it was easy. He had a plan.

He had made his own logical deductions.

Lizzie's farewell party was so well publicized amongst the staff that discovering her date and time of departure was not complicated.

That Amanda had the document, wrapped from the Convent on her dresser was certain. He had seen it with his own eyes. Certainly, if she had any ancient relic, she would send it back to the United States.

She would give it to Lizzie as Courier.

What else do you do with precious relics but get them out of the country first? Chiefly for security reasons. Yes. She would give it Lizzie to take to the United States.

Jacques stared at his message. Or, as the old saying went, kill the owner, inherit the title...

He replied.

> *Is there any other existing example?*

He signed off, and went to dinner. When he returned, there was an answer.

> *"If the images provide the original, we have reflected on the possibilities that you may have more than you think. It <u>infers </u>other ports, if not an entire region as bequest, as well."*

> *"Of course we have work still to do. That is, we can prove that there is linguistically a possible corollary for others ports included in the gift, like that cited on the discovery of other ports like now the ports of Mesa Gawanis, first documented on Queen Hatshepsut's famous engravings of Punt – but now clearly understood to be an ancient port in pre-use; Byblos, where we have commercial accounting, ascribing with God's Holy Authority the asset of the port facility; and possible ownership also of Jaffa whose references only appear later in the Amarna Letters, known as Yapu , possibly inferring home for Japhetch, son of Noah who rebuilt it after the Great Flood, they knew."*

Jacques stared at email. Then he printed it out and sat down to absorb the enormity of what he had.

To own the authenticated first deed to one of the world's most historical seaports would fetch millions in rights; recognition as a founder if not a seat on a Board of a Museum, and tons of

insurance coverage for a long, long time. His finding, as a antiquities expert, just made him a celebrated icon in the world of collectors and philanthropists...whose Trusts he could oversee. The prospect of world fame and serious money sat well with his tastes. This had been a difficult test, but a necessary one. Yes, he had passed it!
He would have a drink.

Bloody Hell.

Fifteen

Amanda was wearing a summery flowered frock and white sandals. She hailed a taxi. She was going out for a morning coffee, some shopping, and then walk to the *Au Francoise*...

It has been a week since the tremor.

She was excited. Today she was buying fabric for a dress she wanted to sew together a simple cotton cocktail dress for herself. With a pink ribbon to remind her of Lizzie.

The idea of losing herself in all that clipping, snipping, basting and pressing to produce something herself felt good. And it served as distraction.

She had sketched the design all night. Emailed her Mother about it and decided what bag and shoes would match. Something to surprise her friends with, at the next party. Haha!

The sun was an orb suspended on the horizon. Traffic buzzed by, an occasional jarring horn for slothful pedestrians, most of whom were perambulating down the Cornish.

It had a calming effect on her nerves, the city in full swing. She paid off the taxi.

She took a short stroll to the market behind the restaurant that had so delighted Lizzie. But almost wanted to choke back a tear at the memory.

Suddenly she missed the girl and felt an emptiness that only teenagers can fill with their many demands and dreamy expectations about life. Perhaps it was the sight of the shops they had visited together. Especially the Boutique of fabrics where they had had so much fun. So today, she was pleased with her selection of fabric. Large white leaf patterns on a field of navy blue and green.

Amanda was not thinking when she stopped walking. Did she imagine it? Was there something recognizable about the woman that just entered the shop? It came as an after-flash picture. But with so many others, the woman was wearing a dark cloth and burka.

But did Amanda imagine that jeweled face or not? Forget it, she decided. Enough of that! She hailed the cab home.

Most definitively it was a diamond pierced nose in a small gold scarab. She recognized it beneath the burka veil of the woman ...

Damn, but she was getting tired.

* *

With repairs being done in the Embassy, she had been asked to lodge at the hotel. Not for all personnel. Just for those Residents living on the top floors of the Embassy. Roofing and re-plastering issues.

It was an effort to regain her footing really, let alone maintain a continuity with her previous life. At least she was online; had her stuff in a suitcase. Plus her sewing machine. And her daily office job. She plugged in her laptop computer and checked her mail.

A direct analysis of the manuscript. Finally!

> *"Your document is an account of a handmaiden speaking about her mistress; a tale handed down as a family fable and guarded by the culture of a high priestess, significant of the earliest centuries of the 2nd millennium BC. It is early and has traveled through Diasporas.*
>
> *"But it was actually committed to words by a later generation in Coptic. The backside writing is Latin, medieval: a translation of the original Coptic text. But that comes centuries later!*
>
> *"The parchment has been damaged with age and fading. You must identify the high priestess...One thing is certain. It is a family bequest of a heritage. And it is signed with a name:*

Amanda almost wanted to laugh.

Who the hell was *Keturah*?

Discovering the "identity of the high priestess"? She closed her eyes, and wondered what business she had even contemplating such a notion. She felt drained.

And had just about had it.

She lay back in the bath tub. She would play tourist. She would become normal.

She heard the door knock, and jumped quickly out to answer in her bathrobe.

The tall, dusty, disheveled figure leaning against the door frame was Trevor. He looked drawn.

"Oh!" Was all she could manage, her untidy emotions in total disarray.

"I want to go home...Lizzie at least, is fine ..." he began without making any sense.

Her feelings wanted to tumble out, both of them survivors.

"I know" she said. Then she paused and eyed him. "Damn it Trevor, where the hell have you...?"

He had stepped in, pushed the door shut and brought his mouth down on hers.

It was a kiss without reserve. Amanda could hardly believe she was responding.

Jesus! What a world.

Nothing platonic or business like about it, she realized. She finally pushed him away.

"Sorry..."he said pathetically "I was so relieved to see you. You're... family...It's been unreal...you've no idea"

She stepped back "Are you alright Trevor?"

He nodded.

Amanda raised her hand to her lips "That was some kiss!"

"Please forgive me... I was out of line. Pack your things. I've got the car waiting downstairs and I've come to take you home. Embassy is All Clear"

"Now?"

He nodded.

She looked at him once in the car. The city lights passed them like dull drumbeats.

She observed the face that was once a happy-go-lucky Trevor now deeply grooved, dehydrated and preoccupied.

She squeezed his hand, and she smiled, recalling an intense kiss less than half an hour ago.

She felt an obligation, now more than ever, to unburden herself of information. But as he looked down at her, she saw a man so troubled that she wondered if this was the right time to add to his distress.

Instead she said "How's everything?"

"A nightmare. Security is spread thin. The Port of Haifa has been shut down. Factions everywhere. Unrest brewing on every street corner…"

Amanda knew that Trevor lived in the world of intelligence gathering: Informants, conduits, communiqués and secret missions filled his files.

But she could be put off no longer. She knew she must tell him. Especially with Lizzie holding the relic.

"Trevor. There is something I want to tell you about. Something that began with Lizzie."

The sirens swarmed by.

The driver slowed down, and police cars followed.

"Shall I stay, Sir?"

"No. Move on!" said Trevor.

They turned along the boulevard of the Cornish and had to stop as they passed by the French quarter where Amanda had been with Lizzie.

A mob had gathered - smoke trailing behind them. As the car passed slowly through the checkpoint, Amanda asked what the commotion was about.

"Another bombing!" said the driver.

Then she saw it.

Where the French Boutique had stood, there was nothing but rubble and burning.

"Oh my God! I was just here yesterday!" she said in disbelief.

"It's the store Lizzie and I came to get a dress made..."

"You brought Lizzie ...*here*?" he said, his face draining of color.

Before she could explain he leaned forward and tapped the driver on the shoulder. "Can we get a move on... through this mess?"

"Yes Sir!" said the driver who reached for a siren that would give the car Emergency right-of-way. But he saw an opening and deftly navigated the black Embassy car through the congestion and left it in the rear view mirror without having to turn it on.

* *

At Tell el-Hammam, the ground had been shaking with small tremors for days, if not weeks. Months even, though ground tremors were not an unusual thing.

In the servant's quarters of Lot's wife, the housekeeper was furious. She wanted to kill the scullery maid.

In the small clearing of their domicile, where they kept the cattle, a milking animal had swollen glands ready to milk, the maid was nowhere to be found. In the back rooms, five looms lay waiting for their occupants to continue weaving cloth, plus ample supply of silk and dye – they had five robes on consignment and seven orders of cloaks to be made still. Lot's wife was known for her domestic industry.

And in two days, a party was arriving from the head of the household's family which required a feast, preparations, and the slaughtering of - at least a few lambs.

But worst of all, she was not happy with the grain supply in the sacks behind the Wadi well, and the ground was parched and cut up with hoof marks from animals at the low trough.

At least she had oil in her jars, wine and bitters from other grains, and spices. Plenty of spices, and lard for cooking. What she could use was an extra supply of timber for the cooking fires, and some yeast for the risings of bread, plus goat's milk in the cool of night.

Where was that girl?

Oh, and that was another thing that annoyed her, the girl had brought insufficient water from the well to swill out the terracotta bowls: Contaminations of yeast for fermentation of yogurt was one thing; spoiling from soiled vessels with the sour curd would fail to congeal...

Where was she?

Dawn, and the household would be up and about soon. The men would want their sweet tea and cakes, plus some for the field hands minding the herd.

She would kill her!

The maid's sister showed up, a maid servant herself. Could she help, and no, her sister would not be lured out of her hole. She took the two staved barrels appending from a yoke stick, and went to the well to fetch water, in her stead.

The housekeeper glowered. But at least water would be brought! She moved to the back of the abode and found dust on the ground from the slight tremors that disturbed the structure overhead beams. She picked up the switch broom and started to sweep the plastered floor. Suddenly she stopped, a crack up the wall at the far end of the chamber surprised her.

The tremors!

Outside, it was more than dust and debris that showed signs of the tremors. It was loose pebbles, and gravel that ran along the surface and gathered at the drainage ditches, clogging and clotting up with dust-driven twigs and balls of straw. What if it rained, she muttered, now cleaning out the ditches around the habitation perimeter.

Damn that girl! So much to do, and so little time to prepare!

She heard the men's voices, and ran to the courtyard hearth to ignite the fire for boiling water.

The maid servant girl came back just in time. But a disastrous argument followed.

The girl barely got out the words...

"The water....No! Don't beat me! No! No! ...The water was so low down, I nearly fell in trying to pull the rope....No! I swear it!"

"You nearly fell in?" screamed the enraged housekeeper. "I shall *throw* you in!"

"No!"

"You...you...useless seed of a whore...Where's the water in this bucket? Half drawn? Half spilled? And look,! How I can cleanse out the dyeing wool with this colored water... It's mud, you imbecile. *Mud! Mud! Mud!*"

"No...I swear it. I tried....No!"

    * *

He had told him everything.

The man in the brown vestments led the caravan northward. He had pushed them for three days. The mule pack train that travelled north was long, escorted by skilled horsemen trained at defending the cargo of overland transport caravans. He had paid them well.

He thought of Abimlebec, and his heart ached with shame. Still, they parted friends.

And he told him everything, their story, all of it.

Still, fatigued as he was, he wanted to get away from the place where humans were sold as commodities for labor; for pleasure; for breeding, for skills - territorialism of their cults counted for everything: The place was a savage place, dangerous, godless - and that might extinguish *his* tribe. His tribe must continue. He was fearful.

He told him that... Abimlebec understood.

He told him that he was a man of conviction.

Of this he felt sure, he explained. He felt responsible. He must ensure its safety and survival. Abraham was now head of his travelling tribe... His thoughts lingered still.

 A water-carrier ran up and offered him drink. He took a swig, and thanked the servant.

Rest, the servant's eyes told him. *Rest a while!*

He turned to survey the mule train following. He was pushing them.

Those travelling on mules and camels were essential personnel to the camp, also principles of the family.

The cargo contained supplies and provisions for an extensive encampment, if not a settlement, which was to occur at the next oasis by the well. They had menservants, maidservants, asses, laborers, tradesmen, stockmen, merchants, managers...

They walked onward.

But in large part, the most precious cargo were the Syro-Phoenecian seals upon the ledgers that itemized the sacks of grain; seed, food oil, fuel oil, dried fruits, and other items for making iron manufacture for hooks, rims, jars, barrels. Plus chicken, cattle, oxen, sheep, goats and other livestock.

He had come down towards Egypt to re-provision. He was now migrating northward again. But the mood was somber. No singing of girls, wailing of women, cheering in the voice of the young. Something had gone terribly wrong.

He thought of Sarah, and he held back his sobbing.

Travelling in a howdah crafted for the back of a camel, she was secure, the curtains offering privacy from the rest of the travelers.

Behind her, the retinue of her household followed. Her tent would be erected in advance, and she would be adequately provisioned and attended by her handmaidens even before arriving. She was after all, a Priestess of Canaan.

And Abram's wife.

Sarah felt alone.

She wept incessantly, her body weak. She had been deeply hurt in Egypt. And were it not for her God and for the fortuitous ruminating of an astute prince who claimed that he listened to his God, she might have been taken for pleasure by him on his bed, the purity of her high lineage pedigree forever forfeit...

She felt betrayed. She was heartbroken. She had been humiliated! How could she ever *forgive* Abram? How could she forget what happened? Would bitterness not bite into her heart, she scolded... Nor could she go back!

She would die in the wilderness, she swore. Abram need not approach her anymore, she swore. She felt herself convicted: She would *not* conceive for him, she said in utter frustration.

For his part, Abram was mortified.

Even as he was migrating north, drought and famine lay everywhere. He was fully provisioned with stock, if not over- filled to capacity. Certainly, he could now survive, or trade from his stocks and inventory; he could re-instate his family camp for at least a year until the new planting seasons might come.

But he felt broken. He had greatly erred.

On the long journey back, his thoughts and memories plagued him. He walked alone at the head of his tribe. He walked alone with his thoughts. What happened?

His father, how mortified he would be! His father Terah, as the writings of the scriptures said, was the tenth descendent from Noah of the great flood - his sons were Abram, Nahor and Haran.

Haran was at Ur of Chaldees, where he suddenly died, and Abram adopted his boy, Lot.

After Abrams marriage to Sarai, they all moved to Canaan. They camped in Haran, where Terah stayed with them until his death. As far as Sarai was concerned, that was their home.

Then Abram claimed that God told him to move to a better land. God promised to give that land to him, and make him prosper and grow into a great nation, ordaining him the leader, and promising in an oath of sacredness, to support him and bless those who would bless him, and curse those who would curse him.

This mandate, Abram took seriously. And with Sarai, his nephew Lot, and all their possessions, he moved to Shechem in Canaan. That is, until the famine struck.

It came vigorously, furiously and with devastating catastrophe. It disrupted all trade; society and stability in the region.

Abram was devastated. He must travel south, he decided. Towards Egypt.

Abram was on his way to Hebron, in Mare, when he even built a new alter to worship his God. But at Hai, Lot and Abram had domestic trouble. Apparently, their herdsmen were feuding; the households' cattle straying and intermingling, disrupting family accounting and belongings.

Abram suggested to Lot that they separate. Lot chose the plain of Jordan, near Soar, near Sodom. Abram told the boy that his father Haran would have wanted him to stay closer with the household migrating southward... at least until things settled down. Here, it was dangerous. The local cities in the Valley of Siddim, Sodom, Gomorrah, Zoar, Zeboiim and Admah were preparing to join forces to do battle with the Mesopotamian kings.

 Lot split off.

The memory of it all was too depressing: It was sad enough parting with Lot, but how could he forget the day that he heard of the rebellion of the Jordan River cities against Elam. And Lot had been captured by the invading forces!

Abram had to turn back and rescue him with a small elite force of 318 men who pursued the Elamite Army, by now walking off with their spoils of war and captives, including Lot.

Abram decided on a night raid, and not only did his men rescue Lot, but they slaughtered the Elamite King Chedorlaomer at Haboh, at a place north of Damascus.

Lot was freed; given his household and possessions. On their return to Sodom, Abram's forces were now viewed as heroes in the region. He could be a new king in the valley. He was made welcome by the king of Jerusalem and showered with awards and gratitude for the rescue mission. Abram refused the rewards, other than his expenses. But word got out. He was a man to be honored; deified and blessed for his valor. Especially his God, a god to fear, said the local populace.

Still, Lot stayed behind in Sodom, and Abram proceeded southward.

As he thought about it, he wished he had not gone.
They met a Prince of Egypt. Abimlebec.
And Sarai, the love of his life, she now wept...

Later in the day, he checked on her. He put his hand up to her bower. "Sarai?"
Her jeweled hand emerged from her curtains, and their fingers entwined.
She loved him. Always.

* *

The village was not without its populations and sources of revenue. It teemed with trans-humanic trade between Sodom and Gomorrah, and had been well-established and well-fortified city. Below them, to the south was Ai and Bethel, with a disc-shaped plain of the southern Jordan valley, a broad alluvial plain just north of the Dead Sea. Beneath them, in the Great Rift Valley, a deep fault line in the earth's crust was ripping apart. Its foreshocks had serious meaning for many.
The rumblings had not ceased for three days, and they knew something was coming. When it erupted in earnest, it measured, as some archeologists would later say, on a scale of 8.0 on the Richter scale.
Fire and brimstone poured down relentlessly, and with such intense heat that everything was incinerated instantly. Those that failed to flee far enough were asphyxiated by the fumes, and by the time the narrow isthmus between the northern and southern Dead Sea basins gave way, the flood

into the southern Valley of Sid dim inundated all inhabitants.

Worse, once the earthquake caused the natural sulfur and bitumen deposits of the Dead Sea to erupt to the surface, large enveloping quantities of natural gas filled the air. When exposed to the fire, it lit up the sky from above, gas making the entire plain a giant furnace of consuming ferocity. Lot was out of the plain with the herds, having agreed to move. It was an issue. To go, or not to go. To stay or to migrate southward, at least until his household reached the southern border of Canaan, east of Gaza. Lot liked the Lisa peninsula. Fertile plains and valleys, well watered. But lately, the ground had been shaking, the wells dry.

The geography would be forever altered.

Sixteen

How long she'd been asleep she didn't know.

Not long evidently, but enough to clear her vision, and she decided on a solution.

She would write Lizzie an email.

> *"The precious cargo"* she could say, *mistakenly put in her bag in the rush of leaving...*
>
> *"Please send it on to the University Department, addressed to: Amanda Wells, c/o Professor Lawson, Department of ..."*

Satisfied, Amanda leaned back. That was simple enough.

If Lizzie forwarded the article to Bob Lawson at the Central University, then he'd keep it there for Amanda until further instructions...She and Bob were good friends, and had shared professional favors many times. With him it would be safe.

At least Lizzie could handle a local New York address: No complications. No super costly postage.

<SEND>

Amanda got up, poured herself some wine, then went out to the veranda.

She would stop worrying.

Enough!

Remarkably, the office life and routine of daily tasks resumed smoothly since the disruption three weeks ago.
The building sustained little damage. Mainly electrical.
In the city some gas lines had burst, fires had ignited and a small protest by alarmed residents took to the streets as a result. Outside the city too there was news of some disunity and disruption.
Further, it was confirmed that Trevor had done the right thing in sending Lizzie off early: All flights were cancelled for 74 hours, and security had jumped up one Level at all terminals. What Trevor did not want was for his sister to get stranded overseas. Especially in conditions that could so easily deteriorate.

At the Embassy, security had not been compromised, but they were busy setting up new firewalls and operations, just in case.
Alone with her thoughts, Amanda was up, logging her descriptions in her notepad:
By sunrise she was certain. Most definitively it was a diamond pierced nose in a small gold scarab. She recognized it beneath the burka veil of the intruder in the photo of the Embassy garage. She put in a call to Trevor before going to work. There was no answer.

* *

* *

The next three days in the office were unbelievably busy.

Communications traffic from the Home Office was copious. They wanted answers. Did the event and its protests on the streets warrant public statement? Was it a threat? Had the host government been informed? What was to be made of a youth from Cairo being interrogated in Beirut by the authorities about a possible assassination? Who was he? Who was he trying to assassinate?

Then she saw that he was apprehended within a thousand feet of the Naval Ship when it was at dock.

By day two, a phalanx of issues were re-examined to go further afield: How had member governments responded? What was the extent of actual political damage? How much divergence could be said of responses by other parties?

On day three, Intelligence surveys had cast a web of world-wide primary, secondary and tertiary connections that might have a bearing on the event: As far as Amanda could tell by Friday, very little new information had been revealed about what actually happened, and it had become the Home Office's decision to keep the matter in-house or, off the record, and without official enquiry.

The conclusion being that no real harm appeared to have occurred to the Embassy and very little political collateral damage could be assessed.

Finally. As to the intruder entering the building ...it was downplayed and kept off the record. False alarm. Period. Case closed.

The evenings at home, following the earthquake had been different.

When Amanda initially returned to her place, she felt a strange need to reconnect with her surroundings as if her world had been cast adrift. But first she must contact Lizzie. She settled to her computer.

"Dear Lizzie" she began, and expressed the fun, thanks and fears that attend relationships and spontaneous vacations. She particularly enjoyed the hours spent together. The "simple events" that turned into fabulous adventure and excitement. The road trip that was so filled with wonder. Lizzie, she remarked, might always have memories of Beirut.

Finally, she referred to the package. Had Lizzie seen anything? Things had been thrust in her luggage that *"in the rush"* had been *"plunged without aim, accidently thrown in...?"*

The following night, Amanda opened her email and sure enough found a reply from Lizzie.

Displaying a non-stop paragraph of verbal graphics, jokes, impressions, abbreviations and exclamations that defied grammar or case sensitivity, Lizzie left Amanda breathless, if howling with laughter.

But there was no mention of a package.

By Thursday night Lizzie's emails showed her disposition as somewhat recovered with a little more order to her thoughts, and perhaps less runaway trivia. But still no mention of the package.

Amanda was getting frustrated. She would mention it again that night.

* *

At three o'clock on Friday afternoon, Amanda was knocking resolutely on Trevor's glass office door. He got off the phone. Of course they had talked about Lizzie's emails in the passing, but this was different. She wanted his full attention.

"Any news from Lizzie?"

"No."

"Trevor, if you don't mind, I've got something I want to talk to you about... when you get a chance..." she added, knowing that it would have to be scheduled if she wanted any control over the event.

"Your place or mine?" he said playfully

"Oh...err...outdoors...preferably" she said, averting any further diversion. Both his cell and his desk phone rang together while Susan popped her head in with "Mr. Reynolds wishes to see you in 15 Trevor. It's an office conference!"

"Oh for God's sake Trevor!" muttered Amanda "That woman is a menace!"

"Right!" he said automatically as he reached for the desk phone and turned off the cell "Trevor here" he began. Then looked up at Amanda apologetically.

"Later" she motioned, and walked away.

"Damn" she muttered. But before she got very far, he yelled out to her with his hand over the phone, "Tonight at Armand's place for dinner?"

"I'm busy" she said shaking her head without turning back.

Later, as she approached the computer room, he took her aside.

"Tuesday morning, a car approached the Embassy driven by none other than *our friend*" he said, producing the photograph.

This time the features in the rear view mirror of the van were more distinct, and the electronic cameras had captured everything.

"We have a person" he said resolutely.

"Someone we're looking for?" asked Amanda, staring incredulously

"No. someone looking for us!" he said, and walked with her holding the classified file in his hand.

"I know the face" said Amanda.

* *

Amanda was indeed busy that night.

She showed up in an appropriate black cocktail dress and found the Ambassador's wife at the head of the Receiving Line.

 Amanda's role was to assist in the general effort of hosting and entertaining of guests. The Fashion Show had been postponed. But the guest list comprised of personnel from a major British Airline.

Mr. Williams and Mr. Christopher were hard pressed *not* to mention the concerns of their flight paths crossing terrorist boundaries, and a Mrs. Anderson was a booking agent pouring oil over company mergers.

"Damned if I ever thought protecting the Holy Land from unholy acts was so hard to do!" said Williams, thinly masking his dislike for a career that had taken him on quasi-military excursions in explosive regions.

It was clear he could be goaded easily into distasteful talk about world politics. And Amanda steered clear of volatile topics of conversation.

"Last week we played tourists and visited Damascus" began Amanda. "It was wonderful!" she grinned poetically.

"Oh yes" jumped in Christopher with boyish chivalry. "More so for the wonders of travel and transportation."

Mrs. Anderson was suitably impressed. They left together, Amanda noticed.

Williams however, was increasingly intractable as the evening wore on, accepting several drinks from ubiquitous waiters -- a detail not lost on his superiors in the room to whom he owed his career as an Airbus jumbo co-pilot.

When finally Mrs. Reynolds approached her, signaling the end of the party, she thanked Amanda profusely. Then she added that she would be thrilled to come to the American "Barbeque at the pool next week. We can have a good chat about Trevor's little Lizzie..." she giggled. "That is, if   ...my Harry didn't make a

mess of burning those confounded hamburgers and chicken parts...err...what do you call them?"
"Buffalo wings" said Amanda
"Oh, precisely!" she screamed with laughter "something Lizzie would know of course! Oh what fun the girl was..."

Amanda had at least had a chance to exchange a few words with Trevor who attended the event, but whose minute to minute demands would have completely erased any conversation.
"We need talk!" he said
"We do?" she hummed.
"Yes. And without interruptions, I promise!"
."Tomorrow then, lunch at Armand's on the Cornish, say 11.45?"
"You're on!"
She made her farewells, and, exhausted, longed for the comfort of her bed, its pale silk sheets and pretty night stand casting light over an assortment of intriguing books and colorful magazines...
Tomorrow was another day.

* *

Seventeen

Amanda was waiting for Trevor on the veranda of the Cornish café Armand. The first day of her memorable false alarm now forgotten, neatly.

She was watching the cars edge by, some very new, some vintage vehicles often seen in third world countries boasting dubious repairs. But not that many, actually. In fact this economy was decidedly on the rebound with clear signs of wealth, and she picked up her coffee cup with a sanguine smile as a new model Mercedes went roaring by.

She did not see the motion at her table in time to respond. Only a lady's hand registered in her peripheral vision; ringed and finger painted, gently brushing itself along the edge of the table, then moving on casually. The black tob and veil of the woman was already turning away and merging into the crowd when Amanda looked up, just one of many local women in the flow that passed the café.

But there was something about those features that sent an unmistakable chill down Amanda's spine. Had she noticed anything familiar?

Paranoia? Suspicion? Of *that* she was a celebrated master, she through ruefully.

"Amanda!"

She decided to play it cool. Trevor called over from across the street.

He reached down conspicuously to plant an affable kiss on her cheek; waved off his driver lingering across the street; and plunked himself down in his seat across the table, all designed to signal safety.

"Sorry I'm late!" he began, "I thought I'd never make it with that damned cell phone ringing like a cyber siren!"

Trevor had been talking for some minutes.

"So what's up? "He began "and by the way, have I thanked you enough for entertaining my sister..."

"No...Not until we spend some time together" she said playfully leaning forward on her elbows.

"Whoa! ..Err..." his said, his ear turning at the hint of badness in her voice "Can we...err...eat first?" he blinked sheepishly.

"You should look up occasionally, Trevor. The sky is wonderfully blue!"

He looked at her jauntily, but said nothing.

The waiter arrived, and asked for their order.

"Why not? But make it fast! "

She ordered a salad.

"Tell you what I was hoping for..." he said after ordering a lamb chop and prosciutto with beer and wine. "Smith is waiting for me to join him for a round of golf. Care to join me this afternoon?"

Amanda smiled. The golf course and pool were within the compound of the AUB. She was one her way to the pool anyway. Anything to get away from the routine just now.

"I'll wait poolside...basking in the sun till you sink your last ball..." she laughed.

 The waiter arrived to produce her Roman salad served in a hand-painted ceramic platter that defied gravity. The hour passed quickly.

Once inside the AUB compound Trevor turned to Amanda.

"I thought you might enjoy these" he said retrieving a package of photographs from his pocket. "There you two are... And here!"

"Thanks"

"Lizzie gave the photographer my name and address to send the bill to!"

"Oh Trevor" she said, taken aback. "It was a hectic time... but *so* wonderful for her. And for me too!"

"You both look splendid" he said, leaning over kiss her on the forehead. Thanks for everything you'd done. She had a great time."

She nodded. Trevor went on.

"Lizzie didn't say anything. But she told me you needed someone to talk to...What's going on Amanda?"

"First, I do have a question. What did you say Jacques de Torraine did for a living?"

"Easy. Adviser to a Museum in France" he grinned. She waited.

"Ok, I don't know which one - consulting or something to do with authenticating artifacts that appeared on the market and bought by collectors for museum preservation, like the Dead Sea Scrolls. Mostly Latin, though. He's an Antiquities Dealer."

Amanda was turning pale.

"Why?"

"Nothing."

Amanda wondered if she were living in a world of imagination or fear.

Nothing?

When finally he took off to the golf clubhouse, she felt relieved. If she had informed him, she would probably have received the blunt end of his professional questioning rather than his assistance...

Nothing?

The worse he could do is ask her write a full report. She was furious with herself!

Where exactly did that leave her?

Unburden yourself she decided.

Jesus!

She marched into the Clubhouse shop and examined the swimwear. She picked up a bikini the size of a bandana. Something new, she thought, although it was probably more suited to someone Lizzie's age than her own.

Another cute one caught her eye, and she tried it on; the color of darkening dusk, small frilly edging across the bust to the arms, but probably a bit too promiscuous.

She moved on and picked a backless solid black mallot trimmed with yellow cord at the straps. On her athletic body it looked like a good fit. She paid for it and proceeded to the Ladies lockers.

Alone at the pool, she dove into the still aquamarine water and relaxed in buoyancy before covering several laps.

There was energy she needed to expend, sending waves across the pool with clear rhythmic undulations that wiggled the racing lines at the bottom.

Finally, with the arrival to two happy boys who bomb shelled the surface, she floated with her eyes closed, giving them lots of room for their unbridled mirth and whale sized spluttering.

Adrift, she wondered how she could pull herself together to give Trevor a more credible picture...let along get the help she needed.

She emerged from the pool, silver water peeling off her lean body, and sank into her sun chair to dry like a garden turtle. Squinting in the sun, she found her belongings still under the Bermuda seating, and shut her eyes.

Almost identical in the photographs, Lizzie and Amanda were pictured at the party, just days ago.

 Photographers at airports were common enough. Pictures of those arriving or departing were good business for soliciting photographs for money. Travel, after all, was no longer considered the domain of the rich and famous, photographs of greetings were still a favorite.

One assortment were taken by such a photographer on the morning of the earthquake. Travelers leaving in haste, no doubt, would make news.

Trevor got them from the airline desk who had Lizzie's name and destination address.

There was Lizzie, in her jeans and packages. She was hugging Amanda, in another. Talking to Jacques in another, then all of them walking down the passage towards their respective gates of departure: Jacques was flying to London by another airline. Then Lizzie waving goodbye as she walked down her ramp for Istanbul.

Amanda swam once again to ward off the heat, toweled herself off and settled under the umbrella. Again she sifted through the images, again they had the effect of putting an indelible smile on her lips...

But then a troubling malaise was rising within her.

It had been two hours since she'd seen Trevor, and she felt suddenly overtaken by a sort of piqued ennui. She decided she couldn't stay any longer by the pool.

She left a message on Trevor's cell -- promising a dinner as a rain check, and packed away the pictures. Impatience trailed her strides as she walked out, head down.

It wasn't until she got home that she breathed with measured relief and collapsed on the sofa, tossing the pictures on the coffee table

* *

Trevor pulled her out of her reverie with a phone call. He wanted to know if she was alright. Could he make good on the rest of the afternoon? No need she assured him. Tonight then? No, she insisted, citing a long week and creeping fatigue, plus the need to clean house. But she appreciated the call. She hung up and rested her head on the pillow. Lizzie's emails were absent any comment about the parcel that had found its way into her bag, so clearly shown in the photos.

Amanda must have dozed off. Not for long, but enough to reinvigorate her energy.

She got up, brought some order to an apartment strewn with a week full of encroaching chaos, and made herself a delectable dinner of lamb chops, rice and Greek salad with pita bread.

With a glass of wine, she strolled out to the veranda and she leaned against the railing, balcony trellises flowing plumb ago and ivy geraniums flourishing around her.

She watched the day close as the sun sank beneath the distant surf, its job done.

"Adieu!" she said raising her glass and touting her pinkish suntan from the day. She watched the stars slowly take their stations as sparkling sentries of the heavens.

She didn't hear the first knocking, so a robust ringing brought her rushing in to open her door.

"*Hey! Hey! Hey!*" said Trevor, two glasses and a bottle of Chianti tucked under his arm. "May I come in or it is *interdict*?"

"Oh I'm sorry, Trevor, I just gave up sitting there in the sun by the pool!"

"No, please! 'Tis I who must apologize. God, what was I thinking... playing golf like a fool with a beautiful woman waiting at the pool?" Will you forgive me?" he said, his performance unfinished "Actually, I came to whisk you off...?"

"What?"

"...And, if you don't mind, Cinderella, you also have your carriage waiting below for... a midnight trot down the Cornish in the Mediterranean moonlight?" he beamed like the burly Scotsman that he was.

Amanda couldn't help laughing. It was a sweet gesture, his gallantry and his curls, his wine and absurd proposal. It must have taken some effort putting it all together.

She was thinking about how to dash his hopes, kindly -- as Lizzie would have wanted her to do . Instead she said "Oh what the hell."

She laughed spontaneously "For you, Trevor, I'll go anywhere... But bring me back on the dot before midnight; mind...that clock has wings for hands!"

He absolutely surprised her. Right there, at the Embassy Entrance, two large Greys stood fast, then stomped and snorted with a full jingling of reins. It was horse-drawn carriage that waited below, and the two Grays were festooned with frills, bells and damask gold braids.

Aghneighhhhh!

"A victory Chariot to thank the lady for her chaperoning duties" said Trevor, "with love, from Lizzie!" announced Trevor.

"Oh Trevor, that's very sweet of you all. Tell her...well... tell her... I shall enjoyed every minute...Wait. No. I'll tell her myself!"

He was taking the reins from the seated groom.

"What imagination!" said Amanda, thanking him.

Perambulations and processions down the Cornish seaside boulevard had brought its fare of traditions...

The traffic, evidently, was used to horse drawn carriages - favorite for tourists and sightseeing.

But at night?

The Cornish took on a new life at night, gradually leaving the traffic behind. Trevor poured his wine in two glasses. The sea revealed itself calmly shimmering under a dark sky flooded by moonlight.

They dismounted just before the inlet that marked the end of the Cornish, and Trevor dismissed the driver as Amanda propelled herself to the beach.

They strolled along the sand.

Suddenly, Trevor was running free, then grabbed her hand and propelled her to the water's edge where the waves swirled into the inlet with gentle swells of ebb and flow.

"Care for a swim?" he said pulling from his chest pocked the dusk bikini she had tried on with the faintly frilly edging...

"...How did you know that I..." she began, then paused "Of course...the err...shop attendant saw us come in together when you bought your golf balls. *Bastard!*"

She laughed, snatching the dangling fragments from his fingers.

"Well I am!" he said suddenly dropping his trousers to reveal a pair of legs in swimming gear.

"I've wanted to dive off that cliff since the day I got here. And now I can, since I'm half drunk and half naked ...And most of all, I'm with you!"

"You're not serious?"

"Just watch!" he said kicking up sand as he spun off

"Trevor!" she said. *Idiot*, is what she should have said, stuffing the swimwear into her bag

"You...can't..."

God I hate babysitting boys she thought, following him across the sand to the rocky mouth of the inlet. Sid, her own brother, was no different. You couldn't keep the kid out a pond if there was one in a hundred miles.

Damn. Damn. Damn. Trevor was half way up the rocks, the dark sea swirling in and edging up the surface with menacing swells before dropping out again.

This was no good, she decided.

He was drunk. She was drunk. They were playing. There was only way to avert, or rather, prepare for pending disaster...

Damn. She would head him off at the base and head for...for the water!

She saw his head above her, still climbing the small cliff and cupped her hands to shout.

"OK Elvis this is not Rio..." but the ineffective words flew into the night air.

He was heading for a ledge over the water. She looked down at the dark swells and saw to her dismay that the drop between rise and fall of the swells against the cliff was easily 25 ft. Could he see the unpredictable fluctuation let alone handle its swirling at impact. *In this darkness?*

Amanda started to work fast, flinging off her blouse she rooted into her back, slung into the skimpy swimwear and slipped safely into the water down a convenience ladder. She could at least be in the water to watch where he landed!

The seawater felt surprisingly warm against her skin. Below the surface, soft glints of luminous lighting reflected off the uneven sea floor, and the moon bathed the surface in soft diamonds and gleaming quivers.

She swam out easily, having sailed as a college graduate; swimming was something that came to her as easily as jogging. She reached the middle of the inlet and looked up.

Trevor was standing on his ledge, his tall form outstretched like a god in the moonlight, the position just before diving. He didn't even look down to consider the point of impact.

"Trevor!" she yelled up, waving. If she made him look down, he could take a bearing from her, like a beacon. But nothing could be heard as the water swirled into the inlet with the soft power of a hunching monster, rising up the sides of the rocks, and searching for fissures before receding for another surge.

Up went Amanda's swimming body, clearly twenty feet higher in surge without a real wave in sight. Then down she dropped with the receding water.

It was just at that moment, when Trevor launched from his platform, that she realized she had neither control over the rise and fall nor propulsion against the strong tow.

Where he landed was a mystery. She yelled, knowing not to panic, yet knowing she was in danger. Easily he could have dived into a sinking swirl. Or a growing swell.

The sea did not crash exactly, its just heaved, confined in the inlet, mysteriously looking for free passage and rising instead in menacing volume. Some places the water was luminous. Sometimes just black.

How far away was she from the walls of the cliff? Where was Trevor?

"Trevor!" she called in a controlled voice, salt tasting in her mouth and nose.

"Trevor!" Where the shadows began and the sea ended along the sides of the inlet was hard to define.

She knew enough from her training to head systematically back from the middle. From there she saw in the moonlight the glimmer of chrome of the convenience ladder that disappeared entirely beneath swells.

"Trevor" she called, carefully measuring her breathing and her level of panic. The idea of an accident --and Trevor gone - was closing in. Stay calm.

She approached the ladder and was still looking around. Swim. Swim. Pause. Twenty feet to the ladder.

"Trevor!"

Ten feet. Five feet. Two feet. Then suddenly she shrieked and choked.

From underwater she felt the touch of being enveloped by something. Up sprouted Trevor, inches from her face. She couldn't decide whether she was relieved at finding the ladder or Trevor. But she was safe. And so was he.

Then his lips were on hers. And with a firm push off the ladder, they were together entwined and lifting twenty feet in the sea swell, his mouth panting and touching at the same time.

She responded until breath and water was wanting...

"God you don't know how many times I've wanted to hold you like that!" he spluttered.

Amanda reached again for the ladder and resolutely climbed out, directing a few choice oaths at Trevor for scaring the hell out of her.

* *

It was well into the early dawn hours when she switched on her computer. There was a message

Re: Locating your Priestess

"After examining the evidence of the cuneiform sources, see attachment for historian Speiser who applies the custom to our biblical narrative and concludes that a close contemporary is found in someone we know in biblical terms: He talks of early biblical females of venerated status. First, of course, there's always Sarah.

"Sarah was Terah's daughter by adoption, which is why the relationship was not duly recorded in Genesis 11. At all events, Sarah had adequate credentials to qualify, in one way or another, as Abraham's sister in the broader sense of the term. The ambiguity of the dual usage of "sister" was used to disguise the situation to Pharaoh – "for he was duped' as Abraham and Sarah and the Lord knew he would be."

"While Speiser has written concerning a special legal adoption process among the Hurrians whereby one's wife "could have simultaneously the status of sister" I am hardly convinced that something isn't

missing here though the text is clearly pointing to that incident."

Well that's a help thought Amanda irritably.
She should have not replied. She should have waited. Instead she wrote:
"Why not dig up the Library of Alexandria and look there?"
She paused. Then added "What we need is a high priestess with a higher moral ground. Not a sister, exactly"
"True" came the sudden reply. *"But I'm exploring the female gendering of that era. Don't get frustrated!*

Amanda pulled away from the computer, embarrassed by her impetuous reply. Bob was too thoughtful a scholar to say any less.
She walked around the room, and settled on the same armchair that brought the photographs to her lap. She gazed at them again. The unsettled feelings of before crept over her, and she couldn't understand why she was feeling antsy.
She stayed up late reading. She got up twice. Drank water. Finally just as she dozed off in the early hours of the morning it hit her. She sat up suddenly.
"Impossible!"
She fumbled for the light. Ran out the room and rummaged through the photographs again. Two she clutched. Staring. Disbelieving.
Now she could understand Lizzie's emails.
In one of the two final two photographs of Lizzie leaving, she was holding her packages. The other,

just as she left down her own ramp, one package was gone!

No wonder the girl was clueless!

* *

Abram must have been devastated, thought Amanda, contemplating the scene. Even as he prayed to God about it. *Sarai, his wife: What had he done?*

He had shamed his father's household!

It must have been too awful to contemplate: Tabor, tenth descendant of Noah, in whose ancient tradition of the extended family and connected households of the tribe from Canaan, had raised Priests and Priestesses from various women, including Sarai. She was related by step-marriage and sometimes called sister in tribe-lineage terms, even chosen for him from his kinsmen as principle wife! *A Priestess of the Canaanite tradition, his wife!*

A beauty of such enormous respect and celebrated favor by their Patriarchs that even strangers and Princes fell for her!

As had Abimlebec, Prince of Pharaoh's household! Even as Amimlebec was made aware of his error, and tried so hard to make amends since those days when he first saw her and made overtures for her acquisition. What if he had broken the Oath of the Great Commission given to Abram by his God? What if…What if…All the people knew of the great Oath? The man's fame and his God were widespread and well known…

Abram had cleverly misled him, intonating that by being his sister, she was available! *Never mind that he meant tribal-sister by kinsmen!* And what if he had impugned her reputation – a Priestess no less -   and laid waste to their revered status, would not the god of Canaanites come down upon Abimlebec? Would not such a rumor devastate his Princely status? How would he be able to trade again? It was all too much, and all because that man Abram was in fear of being killed while sojourning in Egypt? Yes, that was what the scriptures said.

But what, thought Amanda, if he had to replenish his depleted stocks, and his livelihood – as well as all those of his group who depended on him, perhaps waiting further north for those Egyptian-provisions; those items of trade, inventory, elements of economic survival for them all? Was that a sort of death/tribe annihilation that Abram feared if he told the truth to Abimlebec? Was Sarah a sacrificial goat? What was the trade-off?

Perhaps that damned war-rescue for Lot (never mind that he had a wife that liked big city life). What if...what if Abram had difficult options before him: So desperately needing to re-provision.

Amanda thought about the words of the scripture. Sure Abimlebec might have killed him. But what if meant killing *of the greater good?* Killing caused by economic dispersion and destitution without Egyptian re-provisions?

And what about Abimlebec when he discovered that Abram had not been truthful about Sarah? What if he discovered Abram's *true* identity and regional reputation? His position with God? Was that an even worse indictment that Abimlebec most feared?

They had been sent away! Stocked to the gills with provisions - and expeditiously so, sent quickly away, nonetheless. Abimlebec wanted nothing more to do with them! This was a scandal that would never be lived down. It was dangerous. Uprisings? God himself might afflict them all, the locals might say...Life was so tenuous for peasants. Their existence was everything, their beliefs everything. *His reputation....?*

This Abram must have dwelled upon those thoughts as they trudged back north. Abraham embarrassed, lost, alone with his God. Sarah desolated, feeling betrayed by her husband?

She must have wanted to burn all that Amimlebec gave them as restitution. Provisions. Extra. Title for lands, ports, everything to be square with accounting and righteousness! Sarah must have wanted to burn everything given to them! *Everything. Everything. Everything.* The memory, the hurt, the feelings of betrayal...

She might never touch a thing of his. She might either leave everything to Abram to dispose of, or execute. Or she might have given stuff to her handmaidens, as gifts.

At any rate, thought Amanda, all must have been packed and repacked, then secured as cargo for beasts of burden to transport. Even in haste, lest trouble break out from any side. Soldiers and footmen were provided to escort the caravan north. Hastily, they left Egypt.

Even the gifts of title, deed and ownership of ports near Canaan given them by the Prince of Pharaoh, Abimlebec.

Recorded by the great recorders of the Phoenician scribes...

Copies now in sheaves and tablets to be kept safe for eternity - now historical legacies, if not cultural icons! Sealed by the Pharaoh and subsequent occupiers of lands if they wanted trade, shipping and survival to continue: Deeds that must be honored, venerated by peoples. Documents now shrouded in cultural if not national ownership, let alone Middle East sovereign boundaries?

This, in a world of modern terror; conflict, territorial disputes and religious factions.

Who... owned what?

Worse. Who had the *liability* of such ownership?

* *

Eighteen

Sunday morning came up too soon for Amanda. Trevor would already have been on the grounds of the Ambassador's residence assisting with the arrangements for the garden party. They would be discussing the guests and dignitaries - he briefing the ambassador with information. It was his job. There was only one way to find the solution to the manuscript, decided Amanda. And that was to find the source who gave to her.
She had a phone call to make.
She cleared her throat and began her message:
"This is Amanda..." Her voice crackled with apology. She flipped up her head and tossed away the silky folds of hair that encompassed the cell phone
"I err... OK: I hate to bother you with stale news, but I am concerned about a package that Lizzie took with her..."
"What with that morning's crisis to get her to the airport etc...It was a bit harrowing to say the least"
She paused
"Anyway, I am concerned that she misplaced some baggage, namely a package with some essential belongings...They appear to be...well, missing from her hands in the photographs."
She left the apartment and went down town. Finding most of the local souk closed, she walked

down the narrow streets, a soft breeze swirling debris from one shuttered kiosk to another. There was nobody about.

It had long been the custom of Beirut to honor the Sabbath - perhaps out of religious deference, or perhaps out of tradition when native food and entertaining was conducted in the family home, or perhaps out of commercial necessity.

But still, she pressed on, wandering down the empty market, turning a few corners, looking, as if for someone who might magically appear.

She gave up and settled for ice-cream along the strand.

Yes, it was the woman who talked with her and Lizzie at the souk, with the gold scarab in her nose – even if she was a suspect terrorist at the Embassy...

By mid-afternoon, she returned to her apartment feeling empty, and alone.

She decided to make an analysis of the situation and list the items she could ascertain with some certainty; items that needed further explaining.

It wasn't until she had completed her list and was feeling a little more organized with the events that she noticed a message, several in fact, on her answering machine. She had neglected to check when she entered her apartment.

It was Paula.

"You won't be missing our *'Great's'* tonight? Drinks - here first...Or, at 7pm later, at the open air theater. This is the last of the three lectures, and promises to be the best ever. Don't miss! See you!

Oh. Remember. Not far from the gate. *Son-et-Lumiere*. Free to the general public also."

* *

Bill Wickes had earlier welcomed them and made the introductions at the commencement of the show. He especially welcomed attendance by the local community, he said.

"So. Ladies and Gentlemen. In the open air and moonlit spirit of our evening here at the University Evening Lecture Series, I present you *The Greats: Married Maidens of Antiquity*."

The amphitheater was a granite structure, theatrical tiers around a stage at the heart of an assembly cradled. Cradled in subdued lighting, plush seating, and special audio visual acoustical enhancers, the audience of the modern auditorium was everywhere engaged. Even those seated in grassy knolls that surrounded the theater, and in between the stands.

The lights came up, shadows and sound filled the air.
"Good Evening!"
The lecturer came on stage, in a glow of light.
The speaker was the Lebanese Professor. Unusually tall with neutral colors of beige silk that matched olive skin and brown eyes expertly powdered. Her auburn hair was upswept au chignon. It was a decidedly sophisticated Mediterranean look, her drama emanating from a

jewelry set of black opals with canary diamonds, sapphires and pearls in white gold.

"In my talk on the *Married Maidens of Antiquity* I shall address the dietary cultures that shaped early culinary traditions. Also Migratory Trade Routes of food - from the earliest nomenclature of spices and early dyes found in regions specialized for their manufacture."

A burst of belly dancers and whirling Dervish swirled around her intonating the traditions of feasts, food and banqueting.

Eventually, the lights dimmed.

 "First accounts of Egypt come to us in Papyrus.

Later, the earliest married maidens of antiquity known in the time lines of the bible are in the accounts of Adam and Eve; Noah and his family followed by Abraham and Sarah. The women of King David include his wives and the beautiful Bathsheba, who gave birth to King Solomon. Women populated world of Christ, followed by those in the world of Mohammad.

Their imagery and iconography have shaped our art for centuries..."

Darkly, the sound of Greek furies broke in with wailing danger, and the auditorium turned silent.

"The real question that emerges in almost every culture is the rightful role and contribution to humanity that women, particularly the *Married Maiden*, have made to the advancement of humanity."

A harp.

The locals were there. A few came in with their sheroots and traditional vestments, hot from a day's sweat and labor. Most sat on the grassy knolls, entire families with children, all having passed through the Gate.

One man, it was told, had been stopped because he refused to part with his horse drawn cart. The MP's cited security reasons for keeping the horse out, to which the man responded by tying his beast to the wrought iron gate. Over the next three hours, there next to the gold-emblazoned insignia of the American Eagle, the animal stood. A man who passed inspection, strolled in and sat on the grass, not too close, but easily within the line of sight of the speaker's podium.

He little moved. Clothed in the garb of locals, he was well dressed, nonetheless. From his neck hung a keepsake, it was a large girasol signet ring of opal dangling from a chain. In his pocket were the keys to his BMW. The car was not outside. He had come in on foot, not too far behind the man with the cart and horse.

He watched the speaker intently. From here, he knew that... *she* knew... he was there. And gradually, it was clear she was aware of his presence.

Watching, he kept his distance throughout the Intermission.

She knew him of course. He was about to marry her niece.

She also knew that her nephew, the girl's brother...he had already manipulated.

Her voice remained steady, is strained.

Amanda was late. She had left a message to Paula telling her not to wait, she'd be at the auditorium...

The lights were down when she entered and she soon gave up trying to locate Paula's party. The Auditorium was already filled to capacity, and the show well underway.

The name, on the brochure was familiar. But Amanda was feeling itchy and concerned. Sure, they had been introduced. But their paths had crossed, perhaps too many times now? How had their contacts weaved together with her and Lizzie?

First, the girl at the souk whom Lizzie was talking to. Then the fleeting glimpse in the Garage photographs of the girl wearing the scarab? Who was it at the market that she spotted, that day? Then the encounter at the Seamstress' shop.

During the interval, Amanda tried to locate Paula. There were too many familiar faces to get anywhere close to the exits.

"How are you dear?" said Tom Rob of the Australian Embassy. They talked.

"Hey Amanda, you didn't return my calls!" said Sam from the Immigration section "I wanted to invite you to..."

Drinks, waiters, music and dazzling evening clothes could have made it a night at the opera. It was for that reason that Amanda made her move well before the conclusion to reach the Speaker.

Amanda met her in the hallway behind the stage at the rear lobby.

"Mrs. Kristopheros!" she said smartly. .

"Yes?" was the charming if now hoarse voice that had just delivered her lecture.

"I'm...err...Amanda Wells. I believe we have met?" she said, thrusting out her hand.

"I'm very glad to meet you" she said, recognition slowly dawning on her face.

"I very much enjoyed your talk. You are most informed about the role of women in early antiquity."

Amanda stared at the beautiful face, its almond green eyes, and the memory of those moments at the bazaar with Lizzie came flooding back. The woman stiffened, hardly moving.

"What University to do you hail from?" asked Amanda "that is...err...when you are not filling our lives with such interesting joy!"

"The University of Cairo" was the reply.

Those eyes, so magnificently made up with soft liner belonged to a sybarite beguiling. Those cheekbones that mantled a face of pink gloss and pumped lips. The veil was gone alright...

She was the girl's Aunt. The girl, Sophia. And something else. It was she who had persuaded Lizzie to buy the shawl at the French Quarter to give to Amanda. The professor!

"I was wondering about cultural traditions..." pressed Amanda. "There are some things that transcend our differences, like ancient treasures that belong in museums?"

The woman's countenance changed suddenly, as if she saw something. Or someone.

Was it behind...? Amanda turned to look back. The woman was leaving, but not before their eyes met, a look of clear gravity on her face, if not dread. She clearly yearned to talk, but could not.

Amanda's thoughts were a jumble all the way home.

What just happened there? Was it just woman's talk? Idle conversation?

The man at the gate, and the horse, was gone.

She should have gone home, waited for the morning. Within the safe confines of her secure office, she should have typed up an observation report and then handed it professionally to her superior. That's what she should have done.

She was at the door when Bill rose to the applause and thank the Lecturer - Mrs. Alexander Kristopheros who would be happy to answer any questions...

It was another good twenty minutes before the event finally wrapped up. At close range from just behind the platform Amanda had a good look at the retreating speaker. The familiarity was uncanny. The shape of the body, the form, those eyes, but it was not until Amanda was less than two feet away from her that she knew exactly who she was...

Amanda was still lost in her thoughts about the leather bound scrip.

How could she forget that posit?

Only now, even if she wanted to do something...

She had to locate the damned thing!

She picked up the phone. "Trevor... I think I may have some answers..." she began.

"If-you'd-like-to-leave-a-message" said the recorded messaging "... wait-for-the-beep...Bleep...If -you'd-like-to-leave-a- message... wait-for- the ..."

Of course, having not located him at the auditorium, he was clearly still with the Ambassador.

She was waiting for Trevor to return her call when she went online.

She queried "Lost Treasure" on her Google page of enquires.

National treasures were the first assets to flee the face of terrorism. Was it because of its intrinsic value? Perishability? Security compromised?

What happened to these items, she wondered.

Most recently treasures were stolen from the Museum of Baghdad during the fall of Saddam Hussein. These were hopelessly posted on world wide websites for easy recognition.

Amongst the many stolen treasures listed as Missing:

> *IM5572 was a large sand-colored stone statue of a male priest (15.2 x 38 cm), with an inscription on the right shoulder mentioning the goddess Nin-shu-pur, reputedly found in the vicinity of Adab (Bismaiya), datable to the 3rd Early Dynastic Period (c. 2500 B.C.)*

The list was endless.

 Most appalling to Amanda was an EBay scam by bidders trying to recapture authentic articles to peddle their fakes.

One article online by Ettore and Diana Nannetti even described the missing Trojan Gold when Munich fell to the allied forces. This account, Amanda knew had a happy ending.

Amanda knew that history had not been kind to art. Relics and great works of the hand were valued in the age of patronage, when dress and social standing represented access to capital and credit, often to showcase people in the theater of their life's toiling.

But the list was endless. Napoleon, monarchs of France, Spain, England and Holland cheerfully looting treasures on the high seas as piracy!

The pattern was the same. Finally, she found a scholarly article of recent publication curiously citing the looting and takings of cultural iconography as having patterns not dissimilar to Roman conquests and early societal conquests: To rob treasures was to rob a culture of its identity. Hence the defacing of earlier rulers in ancient Egyptian temples and tombs. It was a cultural eraser. A de-humanizing effort at reduction and population assimilation!

Nineteen

"You did *what..?*" thundered Trevor, eyes ablaze. Within the communications center, Trevor had an office.

His office had a fabulous view from windows. Its walls were oyster white; like the stucco vistas of the city below. His door, accessed only from a connecting hallway had glass panels, beyond the central desk. It was secure, a distance from any other communications offices. Today, you could hear his voice across the section.

He stopped pacing, glowered at her, then marched to the door and shut it firmly.

It wasn't long in the telling really, since she omitted most of the dangers and apprehensions that might make Trevor feel compromised.

She was also careful to show that Lizzie was never in danger – should he think so. So she kept her account within the realm of coincidence, almost like historical interest and possible connections.

More than anything, she wanted to avoid being met with questions and credibility and gaps.

"So where is it now?"

He said, standing over her with his hand running through his hair.

"I tried to talk to you..."

He was pacing again, and Amanda looked up at him from her seat of interrogation.

Why hadn't she said something before?

Why hadn't Lizzie?

Why had not the object itself - the very object that sent Amanda off the cliff, come forward for inspection?

Why did Amanda not disclose to her superior officer that she knew the woman in the photograph?

What were the connections? The time to analyze the situation was delayed. How to contain any damage, potential liabilities. These things he would have to answer.

Most importantly, was there any breach of security.

There was much to process. He looked at her, almost a look of betrayal. He had trusted her with personal expressions of attraction less than a day ago...

The *first* incident was lax. Had he been negligent? Finally he sat down.

 "Are you telling me the girl in this picture is none other than a professor espousing peace and cultural good will while moonlighting as a terrorist?"

"Well...not exactly..." began Amanda. Trevor was clearly frustrated.

"...And that she planted some bomb in your bag before she made a patsy out of you with a fake antique..."

"..And a Courier out of Lizzie...for God's sake, who is absolutely clueless about all this?"

He got up, incredulous. He stood over Amanda as if she were Judas himself.

She peered up at the shaken curls on his forehead and blue eyes ablaze with anxiety, almost afraid to respond. "Well...it's a possibility that...."

A knock at the door brought in Susan's face. "Ambassador's Monday meeting in five...err... Shall I have you excused?"

"No need. I'll be up shortly..." He turned back to Amanda

"Look" she said. "I tried to tell you ...but...in fact...on several occasions..."

"Well...what then?"

The phone rang. "Yes? Oh yes! The Jordanian Embassy luncheon at one o'clock. Have Yusef come round with the car if you don't mind. And...Err... Mrs. Anderson, could you field my calls for the day, I'm stacking up here just a bit...yes, thank you."

"Now see here" he began in his official voice when his cell phone chimed. His hand came down on the desk with a jerk and he picked it up to adjust the ringer to vibrating mode.

Damn it to hell Amanda ... What were you thinking?

"You need the full picture..." she said softly. And left.

Trevor glowered at the photographs on the table, his composure visibly unfastened at the threat they suggested.

"Amanda!" he called, fingering the cell phone

"Just be ...careful will you?" He looked like a defeated camp master.

"Yes Sir…" she said. Then added "It would have helped if you were a lot more…*accessible*?"

Susan was all smiles.

Amanda walked all the way to the coffee room muttering, if in two different languages.

 If office protocol weren't her credo, she would have pointed out that this was the best explanation for a possible suspect who had breached Embassy security.

Furthermore, if he hadn't been cavorting all night with the local flavors he'd probably have responded with greater clarity. She threw her paper cup into the basket.

JoAnne waived at her from the far end of the hall.

Only later did Amanda realize that what she saw in Trevor's eyes was more than righteous indignation, it was fear.

Fear for Lizzie.

One thing Amanda knew: The woman in question was no threat.

* *

Amanda got through the busy day and arrived, thankfully, in her apartment with an armful of grocery provisions and a lot of mail in her box.

Her brother had sent pictures of the kids from Wales. Her Dad a small gift from Maryland where he and his American wife lived. Also, she had two postcards from College friends. There were a couple of magazines, a book and two ordered CDs.

She anticipated a lovely evening of quiet at home entertainment. Actually she was exhausted. The weekend had been long.

A steak, French fries, and a salad revived her. And she had a beer.

Instead of listening to her phone messages or switching on her computer she took a long bath and decided to curl up in her silky sheets with a good book for the evening.

* *

She was reading a journal publication from a Biblical Antiquities Scholarship.

> *"So far, we have cited on the documentation the ports of Mersa Gawanis, first documented on Queen Hatshepsut's famous engravings of Punt - clearly an ancient port in pre-use to its depiction but only now being unearthed; Byblos, where we have commercial accounts listing the asset at the port by the Agency Executive (who gave away the assets*

* *

The soft shaded lamp cast a comforting light across her bed as she reviewed an assortment of books piled up for her enjoyment. There were two Elizabeth Peter's books, *Golden One* and *Children of the Storm* – vintage Amelia Peabody Emerson, and *Trojan Gold* Vicky Bliss. Then there was the most enchanting *Charlemagne's Tablecloth: a piquant History of 12th century Feasting*, by Nicola

Fletcher; followed by 15th century novels *Plays of Knaves; Lords and Isaac* by Margaret Frazer. A sanguine account of 18th century *Princesses of George III* by Flora Frasier.

She fingered them all. If she picked Elizabeth Peters, she'd be reading all night about Egyptology. What she needed was some rest tonight. So she picked, finally, Charlemagne, and kept an eye on the time for a decent light's out. But that was not to be.

She dozed off in the white silky comfort of her embroidered pillows, then shook herself awake. She was edgy, as if afraid to neglect something.

The day's events had clearly grated. Perhaps it was that fine line of definition that marks right from wrong, or "us" from "them"...the stuff of intellectual discourse in the age of reason and enlightenment.

The *Journey to Truth* is what man is made of said the great philosophers: Iterative thinking that marked the difference between him and animal.

"Other" as they defined it for academic debate. But who exactly was "Other"? Clearly, those outside the chosen children of God, right?

The answer eluded her, leaving her with a gap of answers in a world overtaken by chaos overlaps.

Perhaps, she mused, if she had a husband beside her he would be offering some lively discussion. if not levity. Or some rabid lovemaking, she leered longingly.

Even a friend to talk to! Hell, she'd settle for some wild-eyed college freak, if he was imaginative enough. She certainly had met a few. But no! *Here* on post it was all work. All business. All talk. She leaned over and turned off the light to drift off.

But sleep, real REM sleep, would not come gracefully it seemed. No. Nothing here was simple. Just ancient. Profound. Genetic material for humanity. She *was* in a bad mood. As if Trevor had the right to ...admonish her!

She sat up, switched on the lights and began rooting around her shelves for a materialized concept that held the key to her insomnia she decided. At least to brooding.

 Connected with memories of early childhood schooling, the soft leather bound book at her bedside, with its frilling edges and gilt title was... *where* exactly? Where was the silly thing? She tucked her head under the bed to see if it had become the dusty victim of a crammed bedside bookshelf. Nope!

But it was here somewhere? Wasn't there a bible in everybody's house somewhere?

She padded across the apartment, ran her finger along the bookshelves in the front room and wondered at the recollections of her untidy mind. She gave up. She switched off the light. Then froze in the doorway and switched it on again.

An orphaned stack of books perched precariously against a box marked "for shelf space when available" held her accusing gaze.

She pulled out the dark red volume and opened it softly, recognizing those inky family words inscribed on the cover page.

"To our darling Amanda on her Confirmation..."

The first few pages were rubric. So: Chapter One, Verse One.

"In the beginning God created the heaven and the earth..."

The ancient words of the first text flowed like a tender brook of fresh water. The rich imagery, tumbling along with timeless storytelling, was captivating, burdened only with meaning and secret wonders...

Yet when Amanda looked up, blinking, she wondered if God knew what he was doing when he let King James torture those early texts with Elizabethan English!

Finally she fell asleep.

**

Twenty

Mozart did not miss a beat on the extraordinary CD recording that Amanda had piping through her speakers. It was a glorious evening outside, and the gauze curtains swirled from the veranda door.

When the doorbell rang twice Amanda had an idea who it might be.

Jim stood against the door frame with his customary can of beer.

"I am your neighbor. Remember?"

"Hello, Jim!"

He walked right in and sat down at the dining table.

"Do come in, why don't you?"

"You forget the Welsh have an ear for good music!"

"Oh I'm sorry. I'll turn it down. I didn't mean to disturb your peace and quiet." She picked up the remote and turned down the volume.

"Can I get you anything?" she said moving to the kitchen counter and pulling out an assortment of sandwich fixings.

"Nope. I was wondering Amanda, If you might need a hooded monk as you slay your vampire!"

"My what..?"

"Just offering. That's all"

"Wait. What are you talking about?"

"Well, you must know that I work in IT...And as such...I must view much of our email traffic. Security procedures, STP, standard operating protocols, as you know."

"Go on"

"Well. You've been doing a lot of research, I see...And I'm getting a little worried about you. That's all."

Amanda was stunned. She was herself a scholar trained in the tools of research. Why would anyone think...

"The stuff I'm examining is purely academic. It's Nothing ..."

"No" he interrupted. "But it's the sources that it's coming from that I don't like Amanda. Some of these responses are coming from strange and not friendly webservers!"

"*What*?"

"Yes."

She had been chopping onion. She put down the knife and came over.

Jim was sitting at her table. Trevor was not.

She decided to tell him all.

"Trevor is no help at all...He, he.."

Jim sat calmly.

"Amanda. I do see the traffic he reads. Well most of it. Much is beyond my grade level. Honestly, he has to read stuff most people would never even dream of. Trust me. He has a lot on his mind"

"You'd never know it the way he cavorts around with women and..." her voice trailed.

"Precisely. That's what makes him such a valuable asset."

She looked at Jim. He was steady as a rock.

"Show him everything. Give him the images you made of the scrip – or whatever it is.... Tell him the facts. He can then write up a report and leave you unburdened." He paused.

"I just did. Well, most of the story, anyway."

He said nothing.

"I...err...I *am* frustrated with it all."

"Right. It's what we do Amanda. We're sitting on a political hot spot. Danger lurks in every signal; communication or event out here. It's unstable. We monitor everything. We must analyze everything! It's what we do to defend our nation, Amanda!"

She sat.

"Of course. How stupid of me.."

"I know you feel embarrassed at that early incident. Plus you were entertaining Trevor's sister, like you could have exposed her to danger..."

Amanda sighed.

Jim put his hand on her shoulder.

"You've...actually had a rough time of it since you got here. But this way it will put you in the clear of everything. Tell him everything. *He does need to know it all!*"

Finally she looked up. "I will. Thank you!"

* *

Trevor, as usual, only had an hour to spare. But he had agreed to meet with her before leaving for his trip. Official business, he said. Yusef was there waiting in the car too soon.

They had chosen the same little open Café by the sea, Armand. At night, it transformed into a magical carpet for Aladdin, tinkling with the soft sounds of Arabia, the odor of jasmine beneath a night sky of Orion."

"I've been remiss, Trevor. I am sorry. Here are the images of the item that is on Lizzie, I believe. I sent them to be analyzed by a trusted colleague. I should have brought them to you direct. Anyway, you should be aware of the details. It appears they might have cultural worth as a valuable...Again, I'm sorry for the all trouble I've caused."

Amanda gave Trevor a copy of the images, along with a complete file on all her findings. She explained the events that had plagued her for weeks.

His blue eyes never left her face. He listened without saying a word.

"It's all in there..." she said. "Read it discretely."

He touched her hand on the table.

Life, away from the Embassy, was personal in places like this. Places for the heart.

"Trevor...I'm so scared. Nowhere on the job description did it say *Religious Training Required!*"

He smiled "I have a grandmother who was Jewish!"

It brought a smile to her face.

"Thank *goodness*..." she said "...that you have a God somewhere in that lecherous heart of yours!"

He drew in more closely. "Let God have your heart...and I'll take your nubile body!"

"Trevor!" she squealed, then laughed softly.

"Look" he said "As diplomats it's not our job to meddle in other cultures. But as humans, we care about others, and that's the best we can do. Not to proselytize. Not to publicize. Not to institutionalize. Just be you - a human who cares. And you'll be fine!"

She looked up at him.

"And you...are beautiful" he said, getting up "But be careful!"

Yusef was approaching. "When I get back..." he looked up "Yes, hello Yusef..."

He leaned forward "I must go" and pecked her on the cheek. He put money on the waiter's tray, and followed his driver.

Yusef had him speeding down the highway before they could devise a plan.

She sat there, alone. Barely able to pull her thoughts together when a waitress, a solid woman in her forties, cleared away the table. She brought sweet Turkish coffee.

"Food...you like?" she had asked.

Amanda nodded politely. But what came next could not have surprised her more

"Your man..." the waitress said unobtrusively "I hope he rests well ...and arrives safely to his destination!"

Amanda looked up. "*What?*..."

She was quickly gone.

She hailed a taxi.

The words did not sink in until later that night. What an odd thing to say. And why did it bother her so?

Perhaps it was her imagination. Perhaps she saw the man in the background.

What man, exactly?

Later she would find out.

The Café was owned by the girl Sophia's family. That was Saoud. The Uncle.

My God. He had just issued a warning about Trevor's safety!

That evening, on her way back from the International Hotel where an event hosted by another Embassy, something else occurred. It was entirely a coincidence. Or she had stirred up the pot, somehow.

Or both?

As the taxi pulled away for the International Hotel, she saw the girl Sophia running from the Café. It was dark. At the corner was a young man crushing a cigarette with his foot. Amanda turned to look out the rear window of the Taxi. She saw them clasped in each other's arms.

Amanda had seen him before! He worked as an Intern at the American Hospital. Emmanuel. The son of Dr. Yani!

* *

Trevor MacDonnell emerged from the Jaffa Railway Station and took a taxi up Jerusalem Boulevard. In Tel Aviv for a debriefing on his special mission in Cairo, he checked into the St. George Hotel. He checked his watch; made his reservations in the dinning hall, and though without his driver, he decided to make his first appointment to a mission school.

The Tabeetha School of Jaffa, founded in 1863 and owned by the Church of Scotland, was actively providing education in English to children from Christian, Jewish and Muslim backgrounds. Trevor was a generous contributor to the Church of Scotland. A promise was a promise. He would visit.

He made his way through Jaffa. Its views of the Mediterranean Sea from the Jaffa Light, not unlike the famous paintings of Dutch master Lebrun from 1675, was stunning. Trevor knew of its torrid past, from a Bronze Age strategic military outpost to its recent Partition Plan made by the English, to establish the State of Israel. Jaffa, from which a Jewish suburb was carved, was now TelAviv. It had been the object of conquests, evictions, divisions and sectarianism. Even today, in a continuing dispute between religions, some quarters were considered subject to drug problems, crime and violence. Plus, Arab residents were complaining about Israeli authorities and their controversial housing settlements.

Old landmarks remained. For years Europeans attempted to find answers for a peaceful co-habitation between Christian, Muslim and Jewish peoples here, each culture having added richly to its history. The Lighthouse; the Greek Orthodox Monastery and St. Peter's Church at St Nicholas.

A Crusaders fortress, Immanuel Church, the Clock Tower. Above all, the Al Hahr Mosque held a commanding hilltop view of the Mediterranean Sea.

That evening, he took a stroll to watch the sunset. The next day began early.

"We had hopes for the Damascus Spring" said Davie Jones, Councilor for the Embassy in Tel Aviv. "Seemed like Assad's son, with all his European background, might actually bring the country into the twentieth century." Jones sipped his coffee, his legs crossed at the outdoor café where he and Trevor had just finished breakfast "...But for all the talk, forums, salons intellectual discussions - nothing changed!"

"A revolt was inevitable. Syria is a mess. Things will get a lot worse before things getting better..." he said. "Arab Spring - and a deteriorating global economy is not helping anyone here!"

"I understand" said Trevor

Jones drained his coffee "... Benny Salurum wants to talk with you before you return to Beirut. He's about as informed on the situation as anyone in the Israeli Authority."

"What's their position?"

"Their position, officially, is one of observation at this point. *They* are keeping us informed. But it's the stuff we *can't* see that worries us! You know, modern criminals using old ways to inflict damage..."

They walked back to the Hotel. "Here are some reports, the latest" continued Jones. "Keep them out of circulation, stay in touch...I want an ear on those border skirmishes!"

Once inside the lobby, Jones shook his hand. Trevor smiled to the Front Desk Receptionist and asked to check his messages. When he looked up, Davie was gone.

Upstairs, he found his room freshly turned out. He lay back on the bed, and began reading the Embassy Intelligence Report, most of which he already knew.

"The Assad family come from the Alani sect, an offshoot of Shiite Islam. They've had a tight grip, he and his father's family, over the Sunni Muslims and Kurds who frequently complained of socio economic inequality, cronyism, and deteriorations of standards of living and opportunities. They crushed opposition. With the country under emergency rule for 48 years, human rights are non-existent, and using a cult of personality, they've had a free reign on dictatorship.

"The central danger from Syria is its arsenal. Syria is thought to have the third largest stockpile of chemical weapons. For use against domestic enemies and possibly - as neighbors point out, internationally. Turkey, Israel, Jordan, Lebanon to name them..."

Trevor got up and poured himself a drink. It was an appalling condition, a loose cannon. The United States and its Allies had issued a Warning on this issues: A red line, if crossed by Ba'athist regime would be dangerous with "– enormous consequences –"

It was Trevor's job to make sure they complied.

He drained his scotch.

"Especially along the border regions with Lebanon. But that little thorny issue was easier said than done. The grip on Lebanon by Syrian Damascus was firm, especially when plots were reported in the newspapers, inciting rage. The Beirut government was allegedly made up of Syrian allies, including Hezbollah. But lately, cracks were appearing as the Hezbollah, once a militant group, was findings its own legs as a legitimate party endorsed by the people, and now voicing its objections to the Syrian grip...

That is, until it hit Israel.

"But trying to keep an even keel in Beirut, without letting the Syrian crisis spill over its borders. Thus even as whistleblowers are demonstrably assassinated, leaders of the Druze are quick to assert non-blame..."

Trevor knew it was dicey, at best, and dangerous as hell. Less a matter of "looking into the abyss" as one newspaper account put it, as it was fatigue from decades of fractional fighting and sectarian differences in Beirut.

Peace was sought by all locals. This, Trevor had to believe, if to verify he must. But something graver was his concern: Local uprising and malcontent was exposing less the failure of the regional conflicts as the inability of the international community to respond. Perhaps because of their ultimate belief that the era of their intervention had come to an end. Or perhaps because policy change in the west was insufficient.

Either way, Beirut would be used as patsy.

Trevor was to write his report. Instead, he packed up and decided to leave an hour earlier for the

Airport. Downstairs, as he checked out, he found a message.

 From Benny "S" for Saleroom.

"Diversion: Package coming through Lebanese transports, major shipment. Watch ports, intentions unknown..."

The only "diversion" coming through was the one he went to witness in Cairo. Something had happened with a change of plan somewhere. What he would have to discover is *what* the shipment was.

He turned around to face the lobby, clearly being watched, read the message, then in full view tore it up for proper disposal into a lobby waste paper basket.

He walked out of the hotel and hailed a Taxi for the Airport. His response was clear.

* *

Twenty One

Today, he was due back in the office. He might had even come in earlier. He had returned from his trip last night, presumably.

Amanda walked into Trevor's office wearing a linen tan skirt cut on the bias that swung at the knees. White canvas sandals on cork heels laced at the ankle gave her the tropical look of a girl on a beach, complete with floral bush shirt and white shell necklace. In the spirit of the day's events - which included an invite from Diane for a poolside Caribbean barbeque - but really for Trevor, she added the last adornment, a straw bag --containing fresh shots of Lizzie from her camera!

She had those ready, photos of Lizzie taken by Paul and Bill. She would show them to him. They were cute.

But she stopped abruptly in the doorway of his dark office: Desk, chair, paperwork starkly untouched since last night's janitors!

She spun around.

Nobody told her he was off for another official visit somewhere?

She marched to the coffee counter and poured herself a drink that managed to spill itself down her skirt.

"God Damn it!"

What irked her most was that she was taken by surprise. Then, in afterthought, she swanned back to her desk, sat with a pen and flipped over the calendar.

Of course it was scheduled! And in her own handwriting:

June 16th *"Official visit to Jordan"*.

June was a month full of visits including Amman...Jerusalem. How did she not recall?

She couldn't decide if it was her own oversight; the coffee spill, or the dark office that stole her morning hubris. She wanted to tear off the stupid shell necklace.

* *

Dawn could put Amanda almost a day ahead of the US on GMT. The email message from Lizzie would be one Amanda wanted to open, if only for its refreshing unadorned and unbridled *joy-de-vivre*.

"So, how's Sophia, (w/diamond in the nose, as in/ daughter of the PhD Prof) She got any new stuff in her store? Tell her I need a silver bracelet to go w/ my necklace! Only I bet she doesn't remember me so...

What yam doing these days A? I miss the club. The pool. The rock climbing and all that blue sea...Wow with all the guys at the AUB. Gees, what a Party, poker and golf, those dudes.

I miss you sooooooooooooooooooo much!!!!
Hey, tell Trev I'm ok. He is so gone on travel .... All the time
Did you find your book thing, or does Jacques still have it? I guess I she/ asked or sd something on the plane.
More later.
Loveya.."
Lizzie."

* *

Monday's dawn had the sun touch the Mediterranean, and as she took in the azure sea stretching endlessly into a pale horizon, Amanda decided that this was the view that made this job worth having; even if it was half way around the world from the sanitized environment of the West.

A world that she must walk into dressed, coiffed and business-like four floors below in just over an hour.

She turned her face into the breeze, for a few minutes more....She thought of Trevor, finished her coffee, and went inside to check her messages. Amanda showered, made a quick effort at tidying up an apartment that had seen a weekend of stretching out, book reading, swimwear, desk correspondence, ironing board, midnight dishes and perhaps a thin layer of dust if not salt carried in through open veranda doors.

Finally dressed, she watered her plants, straightened a stray rug and, picking up her handbag, cast a last glimpse on her space. It was organized, of sorts, imprinted by a life interested in color and curiosity. At any rate, the Janitors came in on Tuesday and they would leave the place dark, air conditioned and squared away like a vacant hotel room.

She got into the elevator and as the doors were closing when another resident from her floor Ian dashed in with barely his sleepwear off, pasting his hair down and jerking on his tie with a murderous knot.

"Morning!" he managed to say in the broken voice of a hangover.

"You need coffee!" she said sideways.

"And food" he added wistfully.

The itinerary on Trevor calendar showed a scheduled stop at Jerusalem. But someone had marked it off. She asked the office manager about Trevor's stop at Jerusalem. Cancelled, she was told.

By whom? She wanted to ask, but Amanda returned to her desk and began to sort essential papers before finding her way to her computer. She opened her e-mail.

The emails were nothing important and she cursed the spam that cluttered her screen a giant block of deletions.

 Lunch came suddenly, it seemed. She set up for a long email to Lizzie, a personal email, something she never did from her office.

She didn't want to sound alarmed about Trevor, but wanted to delineate her concern about his absence. She wondered if Lizzie would sense anxiety at this or accept it as an occupational hazard. She decided Lizzie was a big girl and could handle it. So she decided to show spreading concern:

"The girl we met in the souk – do you remember? – she turned up the other day...and she might be needing some help..." Amanda decided to keep writing, and asked Lizzie by the way, *"what happened to Jacques?"*...What did he say on the flight back, and did he give any indication about what his plans whereabouts? In fact, she urged Lizzie to think hard, since Trevor too would be served by the information. Amanda stopped short of expressing urgency, in case she tripped alarms, but she urged Lizzie to respond, and soon. She hit SAVE.

It wasn't that the matter was immunized, it's just that she couldn't identify the source of her disquiet. Not until she reached the ground floor on the elevator that she caught her breath:

Pushing the button on the elevator again, she returned to her office.

Most personnel had pretty much emptied out. A few last voices could be heard receding down the hallway. Mainly men's gathering laughter before the elevators closed on them.

She sat at the desk and reviewed the Calendar with Trevor's appointments. She examined June 18th.

The page had enlarged punch holes. It had been tampered. The calendar handwriting was her own, the date like all the others. But the sequence had been changed! She looked closely at June 16th: The second denomination had been altered an 8

to show only the peeping holes made to look like
June 16th
Trevor then, was unaccounted for.
She paused, holding her breath as she marshalled
her thoughts.
If so, he had missing for two days!
She returned to her message deferred to Lizzie
and added "Have you heard from Trevor recently?
Just asking"
<SEND>

* *

Amanda put on a raw silk cocktail dress for a
soiree at the Clubhouse.
She sat with the Spencer's in the Pavilion
consuming salty petit fours and club soda with a
twist of lime.
They danced, talked, and finally left. She
wondered if they every tired of the place.
She turned and leaned over the greens and took a
big breath of cool night air.
The air felt silky across her face, and she knew she
was ready to leave.
With a small hand wave here, and a big smile
there, Amanda crossed the dance floor with Jim
swaying gracefully with the music until she
reached the other side.
Jim would have held her to dancing with him if he
could. But Amanda worked her way through the
crowd where she managed to thank the host, and
leave.

The evening, as she applied the key to her apartment door, was uneventful in terms of culling through her thoughts. She sighed.

Nor had the swing of the party appeased her anxiety about Trevor. Come to think about it, she missed him. Damned hero of the night swims! She would give anything to be talking to him right now.

God, what was he doing at large? His duty? Then why the silence?

Clearly he was attached to a sortie of intelligence-gathering of some kind, probably at some dark border patrol post defined by barbed wire and desert hyenas.

Damn it Trevor. Where the hell are you?

She opened her e-mail, and to her surprise an entry came in from Jerusalem: It was forwarded as a message. Trevor had passed along her enquiry on the scrolls.

A translation had been made. In English! As she read it carefully, her eyes swam with soft tears. It could have been a love poem, or a passage from the Old Testament. The words tumbled like timeless roses.

Originally in Assyrian, translated later into Hebrew, it said. Possibly once inscribed on a letter, a scroll, as if to be carried by decree of some official kind. Perhaps later copied to parchment, they reiterate ancient intonations...."

"Behold, I have given to Beth Amanda the House of Pierez...Write it in the king's name, and seal it with the king's ring; for the writing which is written in the kings name, and sealed with the king's ring, no man reverse..."

Amanda's followed the post script.
These are clearly irrevocable words...and yet given to whom exactly? "We find similar language in the reign of King Ahasuerus when he decreed against the Jews in the Book of Esther...

It is a cultural known that women were the slave property of men, and that to have a document of redemption from a man or an owner was not only suppressed by a male dominated society, but a mark of extreme emancipation for the document holder and their family. In this case, it was decree of a political nature. Possibly allegiance of one party against another within the King's household. Clearly, this was a declaration of huge significance! If you consider that a woman's place as slave to the patriarch of the family, disposed of like chattel had worth or not, depending on marriage alliances. But to have a seal so clearly enunciated suggests a great deal of wealth...most probably associated with agrarian wealth of land usage, perhaps the control of a valuable resource, or trade route, by land, or by sea....In this case, over the centuries, we've come to develop some of the ancient routes of trade into modern commercial centers...Such A document rare indeed!
The question is, who? And where?
There is need for more analysis. Possible inscriptions that make it name specific....
Finally the last words of the message sank in.

"If anyone should have an original of this document, and produced it as some kind of deed with agency, it might hold sway in a court of law. Not only because it survived a male dominated culture, but in terms of antiquity value, the belongings of a lady princess or priestess many centuries old. Something to be kept safe for both intrinsic and cultural reasons, if not for the few million in monetary value... Even before the boundary descriptions, and its contested disputes...if any!"

Amanda was feeling that she had waded into things way beyond her understanding. She didn't even really understand her own culture -- let alone the culture of others...

* *

Later, much later in the day, when the waste basket was emptied, all that was found were the shreds of a Hotel bill ascribed to Trevor MacDonnell.

Clearly things on the border were getting derailed and overtaken by events - events that Trevor perceived as the greater threat.

Trevor had called Yusef's wife in Damascus. Her brother-in-law worked in Tel Aviv at the Taxi stands shuttling tourists to airports. Calmly, Trevor passed the written message to him as he loaded luggage into the Taxi.

 Neither was Trevor going to the Airport.

Yusef, Trevor's Embassy driver got the message from his brother. He found the opportunity, the next day, and gave it to one of Trevor's

Administrative Staff.   Yusef had approached her on the stairwell, not far from the cafeteria. He said he had something from Trevor, and she, in polite fashion, took the paper from his hand and inserted it into her folder, a folder that would be placed in Trevor's inbox.

* *

Amanda went through Trevor's Inbox. Confusing enough that Trevor was in Cairo, but this...? What Syria had anything to do with anything now on his agenda, was puzzling.
Of course, her own duplicity to officially reroute Trevor's mail back from London was something else, and short of illicit.
She needed to locate the manuscript, let alone what it said.
So, what *did Trevor want done with this*? Either he was too busy doing something else....or as Yusef put it, he was "in danger." A joke, right?
At first, Amanda was furious. Like all normal females, her feeling about bailing out men's problems was annoyance. What was *this* about? *What* delivery? Going *where*?

She got a message to go the Front Office. She flew down the hallway wondering if a nice boring job in a desk somewhere half way around the world wouldn't be better for her. But no! Here when you are called in to the Front Office, by God, you were being called into the Front Office... Her thoughts were spinning. Damn it all to hell, where was *Trevor?* She straightened her bouncing hair. What err...what was she wearing today? A Thakoon Addition dress in orange and black stripes with the ruffle! Did she look suitable? Yes? No? *Why not a beach ball too...*

Too late. The door opened.

"Miss Wells" said the Ambassador. "Please take a seat!"

She was the only staffer in the room. The two others already seated around the conference table were high ranking diplomats, and one American from the US State Department.

"We have news of a spot of trouble brewing in Syria. Could you find out all you can about the whereabouts of Trevor MacDonnell? Please to distribute your Report to each of us here, Eyes Only?"

"Yes Sir!"

"Err..." interrupted Mr. Thackery Julius "Will that take very long, Ms. Wells?"

Amanda was about to open her mouth and promise him a delivery date, signed, sealed and before breakfast when the Ambassador jumped in "Oh, let's say before the end of the week Julius. I'll pass it along to you all the minute I receive it. Ms. Wells is the best, trained in thorough findings and access to all important information in her office. Trevor recommends her highly." *He did?*

The Ambassador chuckled, by way of offering her cover, she made a dash for the door, and assuring them at the same time, that he was to see the first copy and read it first ONLY...

Amanda nodded politely. He led her to the door by the elbow whispering "Especially related to Iran, ok?"

"Yes Sir..." she breathed, returning to her office where it took her close to an hour to recover.

She had just received her new orders. And while Trevor was mentioned, even using his endorsements for her authorizations to access his material, the truth was, she knew nothing. Neither did anybody else in the room have a clue. That signaled one thing. Trouble. Alarm.

They did not know where Trevor was.

She marched out of her cubicle and into Trevor's office, closed the door, and switched on his computer using his access codes to intelligence grids everywhere. She wiggled about to make herself comfortable in his seat, muttering quietly to herself as the official government files opened up, one by one.

First things first. Game on!

So, Trevor MacDonnell. *Where are you?*

Actually, she should begin with fulfilling the Ambassador's mandate. What did he say ..."a spot of trouble in Syria..."

By the time she finished reading, her heart sank.

Damn right, a spot- of- trouble...Jesus!

Aleppo was now the site of staff treating injured rebel fighters and civilians... How was this possible, she wondered? Syrian had earned a place of respect amongst nations, right? According to the Human Rights Watch reporting to the United Nations, the government had created assault and terror centers against civilians... Death tolls were high, though it was hard to determine who were "Armed combatants" and who were rebel fighters.

She flipped on Trevor's button for the Cipher room and requested incoming message traffic from other Governments.

Intelligence reports cited the deployment of troops to zones within the border, and along the rims. The United Nations had already issued statements that said 2.5 million people needed help in this civil war – with over one million displaced. Thousands of refugees, and their children were fleeing to neighboring nations.

God, Amanda thought of the local Orphanage. For her part, Sister Margaret and her mission would be filling up with refugees. They would be under lock-down, she knew, for security reasons. Perhaps she would call them later...

Overseas, there were "consequences" for Syrian dissidents including those living in Canada, Chile, France, Germany Spain, Sweden the United Kingdom and the US.

Amanda scrolled down the e-list of heritage sites now damaged by shelling, many of them listed as World Heritage Sites, including the places...the places...*Oh my God!* The list went on.

...Places where Abram and Sarah had made their epic journey, a journey recorded in multiple Holy Scriptures charged by God's with a promise that would change the world. Destruction of antiquities had occurred because of bombs dropped by Syrian forces, or military entrenchment -- looting at various tells; museums and monuments now casualties of this conflict. Sites once monitored and recorded by archeologists.

The door flew open. "Amanda! I was wondering *who* would be in Trevor's office..." said Susan.

"Oh! Of course. Susan! I am sorry. I should have checked with you first. Just got a request to update the passwords and clean up administrative housekeeping, that's all. Be done in an hour!"

"Oh...Alright then. Carry on!" and she slammed the door.

And who made you Trevor's keeper? Amanda looked at her watch. Time was short. Queries, clearly.

Just then the fax machine spewed out fresh message traffic... (Hopefully Susan would be distant enough not to recognize the sputtering sound of the thing) That's when Amanda read what it was the Ambassador was most concerned about:

"Syria under pressure from Iran, leading with technical support and combat troops, especially the Revolutionary Guards to bolster Syrian military operations. Fighters trained in Iran for the Hezbollah, militants group based in Lebanon, deployed to attack rebels. Shipments of Arms and Troops coming going through Iraq – travelling across Iraq from Iran to Syria - include flying over their airspace still defense under Americans..."

Amanda shuddered. How could this be? Surely the Americans knew this..."Analysts in US State believe this conflict to be part of a regional proxy war between Sunni states - Turkey, Saudi Arabia and Qatar supporter of Sunni-led opposition, - Iran and Hezbollah, now pro Alawite-led government of Syria....ALERT. ALERT.."

Amanda waited. The machine started printing again "Christians in the area in extreme danger. US Personnel Alert. Evacuations underway. Commercial targets for overt aggression. Recommend cautionary warnings issued to leave the country and environs..."

Shortly after leaving Trevor's office in total darkness, Amanda saw Susan in the hallway who passed her with a haughty air of suspicion, silent. Had she cleared up thoroughly? No risk of exposure? No intelligence sites on the browser... None!

Amanda knew that by morning, the staff would be informed to start a program of purging personnel. Only essential personnel would be in place before the end of the year, she knew.

Amanda had delivered her reports to the Ambassador who thanked her profusely.

Still, she felt so helpless as she made her way back to her apartment, her thoughts of Sophie and her family.

She felt surrounded not by colors or meanings in the surroundings of life, but by an endless silence.

A deep, dark and empty silence.

Trevor? Where was *he* now?

* *

Twenty Two

She managed to get through the night, somewhat. Perhaps there was a storm at sea, for the night wind was filled with haunting lifts of hawk screeching and surges of gusts. In frenzied flailing, the curtains blew down a vase, and Amanda shut both veranda doors.

She toiled the sheets of a note-taking report into organized thoughts. Then into a large ball, and unfurled them back around her again. She opened the shutters. Now what?

And the question never left: Sleepless and weary she wondered how the effects of another issue would matter still. Clearly, it was related. Perhaps distress at the local level was already seeping into the mainstream? Conflict was known by its family of attending problems, like loss of standards, security, currency, authority...It would not be the first time that a local appealed to a foreign diplomat for aide on a personal level to solve personal problems.

She attempted again to align the possible connections of the sequence of events:

Why would such a document/or relic, if it hand any value, have been placed on her person...For its commercial worth. A theft? A mistake?

People would have been interested in preserving such a document. Perhaps it had been placed on her for safekeeping!

Yeah, right...some "safe-keeper" she became -- standing on the end of the jetty waiting for King Poseidon!

Clearly Sister Margaret saw something remarkable in that significance. But where had she gone to since those early weeks?

Amanda got up several times. She re-opened the windows and let the sounds of the night sky seep into her consciousness.

And the more she thought about it, the more she sensed a sinister meaning behind the actions. Was it a danger by default? Or a threat?

Would someone steal it on purpose?

She sat bolt upright in her bed. They would go for its value on a European market if they were antique dealers: In fact, it could be the deal of a lifetime!

Or they could steal and damage people for it.

Had she been placed in danger when the article was planted on her, like a bomb? Yes! The package was worse than a bomb. What possible connections to endangering her, but also sending a message...and then losing the evidence in a ...

Impossible!

Who would blow up a whole damned Embassy to bury such a document? If that *was* a plausible theory?

No. Surely not!

But had she placed *Lizzie* in danger when she gave it her? Who would steal it from Lizzie? Who would have known?

Jacques?

The thought was barely out of her mouth when she realized that not only Lizzie was a target but Trevor: Who had driven him off with the copies of the manuscript?

What if it wasn't just money?

What of its *cultural* significance? Had she inadvertently trampled on something that could upend religious doctrine or patriarchal domain?

Somehow, that didn't fit with the sweet nature of the Muslim characters around here... although it might suit Fundamentalists?

No!

So. If the Aunt placed it on her, then surely the matter in question was Sophia...

But what about the girl, Sophia?

How could such a lovely happy girl having to marry such an ugly old toad? Unless it was arranged. Why? He was after her for another reason?

Such as, *what,* exactly?

Documents of value had to say something of authority that was binding... in order to give value. That is, records of an event, or accounting of wealth, or had covenant ties with obligations, rights and agreements.

Clearly, the Professor had placed the item in Amanda's handbag. There was opportunity, motive and thought.

Where did that leave her? She needed authority for a thing to have value: So. Priestess implied things spiritual. But this might hold temporal value also, as in title of ownership?

Unless it was the Priestess who had the authority to bequeath something temporal. But then, if only men could write writs...

Unless the *name* of parties on the documents held legal tender of some kind...Or particular locations, like the rights to a location.

Ridiculous!

Priestesses belonged in the past ...After all, a name was cited, yes? No!

Eliminate what...emancipation for woman in the historical record? Surely not! Surely there are lots and lots of records, references and traditions and... This was getting nowhere.

Yet something was nibbling on the edges of a framework she could not put together...It was annoying as hell.

If not dangerous. Deadly.

Tuesday:

"Lizzie" she began her email. "I need to locate that manuscript you must have had in your bag on your way to the airport – you know, the thing I thought was a b..."

Amanda froze and looked at what she had written. That was no way to manage a problem. Not the direct approach. Especially to a teenager with colored hair whose brother was now missing...

"Lizzie" she began again. The rest came easy.

"Remember the girl in the souk? Sophia, daughter of a professor of ancient Middle Eastern history ... at Chez Francoise...the trousseau... marrying...etc., etc...

Dawn! She turned over, stretched, and realized that exhaustion, if not stress, had clearly caught up with her...She decided to snooze for an hour. That was hours ago!

Her mind was awake, and it wasn't long before she was up making coffee and plugging in the curling iron to straighten her hair for the day, now well frizzed.

The computer, she noticed, was still on. Moreover, there was a message. It was from Lizzie.

"I don't know what you mean... Amanda, I have seen no manuscript. Jacques disembarked at London but never came back up for the rest of the flight to New York, which he said he was going to do. Anyhow. That's all I know.

Tell Trevor to email me. I need money! Yes, I'll go to Baltimore if the thing (whatever they are) shows up. Yes, I know where BWI airport is. But please tell Trevor I *really really really* need money for school clothes OK?

Oh, Amanda, I need to tell you, I met this really cool guy... he's got a great ass...ok I never said that, Italian or something I think...loveya

Will talk later gottago. Lizzie"

With a college education costing close to $100,000 Amanda decided she needed to talk to Trevor about Lizzie's career track. *As if it were any of her business!*

But as she started her day, she decided she'd talk to Trevor about Lizzie's courses anyway. That is, when she next saw him. Where was he?

Trevor's absence was becoming seriously disturbing. Damn the Embassy protocol. She decided she would chase down his political contacts, if necessary. She sipped her coffee. What if, at the end of the day she was still no clearer on his situation? Time to press home to Lizzie about her concerns, security be damned. She wrote:

> *"Lizzie, I'm a little concerned about Trevor. I don't know where he is just now. Clearly, he hasn't contacted you. Anyway, I'm asking...*

Time passed quickly, and she returned to her flat for lunch. She searched for a reply to her email. Evidently, the 7 hour time zone difference to the States had found Lizzie up and responding.

> *"No. I don't know exactly. But I've gotten in touch with a girl on the plane that sat next to me and knew Jacques personally. In Istanbul, she had to change flights, and boarded for London, and she travelled in his company to London. She just emailed me something about he was asked aside at Heathrow. Perhaps about customs and security stuff. He is a known Antiquities Dealer with some issues that they wished to see him about. They confiscated all his baggage at Customs. .*
> *Let me know when you hear from Trevor."*

Amanda spent the rest of the afternoon using Trevor's authorized title and rank to make official enquiries about the passage of a certain Jacques de Torraine on a flight to Heathrow, the 7th of the month, from Beirut. Not exactly an official enquiry, nor a policy investigation, rather, for socio-diplomatic reasons of logistics related to the French.

It was not difficult to do on his behalf, since she frequently wrote up his communiqués.

But on this occasion, with Susan and half the office watching, she decided to send the message as coded and secure – one way of screening out non-secured staff from reading Trevor's traffic.

Next, she took the plunge.

Citing the need for matters of local culture and delicacy, she asked that any confiscated materials confiscated at Customs be returned to Beirut by delivery of the next Queens Messenger Service.

> *"Query Re A certain party arriving London from Beirut..."*

All afternoon she expected a call from the cipher room asking for confirmation about her point of authority for the message. Trevor should have been the one to sign for the requisition.

None came.

Upstairs, in her apartment at dinner time a message pulled her away from her reading. It was from her colleague, the professor.

Only one line. *"You have the real McCoy!"*

Amanda poured herself a drink.

Clearly, the scrip had been put on her person for a reason. It wasn't intended as a threat... not a bomb threat at all. She had been picked as a protective host.

But by whom? Why? Who from? She took another drink and realized that if someone was that desperate...someone *else* was after it.

Did that explain the woman in the garage...?

Desperate for the safe sound of familiar voices, Amanda moved to her telephone and punched the button for messages.

She let the messages roll on, sitting back. One message, a little odd, was Peggy saying that Bill had something he wanted her know about her "research"...

She relaxed, her head down between her knees to relieve her stiff neck. She rubbed. Then lay back on her sofa. A reality was sinking in.

She was the first in the office, and the midweek work load was little lighter than usual. She called down to the cipher room: Anyone know when Trevor was due back? They hollered around asking, and nobody knew. Someone said they weren't aware he was gone! No. Just kidding they said.

Trevor's Superior Officer, officially, was the Charge D'Affairs, Mr. Benton, ex-military engineering corps, a tall man of balding head who wore tan suits almost without relief. As far as he was concerned, he was in the Tropics.

She walked into his office and stopped. Today was no different, except perhaps his tie, a rusty terracotta color that actually harmonized with his hazel eyes.

"Come in my dear" he said perceptively "I hear you've been running the Section without Trevor!

The cipher rooms tell me you're pestering the hell out of their incoming box. Is that zeal or what?" he laughed.

OK she mused, let him smooth the way. "Yes, I'm sorry. But it's been busy and we all want to pitch in for Trevor in his absence. You know us women; we'd like to know where our hero is!"

"Ahah!"

"Trevor, I mean, we'd like to know when he's coming back... precisely..."

She saw his eyes glance at the batch of communications just placed on his desk. Had he noticed her messages to London asking for the QM to deliver materials ...

"Oh tomorrow I should think... Is there something troubling that has come in for him, perhaps I can help...?"

"No!" said Amanda, her eyes leveling with his. "We're getting a little nervous not having him in the office, it's a tight ship we run, and there are some issues of priority that we're quibbling about. His absence is getting to us..."

"Oh, I see. Well if it helps to know his itinerary, I can tell you he's parlaying some negotiations about security at the port of Haifa."

Amanda was no fool - and he was being told as much by her continued gaze.

"We're a little concerned about the Palestinian hold on their unfettered radicals, and they're straying all over the place without security checks...We'd like to see some movement on new port construction..."

Amanda stalked out and went into Trevor's office. She sifted through a pile of recent papers on his desk and finally looked up, her hands spread on the desk.

What port construction? There was no "new port construction" in the works!

Abruptly, she walked out and pressed the elevator for the third floor.

"Hi Amanda... You know we're on..." said Susan passing behind her with cute hand wave. Amanda was in no mood to socialize. Susan got ignored.

In the elevator was Mr. Schultz of the Trade Office accompanied by the German representative for Deutsche Bank. Behind him was Sam from Immigration downstairs carrying passports, travel brochures and a pile of visa applications.

They all nodded, smiling politely at the muted sounds of elevator dings. To their surprise Amanda marched out behind them on the third floor and headed directly to the great double glass doors that marked the waiting lounge of Ambassadorial suite.

"Can I help you?" said Catherine looking up from her front desk.

"I'd like to talk with Mr. Reynolds, Cathy" she said plainly.

Catherine de Rockport was too well disciplined in protocol to show surprise.

"He's on the phone to Turkey right now" she said, without prevarication.

Amanda glowered and agreed to sit and wait. The minutes passed slowly, and she wondered if she was making the right move.

"Is there something I can help you with Amanda?"

"No"

"Perhaps Mr. Simmonds can see you?"

"Catherine, I want to speak with Mr. Reynolds. It's personal."

Catherine opened her mouth to say something but changed her mind. Instead, she smiled, skillfully. "He'll be done in just a minute or two. I'll tell him he has a visitor!"

* *

Emmanuel, older than his friends by four years, stepped down the granite steps of the Kellogg School for business at Washington University and headed to the Quad where Shamir, Yakima and Sutti sat waiting.

"So?" said Sutti "Are you coming?"

"Oh Yeah!"

They approached the cafeteria, scattered across the food counters and collected again at the check outs carrying trays of Pizza, melted butter pretzels, pita sandwiches and power drinks.

Ani came over, a Muslim headdress scarf over her head, and she smiled at them. She had two friends with her. With red painted fingernails she waived "Hi Guys!"

"Hi" they said, and she moved on, her dark eyes and make- up belying a fabulous body beneath that somber headdress. She was from Lebanon.

Shamir dug Emmanuel in the ribs. Emmanuel glared back at Shamir with a fierce *What?*

Ani was Emmanuel's cousin, she was in America completing her Bachelor's degree in biology as a pre-requisite to Medicine - a degree that Emmanuel already had, along with most of his medical program except for his Internship and some missing graduate electives which he was now taking. In fact, he already had been scheduled to start at the University Hospital next semester.

Shamir shrugged. Just saying. Here was Emmanuel with this drop-dead cousin touting her stuff and he *ignored* her! Huh? *He and his family were something else*. Girls. Money. Cars. Houses. Yet he was pinning over some girl back home... poor shmuck!

"Hey Guys!" interrupted Sutti, checking his I-phone "Check this out. Some chick wants to sell her surf board for $400. It's a long board, says here it's had some wear, but available downtown...We take it?"

"Where?"

"Southwest waterfront area"

"Sounds unsafe place to be!" said Yakim, always the conservative. They all looked up.

"That's Capitol Hill, you idiot!"

"Get it! I'll pay. That makes three boards between the four of us. We leave Friday at 4pm. I'll book a hotel room at Rehoboth Beach"

"Dewey"

"Dewey Beach then"

"You're on! Four o'clock. My car. We go together and load the roof rack on the Jeep!"

"I'll come with you to Capitol Hill" said Yakim "I want to see what the neighborhood looks like"

They rolled their eyes at him.

"I got to go!" said Emmanuel "Psych 401, then History thru five o'clock. My place at six, okay everyone?"

He left for his class. When he emerged from his classes, he was a different man. He had received several messages on his iPhone from his Uncle in Syria.

Yes, he would be with his friends for the weekend and enjoy their surfing... But by Monday, for him, it was all over. His father had been arrested, his mother and sister gone. He was to fly back to help out on the civil war front with his medical skills... He would have to inform Ani, only.

And BTW, he could tell his cousin Ani to specialize in *Dentistry*, goddamn it!

* *

Twenty Three

In a world of international sharing of intelligence, branches of old sections were merging increasingly with highly integrated information gathering.

The collections of evidence from outstanding cases were well archived at the Customs Division of Scotland Yard. Some cases had special places, like security or international concern. That was the E Section supervised by the London police officer DeLaney.

He retrieved from the shelves the envelop in question. Evidence retrieved from Jacques de Torraine, April 8th, Heathrow. He read down the checked boxes: Contents nonflammable. Non-threatening. Ownership not yet fully identified by the Inspector's office. Investigation pending.

In the Inbox came a Special Permission Request of a letter dated May 2nd, the contents were to be handed over to Mr. Smith, Queen's Messenger, for personal courier service. Request approved, signed and endorsed by his superiors at the E Section. Before handing it over the counter to the tall young man asked Mr. Dupery to sign on the clipboard, dated it and kept a copy of the receipt.

It was not the first time that Special Permits Requests were issued for requests from the Foreign Office.

"Thank you" said the young man, and exited the building into a waiting cab. He disappeared into the traffic, and two people in the crowd who witnessed his movements, followed. Security precaution.

He never noticed that the package had been opened and resealed. It was an imperceptible alteration to the package.

Amanda was getting frustrated. She missed the academic rigors of testing prevailing wisdom recognized by a body of peers; collegian scholarship of enquiry was without prejudice or ridicule. She could use ten hours of research in a desolate archive for all this ceremonial bowing and scraping, she thought.

Harold Reynolds came out, sweeping away all formality. He had a strong, reassuring presence about him, and she could see how leadership came to him naturally. He led her to a casual seat by the window. He pulled up a chair in front of her, his back turned to all formal and gold embossed leather and mahogany desk of his official authority. She felt suddenly at ease.

Embassy staff, he said, was family. "Now, what's on your mind?"

"Trevor" she said simply. "He's been gone too long. I...err...we want to know why"

"His absence is causing you some concern in the Section?"

"Yes"

He got up, took several steps to his desk telephone and punched a few buttons.

"Hello, Ambrose? What's the status with Trevor? Oh....um...yes...I see...right you are then....Fine."

He returned to his seat and looked at Amanda. "He's at the hill station on the border, on post as an observer for us. There's been some trouble with insurgency combat. They've been pinned down, and we don't know the damage yet, or when we can extract him."

His blue eyes never blinked as he waited for Amanda to respond.

"Sorry to ask..." she began

"No. It *is* serious. I understand your concern. And I respect it." But he raised his finger to his lips to indicate silent running with the information.

Understandably, she was not on the Need-to-Know list, and she knew the interview was over. As she got up he said

"I know how much my wife appreciates your hand with her fashion show. It's on for next Sunday...yes? She really likes having you around, mainly because she doesn't have a clue about fashion!"

Amanda smiled "I'd be happy to help"

The Embassy car was waiting outside for the Ambassador as soon as she left the room, and she returned not to her office but to the Cafeteria on the ground level, beyond the hallway that flanked the Embassy security desk, partitioned off by bullet resistant glass.

There she spotted Yusuf, Trevor's driver and waved.

"I'm missing Trevor!" she mouthed through the

glass that separated him from the flow of people. Predictably, his face lit up, and he came out from behind the desk section to acknowledge her conversation.

"I'll be bringing him back on Sunday. Special assignment to the Ambassador" he added grinning, and she wondered why she had troubled Mr. Reynolds's office with her question. Yusuf knew everything!

"Going home this Friday to your lovely wife and children Yusuf?" she asked "We so enjoyed ourselves. Thank you again for your hospitality on our tour!"

"Oh not at all" he said grinning across the light brown face that everyone liked.

"No. I'm on duty this Friday. QM arrives tomorrow. I'm to pick him up and deliver him safely to the Embassy. " he added with somber responsibility.

She smiled.

"Thank you Miss Wells" he said, bowing slightly.

The lunch line in the Embassy Cafeteria was not long today. But since Amanda rarely came down for lunch, she feasted her eyes on the buffet anyway. Stuffed cabbage. Meatloaf. Green beans. Zucchini. Garden salad. Pasta primavera and tandura Chicken with rice. Bread rolls, and deserts galore. God, she'd have to run for a week if she ate all those delectable carbs and calories. Still, she knew that as staff, they were spoiled for choice.

There was Susan again.

With a tray amply loaded, she turned and spotted Sam in the far corner on a table for four. He was alone, and she walked over.

"May I join you?"

Sam looked up, and with sudden pleasure on face, waved the green apple in his hand, moved his paperwork over to accommodate her.

He swallowed.

"We're going on a trip to the mountains this weekend, Jim, Betty, Sid and I. Any chance you'd want to come?" he said.

Amanda laughed. "I'm afraid of heights! Besides, I'm not sure I can endure your jokes, Sam" He howled.

"Well, so that's why Jim gives you aid, succor and comfort on the top floor as your neighbor?"

"Just the 'Aid' part. And *I'm* usually doing the aiding! See, he forgets to buy food. And if it weren't for my sugar, ketchup, bread and water, he'd have perished long ago!"

Sam was easily entertained. Then she asked "Any clearer information on the intruder of the premises of two weeks ago?"

"What? Oh, that! No. No intruder. False alarm it turns out. The girl supposedly lurking in the garage was no other than a Sophia DeBrisieh. She's a student and was applying for a visa to study in London. She was here applying for a passport!" He munched. "Or her aunt was."

"Oh?"

"Her father was English. Her mother is or *was* Lebanese. Her brother was killed in a car accident.

Her aunt is a professor. She got caught on tape wandering around, looking..."

* *

She waited all day. The office staff were busy. The work was endless in communications traffic, much of it related to the recent conflagration of conflicts in the region. All of it requiring information processing, interpreting, assessments of damage control, political liabilities...
Then there were internal affairs. Staff meetings; personnel changes; rotations of duty, new directives, functions and time schedules.
Moreover, government officials from other nations in the diplomatic colony were calling; asking and seeking advice, guidance and information.
Finally, the day done, Amanda got up and stretched her legs. She did not relax in her apartment for the evening.
At the AUB Hospital, she was searching for the Intern, Emmanuel, who had examined her on a previous occasion. At the desk, they said he was "away" – tending to medical emergencies "elsewhere." Maybe later, in the Emergency room...
She was thinking.
Trouble on the boarder stations with casualties?
She sat outside the Emergency Room. He came over, long enough to smoke a cigarette. A casual chance outside encounter.

Amanda said hello.
He smiled shyly. She offered her hand, recalling her visit to the Emergency room following a car accident. His father saw her, he attended.
He remembered.
She said she was a friend of Professor Khristopheros. And Sophia, her niece. Did he know her?
The girl ... was being set up, he said brusquely, stubbing out his cigarette. Then he left abruptly,

Later, as Amanda pushed on the great brass handles of opulent glass doors to exit, Amanda felt her options closing.
She would walk along the Cornish for an evening stroll.
The staff had long left, and the gate guards were somewhat relaxed. They greeted her, jovially, and out she walked, crossing the great highway lined with palms and pines.
She got midway, tropical date trees boarding the tiny islands that gave pedestrians a break in the boulevard. The moist air blew, fast cars ripping past.
Eventually, she made it to the pedestrian Promenade of the Cornish, and walked.
 By dusk, local girls in pink lace dresses ran ahead of their families, boys on bikes. The women, wearing black skirts and frilly blouses, walked slowly in deference to the father whose evening treat it was to take them out.
Amanda just strolled, her athletic wear a clear indication that she was not local.

The information that she had garnered for the day was consistent.

Trevor's driver Yusuf expected him back. Ambassador Reynolds said he was on the boarder somewhere expected to be returning soon. He also said it was dangerous. Meaning what? *Had anyone been damaged there?* What business might the staff have with outposts other than collecting information on who was crossing and what?

Were there any recent suspicious movements, traffic, troops or arms crossing Israeli boarders? None. Besides, if there were, surely there would have been some commentary in the intelligence traffic. Nothing! Yet something struck her as inconsistent with the day's findings. Where?

She paused.

The woman?

Fortunately, no one challenged her official requisition for the contents of confiscated materials taken in at the Heathrow Customs office from Jacques de Touraine!

The internal investigation departments of the police units nearly always worked in tandem with State affairs and foreign requests: Amanda had made such a request using Trevor's authority.

Jacques had been spotted on his arrival at Heathrow Airport in London. Whatever he had on him, assuming he had lifted it from Lizzie, would be returned to her in Beirut by courier. A secure baggage of the QM on his route to Beirut, for *Eyes only* - and sealed within a special security pouch – authorized for release only to Trevor's office.

The QM, she knew was arriving Saturday. That would put the leather script back in her hands by the weekend...

Back she went to the Embassy, pressed the elevator button. She smiled a lot. One of the disadvantages of living on the top floor of the building was sharing the elevator as a resident with every professional who had to go up or down. Finally the thing rang out at her floor the elevator chrome doors opened. She walked out of the elevator impatiently and rounded the corner where she hit Jim head on in the stomach. Dazed, he rubbed his chest, and took a few steps back.

'Oh Jim, I'm so sorry...did I hurt you? I wasn't looking where I was going...are you alright?"

He looked at her, and grinned. "Want to make it up to me?"

"Really are you alright?" she was bending down trying to examine the damage.

"Relax... I'm OK!"

She straightened up, waiting for a little more assurance that his wits were still with him. Finally she said, "Sam invited me to your weekend trip this weekend. I know it's going to be a lot of fun..."

"Oh he did, did he?" said Jim still rubbing his chest, more for effect and sympathy "And you told him you'd come?" he added hopefully.

"No! I'm sorry Jim...They say it's dangerous on the boarder these days" she said.

"Nonsense!" he said brightly, if disappointed "It's that you can't stand to be confined in small places with me, eh?"

"Not at all. I'd come in a flash. Just some local socializing to do...promises to keep..."

"Oh. I see."

Once inside her apartment, she let out a deep breath and smiled at Jim's good nature.

Except for a... *No troubles on the boarder*? That was strange. Then he should know. He worked in the cipher room and had Top Security Clearances. He wouldn't be going on a weekend excursion. No. A thought struck her. Sam.

What was it Sam had said earlier today?

The girl Sophia was getting a visa? Why was she going to... *London*? What was she carrying? That was what had been troubling her all day. The girl had some connection...

The thoughts raced through her mind like a freight train. Why? She would find the girl and talk: Amanda might just have Trevor's whereabouts within her sights. Better than a rifle aiming for his head.

Border troubles my ass!

Or ...Or whatever that beast was doing before that wedding. She must go back.

The thought was barely grazing the margins of her consciousness when Amanda found herself flying down to the lobby and out the door for a cab.

She walked half way across the boulevard to stop a Taxi burning off a pair of skid marks to prevent hitting her. Her jacket, if it was fully on, was inside out, and she really didn't much care what her appearance one.

"The souk!" she managed to indicate, and only then did the taxi driver allow clarity to clear the expression off his brow. *A deranged woman!*

"But madam...."he began.

"Quickly!" she interrupted.

It took four minutes to negotiate the main boulevard on the Cornish, and then another ten to approach the souk from the highway filling with sidewalk strollers, restaurant tables for alfresco dinning and Cinderella ice-cream parlors. Cars were bringing people in, the street become a sociable balustrade rather than a market's throughway.

Only when Amanda tore into the souk did she see that the steel shutters and corrugated metal sheets that barred the open stores were padlocked. Of Course. It was all closed. Sunday! *Whatever* she was doing here, or *whoever* she wanted to meet...was ludicrous!

She walked a little, the sun setting upon the city of the ancients, and her thoughts settled into calm rationale.

She enumerated her options, and thought carefully over the details that had so eluded her.

There was a link lost on her. Somewhere, somehow, it was connected to the girl. *What was it?*

Moreover, if there was trouble on the Boarders, only the intelligence communities would know, right?

The Ambassador did say it was "serious." What did that mean, exactly in Embassy parlance? Did that mean *casualties*? How distant were those boarder troubles anyway?

So, why didn't Jim know about anything strange happening, when she saw him?

Perhaps the Ambassador was right?

Why would undercover operations become current content for communications traffic anyway? If that sensitive, then critical information was done by special coded communications, perhaps over phones...

No wonder Jim knew nothing: He had *seen* nothing!

She took a big breath.

Time to go home, she decided. She was wasting her energy out here.

She got into a taxi, and gave the address to the Embassy. But as he approached the familiar road, she asked for a sudden diversion, up the street to the entrance, not far, of the AUB.

The gate at the base was just opposite the side entrance of the British Embassy. And from the gate she walked onto the mountainside campus.

It was dark - a wilderness at night, but it was American guarded, and she enjoyed the safety of the place as she wended up the steep streets to the summit.

There, lit by an array of blue and white lights for emergency vehicles was the hospital of the AUB.

She sat outside in the dark, not far from the Emergency Room entrance.

There was a park bench.

She waited. One hour passed.

Two camouflaged special ops military American vehicles pulled in then backed up to the Emergency Room. Obscured from view, Amanda realized that they were unloading injured military combat personnel.

At one point, she spotted Emmanuel. He was taking them in, two on the stretchers. Others were in rough shape.

Maybe he knew the locations of where Trevor might be, thought Amanda.

Within a half an hour, another two vehicles drove up and delivered more combat injured.

It was dark, quiet, and in the night, almost happening without a ripple, the palm trees thrashing from a tropical dust storm.

Where were these men coming from?

* *

Trevor could hardly move his body. His muscles were stiff and his necked ached from the night vision goggles. Benny lay besides him in full combat uniform, the Insignia of the Israeli military divisions on his epaulet. They had been perched themselves behind desert boulders for two and half hours.

"How long have you been doing this?" he asked the man lying prone beside him.

"A couple of years, really..."

"So much for being a French archaeologist!" said Trevor sympathetically.

"Well yes. And no. My family 'ave been helping this cause for several generations, really. First watching the fundamentalists during the last century in Egypt. Then Syria"

Trevor squirmed and shuffled his body to lay on his back for a little relief from lying on his belly. He would have like to smoke a cigarette, of course. But that kind of light was visible for miles.

And in these desert regions, insurgents trained by Revolutionary Guards had possession of infrared technology way beyond most local military equipment.

"You've seen a few changes then, generationally speaking?"

Benny put down his hands and lay down her head.

"If you mean that my family is happy to have witnesses the inauguration of an Israeli state in 1948, then yes. It was a gratifying moment for us in Europe. Even if it had to come on the heels of WWII and at such a high cost..."

"I see."

"Well, I doubt that you do. But here you are, helping me on my mission as an Observer. God willing, we might survive to report the observing...Here, have some water!"

Trevor finally turned back to his position and raised the night vision goggles. He wasn't sure, but had a spec on the horizon shifted somewhat, or what...?"

Benny Salurum took a spell to rest facing upwards. "We live on the surface, so to speak, and have to keep our mouths shut. But there's one hell of a lot we can do to help *beneath* the surface." He said. "Like this...damned convoy"

"How did you get your Intel?"

"We have a source, in Cairo. An Indian by the name of *The Learned Unknown*, if you believe...Only he provides us better information through the commercial channels of arms trading than we do!"

"Sounds like a code handle to me...I wonder if I met him" mused Trevor, intent on his focus now.

"He's motivated because he makes money at it. He is, so far, entirely reliable. So here we are. Waiting on a shipment of Arms crossing over Iraq from Iran to Syria. That's what we do best, the Israelis. Waiting. Still, my job is to report to the French Government on their use of chemical weapons. "

"The French Government?"

"Yes. They have a colonial history here, long vested commercial interests and now a few political statements on the line...They're working with us."

Trevor focused upward and noticed a discoloration in the sky.

A reddish dust rose from the naked landscape.

"It's a convoy!" he said "A full-length convoy kicking up enough desert dust as to change the ambient color of the night sky"

"*Jesus!*" said Benny

"Yes. Here they come. Troop carriers, transports, flatbed, escort convoys...the lot...All coming over the hill. A small brigade, I'd say!"

"I'll transmit..." said Benny. "That's all we are to do. Witness, transmit the details, weights, tonnage, estimated cargo and number of force. Got it? So, stay low, they can see by radar. Hopefully, we've become part of these goddamned boulders by now on scanned imaging!"

"Got it!" said Trevor.

They grew in size, number and force. So many in fact, that Trevor wasn't sure if they had mistaken this mission to observe a "shipment" to a full scale Army supply line.

"All this mess is going to Syria?" asked Trevor

"Yep..."

"And across Allied territory?"

"Yep"

"What the hell does this mean? This makes us complicit parties in the conflict of Syria?"

"That's what I want you to report, Sir!"

"*Jesus!*" said Trevor.

"I already said that once" said Benny "...and I'm Jewish!"

They almost an hour to pass, and it was all they could do to keep from choking on dust inhalation. They lay positioned in a vale from which little air was rising as ventilation, crouched at the base of a twister spewing dirt, twigs, sand, gravel. The freight train whined by, grunting, stopping, grinding through gears and rattling with loads of arms, liquid barrels, short range missiles, towed-tanks, Arms cargo and ammunition crates. Punctuated throughout the convoy were troop transports full of soldiers carrying weapons, often flanked by lighter machine gunships as escort, each revving and shuttling around the slowing moving procession, headlights sweeping the trail continuously.

 What puzzled Trevor though, where the sealed tractor trailer trucks. They were moving vans, eighteen wheeled transportation trucks moving containerized shipping crates. It was a wonder their wheels didn't sink into the sand.

"What's in those trucks?" asked Trevor

"It better not be what I think it is..." whispered Benny.

Some stopped, evidently allowing men to jump off and relieve themselves before catching up with a short run to their armored vehicles.

Trevor and Benny had removed their goggles and duck frequently from roving headlights that grazed over them. Clearly, they had not been spotted.

The procession was almost beyond them when one set of headlights lingered. It switched off, in fact, and, staying in silence, waited, the desert night delivering its own echoes of time across space.

It waited an hour.

* *

Trevor and Benny were to be airlifted back to Tel Aviv where a debriefing would occur with the authorities. Verifications had to be made; observation from other sources had to be synchronized. When Trevor finally had his report prepared, they had been at it for days.

"What was in the convoy? For whom? Why? *Intention*?

An Israeli counter-assault? From where did they come?

The name of Saud came up. He was being watched, a Lebanese. His phone had been hacked. He had made a call to someone:

"And if its chemical weapons you're wondering about, then the answer is yes. We shall use them in abundance, if need be. But we would hardly bring them across the terrain like this, would we?" Saud, evidently, was not entirely convinced as to the severity of their conflict. "Besides, it's the vehicles of delivery that we have to transport like this. Hell, the chemical compounds could be brought in canisters, in the back of your own BMW..." laughed the caller.

Still, the question of the convoy was not entirely understood. *Why those tractor trailers?*

The answer came from Benny: Iran wasn't just shipping equipment and supplies to Syria, its ally, but it nuclear lab operations.

Everyone's eyes opened wide, the implications now grave.

Still, they agreed that the purpose was not even for use, but for now, simply for storage "

Why?

"Sanctions!"

Iran needed to have the sanctions lifted. The West had imposed sanctions on Iran for its nuclear program.

It was left to others to report that Iran was taking advantage of this crisis to remove its arsenal. Like Saddam attempted to do.

Such a theory did not surprise Trevor. Rightly or wrongly. It did worry him, however, if these decisions were no longer regional but strategic. This, the West already knew.

At any rate, his mission as observer was done.

He was exhausted.

That night he was abducted.

* *

Amanda walked into the AUB Hospital.

She strolled about, left towards the Emergency Entrance and on up to the waiting reception room. She knew the office of Dr Yani - the same who had checked her after the Earthquake. She saw a technician sitting in the lab across the hall. No, the doctor was not in. After hours...it was now. Could anyone else help? No? Would she like to leave her name with a message for Dr. Yannni..? He would be back in a few days...

Amanda suddenly realized that she hadn't eaten all day. She asked if the hospital coffee shop was open, and took directions.

She was sitting with her back to the entrance, coffee and toasted bagel with cheese on her plate when in walked the young Intern that had aided Dr. Yani, Emmanuel.

She nearly spilled her coffee, and watched him take his order from the counter. He was clearly doing a night shift. The blue hospital gown and cloth covered shoes belied little of his native features.

"Who is Assisting...?" said someone from outside. "Our Intern" came the reply.

She waited. This was one opportunity she would not loose. He recognized her the moment she sat at his booth.

The social exchange was short, one of remembrance, and polite.

Like all young professions making their statement he had shaved his head and wore dark Groucho spectacles.

"No latent symptoms like post trauma are there Miss Wells?" he said jovially.

"No. None at all." She smiled. "Better safe than sorry" she added loudly, acknowledging preventative action as legal defense.

She sensed his discomfort. Perhaps Sophia had told him about her?

Regardless. She would press at this opportunity.

"Look...err...there is something I wanted to ask you." She leaned forward.

"Do you know where Trevor MacDonnell is?" she asked, softly.

She watched for a response. Anything, if not some lip movement from the young man's expression.

"These wounded...where are coming from?"

 He averted his eyes, paled a little, then gestured with a general wave that implied another doctor, Dr. Zoe as the attending physician on duty... general procedure somewhere.

 But the gesture was not natural.

He looked up with a shrug against her unblinking stare, and he knew she was not fooled.

She leaned forward, invading his space and said in a quiet voice that gave him no quarter

"*Where?*"

He squirmed and looked around the cafeteria, cornered.

"He's at another location ...requiring medical attention..."

"At the border you mean, the military check points?"

"*Yes...*Yes. Hello! How lovely to see you" he said loudly, to a fellow Intern passing by.

She pressed, sottovoce "there's been trouble?"

"Some...err...Look!" He moved from her confrontational stance.

"When is he due back?"

"Stop! I'm not supposed to say..." he ripped the eyeglasses off his nose, and replaced them for a fresh start, his forehead wrinkling with anxiety.

"*When?*"

"In the next day or two..."

Two men, a technician and a nurse approached. Amanda looked up at the doctor, and smiled casually as they passed.

"with patients?" she asked.

He turned away and made to walk down the hallway. She brought her shoulder forward, then suddenly let out with a voice that made him turn, her hand reached for the collar of his scrubs "*When?*"

He made a big "shhhh..." with his fingers to his mouth.

She leveled her eyes with his, and reading her reckless despair said quietly.

"OK" He led her to a side room, a broom closet really, and closed the door. "Casualties. Two Americans, one French, and ...one of *yours*. They are being transported in a military airlift Saturday to Frankfurt for surgery ...if they survive!"

"Trevor MacDonnell?"

A small crowd of doctors ambled in followed by chattering nurses and staff. The boy saw them come and changed his expression in an amicable nod. He leaned forward to slide down a bench, and with a broad public smile he whispered hoarsely for only her to hear

"Critical condition...Shot"

"*Shot..?*"

What he said next shocked her even more.

"If we turn him over to the authorities, he will not survive. I can promise you that. He was targeted."

Amanda had stopped seeing.

Somehow raising the bottle of water, she took a sip, and had walked outsider. She raised both arms against the brick garden wall, eyes clenched. *Trevor?*

* *

Trevor was in his cell. Actually, it was not a cell, nor a prison. He could hear children's voices singing.

He met Saoud.

"You're at my school" he said congenially.

"I am not one to play at hard combat, you see, I'm only a shopkeeper..."

Trevor was not surprised. He had been held hostage for two days. There was more coming. He could guess what it was that they wanted, having observed the markings on the walls around him. It was a command center of some kind. Not for military strategy, but highly refined scholarly work.

On the walls around them wall- sized charts hanging the Phoenician alphabet and their corresponding letters.

One chart showed clear syllables of the Proto-Canaanite Alphabet for inscription, older than the first millennium BC. A non-pictographic-iconsonantal alphabet, or abiad - a Northern Semitic language of the Phoenicia, used by tradesman because it recorded only consonantal sounds, plus some meters selections for some vowels.

He knew it was the language of the manuscript, or an earlier *form* of the manuscript. The language on a manuscript that Amanda had given him just before he drove off.

Saoud backed off. "What do you think of our work?" he asked.

"Impressive!" said Trevor, his throat parched. He had examined some of the geometric symbols and letters. A beautiful circle that mean "eye". A delta shape that meant "door". A tall Y shape that meant "hook". An erect line, capped at the top and bottom, like the modern capital letter I meant "weapon". A three-tiered telephone pole meant "fish". A circle containing an X meant wheel...

Next came the Aramaic alphabet, a modified form of the Phoenician ancestor to modern Sybaris script. And of course, Hebrew script a stylistic variant of the Aramaic script was also charted on the wall.

But as the dates scrolled downward those angular and straight shapes gradually turned into the cursive versions of later times that came into the Neo-Punic alphabet of the Roman era of Northern Africa. Notably, the Greek alphabet and Latin, Cyrillic and Coptic letters, which Jacques noted resembled the exact lettering on the script that he saw. He searched for some letter values, changed to represent vowels as descendants of the Phoenician.

Trevor knew what they were after.

Saoud walked around the walls. "If we were to look at authenticity, we now can look at the evolution and translation itself as a measurement." He paused. "When we see distinct variations in different parts of Greece, evolving from these Phoenician characters that did not match Greek, we know it's on track for descendants. Then, when you get to Greek alphabets that evolved into the Latin alphabet, we can actually say we have some pedigree of lineage, an evolutionary accounting for the differences. Yes? For example, Phoenician shorthand was a short dash symbol as a world separator. Some habits seems to die hard, even as they crossed over and descended to younger generations..."

"Who do you represent?" asked Trevor.

Saoud ignored him.

"When first identified in the 19th century, Phoenician was considered a variation of the Egyptian hieroglyphs, even as hieroglyphs were being deciphered. Some even guessed at Hieratic, Cuneiform, theories that ascribed its creation to a single man, or the Kyksos people forming a sort of corrupted Egyptian form of language."

"What are your interests with this, other than antiquities theft in the Holy Land?"

Saoud looked at him, and pointed a wagging cautionary finger.

Trevor got the meaning. He was the one whose hands were tied. He was the prisoner here.

He had not wanted to alert the children, and quietly, he had sat.

"The Proto-Sinai script was in use from 1850 in the Sinai by Canaanite speakers. This particularly resonated with Jacques. This might be closer to anything in the room to what he saw in the scroll of Beirut."

"The rise of a new Semitic kingdom in the 13the centuries BC...?"

Saoud looked at him. "Water?"

Trevor nodded.

"I own a Restaurant. Maybe you have heard of it. Armand. So, I give you Peregrine, for drink, yes?"

He pulled out a bottle and placed it on the table.

"I show my precise as a humanitarian!" he said, cutting the electrical wire that bound Trevor's wrists.

"Fahdal! Please drink!"

Saoud continued. "Everything *before* this period.... is pretty much called "Proto-Canaanite", like stuff found on bronze arrowheads, yet "Phoenician" *after* 1050 BC."

He looked at Trevor. "The Phoenician alphabet succeeded in large part to develop into the Greek, Old Italic, and Anatolian and Paleohispanic scripts: One sound equals one symbol."

"Its good to have this school, here" said Saoud "Is simple to read. Simple to understand. Cuneiform and Egyptian hieroglyphs..."

"What is this? What is you want?"

"I want the original source of that text that was given to you by your administrator Amanda Wells!"

"Why?"

"coming from the maritime trading culture of Phoenician merchants - who spread the alphabet into parts of North Africa and Europe on their ships of trade goods. Their inscriptions - and indeed papyrus have been found in numerous archaeological sites, particularly in the former Phoenician cities and colonies around the Mediterranean, such as Byblos, Lebanon and Carthage in North Africa."

"So, on an original, it's pretty much marked in stone for eternity without disputation rights...?"

"But when the Phoenician letterforms are idealized, this meant something of significance relating to *titular ownership and proprietary* authority in the hierarchy. Yes?"

Twenty Four

One thing about the large compound of the American University of Beirut was that it was private and entirely self-contained. Also secure. Patrolled at the gates, it held teaching facilities; the hospital; park grounds and even apartment housing for Embassy personnel serving in Beirut. It was a sprawling mountainside campus, cared for in manner as to allow nature to have her way down the craggy rocks and tree falls that made a wilderness. Other areas where manicured and kept moist by sprinklers. For youngsters is was a haven.

One of the buildings housed the student interns, and sooner or later, the Lebanese- born Emmanuel would be traipsing through the courtyard lobby, Amanda knew.

Amanda waited. His ER shift might not end until midnight. Or three in the morning for all she knew. But lie in wait for him she would, crouched in her parked car, across the lane, and coffee in hand.

Promptly, at exactly fifteen minutes after midnight he appeared, gown slung sloppily over his shoulder and his shirt unbuttoned at the neck.

Amanda got herself into the central hall sitting pretty like a patient in a waiting room as he came through the glass doors. He stopped, surprised, and, looking up at the security monitors in the lobby, calmly made for the elevator.

She strolled up to him, all smiles, and apologized for bothering him, but wanted to ask him some questions. He looked around the empty space, hesitated, and then smiled suddenly.

"But of course Ms. Wells!" he said. "I am happy to help...shall we step out to the courtyard veranda?"

The night air was warm, and the open courtyard that served as the building entrance was softly lit by floor lights. They found a bench between eucalyptus trees...

Amanda decided to get to the point of her suspicions immediately. "I saw you with the girl Sophia?" She paused.

"You are Emmanuel. The girl's lover..."

He stared at her, searching for connections between his own attenuated world and Western assumptions. Perhaps the Professor Sophia's Aunt had informed Ms. Amanda Wells of her niece's betrothal to Saud?

"Oh that's OK" Amanda said quickly "It's just that I met Sophia, and she's doing a little research for me. She has quite an understanding about her heritage and ancient languages...Bright girl."

"Oh yes!" he said alertly, "She's a bright one that one, she should be studying..." he broke off, his ground unsure again.

Amanda smiled. "Yes I agree. Pity she can't go to school and study as a foreign student isn't it?"

This was too much for the fellow, he looked up with eyes full of words he felt unable to say, and he dived unsteadily into his pocket for a packet of cigarettes.

"Do you mind if I smoke?" he asked.

"Lizzie and I met her once, briefly. Lizzie told her she'd be delighted to have her if she went to the States...you know teenagers!"

"Really?" he said lighting up.

"Yes." said Amanda with emphatic deliberation.

He threw off his cigarette "That beast...he's going to send her to the border and set her up for a mission from which there is no return!"

He looked at her in utter frustration. "Why he picked her I don't know!"

"Let's make a deal. If I hand you Sophia, you switch over another patient for Trevor. And they both take off to Frankfurt?"

She told him everything.

Amanda left as soon as the conversation ended. No sense lingering. The exchange would take place on Saturday. That gave her two days. Tops. The guards at the gate knew her vehicle and she left the compound just before one o'clock in the morning.

Next...Yusef.

Yusef knew what was going on. He even knew of Saoud.

"He has a school" he said "not far from Damascus."

* *

It wasn't the easiest day to get started. Midweek at the office never was.

The Ambassador wanted his morning briefing with his staff. There were some issues that might need attention by everyone, he said, particularly on Border disputes. Plus there may be some local trouble, which everyone knew was euphemism for local terrorism. So he admonished everyone to be on the lookout, to take no chances, and be watchful for everyone else. He glanced briefly at Amanda before closing, his duty executed. He said nothing about Trevor.

A ton of communication traffic stacked up with a vengeance, stuff that without Trevor's decision making, left many in a quandary about who to re-route to.

Worse, workmen were everywhere installing new systems for staff security. Alarm pulls on each floor; disparate stairwell pathways; firewall procedures of extra security; independent air conditioning units on every floor.

They grated.

Everyone was feeling caged in their Embassy white marble building - once an open nest of *esprit de joie*. Amanda suppressed a momentary dislike for governmental authority doing less to allay fears than strengthen bars.

Still, he had to take every precaution.

It was raining outside, and steadily. That meant no promenades; no roof garden drinks in the evening and no veranda uses during the warm night. *Think of the good side, as her mother used to say, the plants need the rain!*

By the time she found Yusef, he had already delivered his charge by special pick up at the airport. The Queens Messenger had arrived and was already upstairs in the executive lounge, his briefcase doubtless with him.

"I'll take that!" said Amanda in the Mail Room. He acknowledge Amanda's position in Trevor's office and conceded.

She pulled over the small mail cart of cargo boxes marked Communications Section into the elevator and wheeled it right into Trevor's office, still dark, and unhitched the dolly. She left the dolly in the hallway, and closed the bars. She did not go into his office until lunch. The clerks would take care of the rest out there.

Susan came by. She smiled.

"Oh Susan. I wonder if you would mind that mail." Of course, she said. She hoped Trevor would be back soon, she said.

It still came as a surprise that her parcel was still unopened. Evidence in London had been left untouched unless by specialized authority once the investigation began. Luckily she had preempted their procedures by diverting it back to the Embassy.

So far, she thought, so good.

To pop the pretty parcel into her straw bag was easy enough to do, and while it was tempting to go to her apartment for lunch today, she decided, instead to go down to the cafeteria. There in arboretum section of the dining hall was Sam.

"Hia Sam!" she said with her food tray "You like your little corner under the banyan tree!" she said, flopping down.

She wondered if she should have just gone to his office. But why stack the odds with all this illicit maneuvering. So she kept things simple, and the conversation was coming along nicely.

"So...err... what exactly was she doing on the premises?"

"Who?" he munched.

"Sophia Antonella Kristophoros." asked Amanda without stating the obvious

"With an English parent, she's entitled to a British Passport...Only, I can't understand it."

He took another bite. "She was so damned excited about filling out the paper work and checking in to see if was ready every two days that I was really surprised when she failed to pick it up!"

"You mean you still have it?"

"Yes!"

"Look, I know the girl. She's professor Kristopheras' niece. You know, Bill Wickes has her lecturing at the AUB. I'm going to see her tomorrow! Shall I take it to her?"

He looked at her, even stopped chewing a tad, then resumed with gusto. Why not? Embassy staff were are security-cleared and reliable as couriers!

"OK. Sign for it, and it's yours to deliver!"

* *

The eye that greeted Amanda definitely belonged to the Ambassador. An enlarged specimen, it met her as she walked in on him inspecting an item under magnification light, an item from a pool of glitter on his desk.

"Oh! Excuse me Sir!" sputtered Amanda.

"Huh?" he said.

"Mrs. Reynolds...She, err...sent me in to ask that you consult with her about the seating arrangements being set up now in the gardens Sir?"

He looked up at a man in the darkness standing behind him and dimmed the magnification apparatus. "I shan't be long, Wilkins" he said, exhaling.

He got up and switched on the desk lights. Everything returned to normal. Amanda averted her eyes, but even as she did so she noted a dark felt draw-string bag sticking up, clearly open.

Damn! She had knocked on the door. Twice! Evidently, he was deeply engrossed in what he was doing. But his wife *had* tasked her to fetch him...

Amanda returned to the gardens and moved to the patio where orchestra and buffet were being set up. She checked the invitation list. She would stay away from the lawn area.

The fashion show was turning into quite an anticipated event, many invitees having accepted. The phones would be ringing for another hour yet, a last minute rush of responses to accept and get reservations.

Next, the flowers arrived, and also the presentation gifts. Amanda saw to them.

When the Ambassador walked out to consult with his wife on the lawn, they stepped away toward the stand of ornamental trees and talked, sometimes quietly, sometimes not. She was in a fluster evidently. He walked away, his face dark.

As the event preparations proceeded, Amanda turned to backstage dressing rooms; the communications systems, and especially the lighting for the runway stage to coordinate with the sound system. No one else did so.

The Banquet food buffets started to light up. Musicians arrived. They were to perform for the guests dining, and for the dance floor part of the show. As the string quartet unloaded its gear and arrange its electronics, the pale blue sky of the alfresco event deepened to cerulean blue. Soon it would turn to dark purple hues of an exotic Mediterranean night. Amanda pressed on.

The floor plan was for dinning on the lawns, dancing up on the great balustrade terrazzo of the grand villa, then the Fashion Show.

Amanda was pleased. It was going to be a beautiful night. She surveyed the food, bars and decorative flower arrangements, including the guest seating areas soon to be populated with crowds in gala jewels and tuxedo.

So, following the receiving line, she told the waiters, the Ambassador and his wife would be clearly at front and center - Theirs was the head table, from there a field of candlelit tables were to be served carefully, each table decked with yes, the silver, crystal glass, fine bone china flowers - and always to serve the ladies first...Timing was important, she insisted, as was wine and special orders.

Dancing would be concomitant with dinner. From there, they would all have an excellent view of the Fashion Show, and the fundraising would begin.

The Maître D' approached to ask if his stewards could begin lighting the lawn torches for the evening. Amanda got a call from the Ambassador's wife.

"Amanda dear, you've been wonderful. I knew I had asked the right person for help! It will be such a fun evening, you have worked so very hard today. Please check with me from time to time, I do get so hopelessly cornered and would like you to make sure I'm circulating nicely!"

"Of course Mrs. Reynolds"

Amanda chose a simple black Bottega Veneta dress for the evening, and notched down her footwear to dark Castaner espadrilles for serviceable duty. She had packed in advance, and changed easily for the occasion after a quick shower in the service quarters of the residence.

* *

Whatever misgivings she had about British bureaucrats during the day quickly dissipated as they entered the gates to the cypress gardens of the Chancery, official home of the Ambassador.

Lined with Toulouse-like trees swirling in the breeze, the red stone gravel driveway curved gently around Roman sculptures, Greek fountains and English topiary. To pull up to the Mansion had quite an effect.

It was private, safe, and under flood lights variably colored in the shimmering reflection pools. Inside, it was enchanting.

Most delegations had such retreats for their staff. Even the Russians, during the cold war years, had a special compound on the shores of the Chesapeake Bay not far from Washington DC.

Such places made people feel human again, if not rested, and this was such a time for the staff at Beirut.

Further, this evening's occasion was also one for entertaining other Delegations.

 Cocktails and hors drovers were served on the grand stone terrazzo. For fun, the Roman statuary were clothed in togas and laurels.

She felt the absence of Trevor.

Mrs. Reynolds kept taking Amanda by the hand to welcome a younger lot of new arrivals, one set Belgian, the other Spanish.

Amanda became aware of a conspicuous absence of many. But judging from the number of diplomatic cars in the parking lot, there was a clear assortment of nationalities present.

* *

Damn! Damn! Damn!
Someone must have alerted customs...?
Jacques did not like the response he would have to send back to England from New York.
Worse. The Metropolitan Museum of Fine Arts was expecting to receive the script as an endowment! It would have a Deed of Gift for a temporary exhibition. Its intrinsic value, rights, monetary valuations for insurance, ownership and entails would be reserved and recognized for the owner once it came onto American soil. He got the information from an informant within the staff administration...At some cost.
That implied that either the script had found its way to America, or was on its way to America!
Thank God!
Jacques went through the options. If the Metropolitan Museum was getting the benefit of the manuscript to augment its mission, then that constituted a donation of sorts, perhaps to mitigate the capital gains valuations expected by the Government if the asset reached America.
Further, by implication, the rights of ownership would also be recognized and legitimized *de facto* by the United States. Even if the actual valuations of the assets themselves remained un-monetized, and overseas.
So, if it was intended to come *into* the country with Lizzie, then, what he had lifted from her - and subsequently had had confiscated by customs - was not the authentic deal?
 Something had happened. What?
What irked him was that he never got a chance to examine the script for authenticity! Something

had been switched by someone who knew exactly what its worth and value was, the entire delivery pre-planned and *manipulated*? If so, who would be doing that?

Moreover, they knew what they were doing - even under duress of an earthquake Emergency. *Who*? Perhaps the Convent Orphanage - whose copy of the script he had seen in Amanda Wells' apartment, and which he had lifted off Lizzie. But he doubted it. Knowledgeable, yes, but willfully deceitful was not their style. That could get the Vatican in a lot of trouble. Although he knew that they had a veritable collection of antiquities within their vaults and interspersed amongst their repositories around the world that was unequalled.

No, he decided. It was not the Convent. That was something he could rule out with confidence.

So, perhaps Lizzie would be quizzed by Amanda, and perhaps the delivery would be getting *to* Lizzie, now that she was on American soil?.

So that left Amanda Wells possibly still in possession of the item, or well informed. He should have taken advantage of the situation while he was in Beirut! Dealing with a woman was one thing, and she was remarkable, true. But when it came to items of incalculable value with long term and lasting monetary revenue, well now that was something else. For Jacques it was all business.

Jacques knew what the consequences were: Not only for him and his London cohorts dealing in antiquities, but for corporate strategic investments counting on that revenue stream from commercial contracts – and big commerce it was – could be affected by its title of ownership, or liabilities from claimants.

 Above all else, he must keep it from getting on American soil.

Yes, he had definitely been too soft on Amanda Wells. He picked up the phone, and dialed London.

"We need to follow Amanda Wells. She is the key. She has the item, I'm sure of it. So far, she has been clever, very clever. It's time to apply pressure...."

"Umm..." Jacques listened, his face red with a hotness that left him uncomfortable.

What he heard next shocked him: *We have Trevor*

"I see..."

His instructions were not pretty, the phone call went on. He knew that when it came to doing business with contacts in the Middle East, an entirely new culture of operations was involved.

"Well, use whatever pressure you must...I'll call someone else to follow and track it down..."

He put away his cell phone and took the subway, his thoughts unsettled.

They had anticipated his dilemma and already planted a man within the staff. He was from London. He knew the Ambassador, had him well invested and compromised!

Jacques was uncomfortable. Dealing with antiquities merchants was one thing, but rogue members of the British Government was quite another.

The man's name in place was Wilkins.

* *

Saoud swatted a fly off the table. "I represent the strategic corporate interests of a large shipping company. We want the clear title to a port on the sea that is embroiled in nationalistic border issues.

....."It is in fact a deed legacy handed down to the high priestess of a people who belonged to the port regions of the Suez, and Caesarea and Tarsus..."

"And the owner is...who?"

Saoud strolled about. "The owner is me!"

"Really? So, why tell me this, your hostage?"

"Because I want to make sure that I get this title upon the marriage of a girl to whom this legacy is a bequest."

"How am I in your way?" asked Amanda, her throat dry.

Saoud grinned.

"You are a diplomat intent on securing commercial continuity for the West..."

"Where am I?"

"..just a few miles outside Damascus!" he laughed. "They will never find you. Especially if you are wounded. In these parts, nothing is truly accountable."

* *

Guests arrived on queue.

They turned the place into a fantasy magical land where people in gowns, glitter and full of laughter filled the air with excitement. The logistics moved beautifully, Amanda thought. Synchronous, without a hitch, the food, service, music, tone and lighting charmed everyone. Even the night air was filled with the scent of blossom. "Beautiful! Just beautiful..." extolled Mrs. Reynolds, sweeping by.

Amanda was beginning to relax just barely, even as she knew the moment of the Fashion Show was still ahead. Many were up and dancing when suddenly a hand at her elbow pressed gently. "Miss Wells? May I have the pleasure of this dance?"

It took her by surprise, somehow, the hours having flown by with success and grace. She looked up, and it was as if a small cold chill went down her spine. There was no mistaking the resolve in this man's eyes. Nor could she forget the *incident* of the earlier hours when she caught the Ambassador unawares. Here was the man who had been standing at his side!

He introduced himself and held her firmly, as if a child needing severe leading. Wilkins, he said his name was.

The moment passed quickly, the dance over. It was nothing really, just an innocent dance with a tall lanky gentlemen. Nobody would have noticed anything unusual about it...

The lights dimmed. Showtime.

An uneasy pause filled the air.

He had left his sting.

He knew where Trevor was.

He would like to question her later with regards her assignments, he said.

* *

She opened the show.

"Let East meet West" announced Lady Remington. "Let the fashion show begin: Ladies and Gentlemen, this simple effort is to remind you of the talent and tradition of this region's clothing industry and to also rise from this exhibition, a charitable donation for the victims of earthquakes... Please give generously, and buy, buy, buy!"

Amanda had spent hours rehearsing with the crew, and by now, the routine was set, except for the cables for the lights along the Runways. Mercifully, the show was going well. She had done all she could backstage. So she took a moment to sit down in the audience.

The show began with a soft tingling drumbeat.

A woman emerged from the shadows with traditional Eastern anklets tinkling with delicacy, her sari folds gentle as a mirage to the distant harmony of a hillside flutist.

But as the music mounted, she let the silken threads slide off her shoulder and trail with billowing drama, her silver bodice now a glittering sea of refractions in the moonlight. The music quivered.

By the time she danced to the end of the catwalk she had been embraced by wind vanes that sent her hair --and what remained of her saffron folds --flailing in fiery tempo to the drumbeats...

Then from the rafters two turbaned men leaped forward, and wearing dark suits, bow ties but no shirts stood dazzled by her beauty, and rushed to her feet on their imploring knees for a grand finale.

It brought the audience to its feet with applause.

It was a stunning success!

Except when Mrs. Reynolds turned to her once more for help entertaining, she looked pale with fatigue, and asked to be unofficially excused for the night.

And there was something more. She alluded to something that caught Amanda's attention. A comment made that surfaced innocently. Trevor's name came up. The MacDonnell lairds were not only in the line of royal succession, but a family, she said, that had a long history of aiding the cause of the Crown. Oh! How she would miss having Trevor around!

Clearly, decided Amanda, the woman was drunk. She had the wrong MacDonnell in mind. And she was losing it. Something the staff must shelter.

Why did she say she would miss having Trevor around unless she was already briefed on something...

Amanda finished her drink of ginger ale with lime and was thinking of leaving when she spotted someone off to the side whom she recognized as the Queen's Messenger.

He looked like a man being kept at bay for a while. She approached him and started a conversation which he was glad to engage of, Welshman that he was.

His return, he said, was anticipated to be Saturday, a German flight back to London.

Amanda listened politely.

"Yes. My son is getting married this week, and wants to be back in time...And yes, as always, Lufthansa is a very comfortable flight back with plenty of room for him and his baggage..."
It was all Amanda needed to know. She left shortly after ten o'clock.

* *

Twenty Five

She was herself exhausted when she returned, but she smiled.

It was inconceivable that the relic scroll had managed to get itself put into Lizzie luggage then lifted by Jacques – a thief? Perhaps he was under pressure of some sort? Perhaps his life had gone astray. Certainly his manner never showed any signs of stress. But then again, on recalling the conversations of the evening at the French Embassy, he had shown particular interest in the bound libretto, joking even about teenagers reading ledgers. ..

He was an antiquities dealer and had been perhaps followed and turned over to the police. Set up? But if that were the case, then Amanda -- and Lizzie for that matter, had been under surveillance?

She switched on her computer and composed a letter to Lizzie.

"Please pick up a friend,. You remember the girl...She needs a chauffeur for a few days. She has things to do. Help her find her way about, will you? *All expenses paid*, as reward, NYC!"

Amanda grinned.

"So be ready!" Amanda stared at the screen. Exactly what do you say? How could she be secure?
Finally she pounced on the key board.
"Trevor sends his love!"
 "*Be at BWI Sunday 8 AM Redeye from London. Your FRIEND.*"

She hit the SEND button sooner than she could think, and with that collapsed into the bed.

* *

It was Saturday. The Immigration and Visa Department window was open to the public for a few hours.
Sam clearly loved having her at his desk, and picked up the phone to dial the number to Sophia Antonella Kristopherous. Her Aunt Professor Kristopheros picked up. He introduced himself and said that Ms. Wells would like to speak with her. He handed Amanda the phone.
Amanda asked if was convenient to drop by around the lunch hour, and the Professor was effusive. The Mid-day hour was excellent she explained, because at that time they were all together and would be delighted to receive her. But when she explained, chiefly for the benefit of Sam, that she wanted to deliver the passport, what Amanda heard was not so easily concealed.
Amanda kept a gamely face and would not be put off.

Once again the word *passport* sent the professor into spasmodic intransigence: But why...Now that her daughter was getting married in a month...She spoke in rapid succession both languages, chiefly, it seemed, for the benefit of her own audience of listeners.

Amanda understood. There was pressure. It was public.

Amanda interrupted her in mid-sentence, and with a touch of laughter added "besides, I wanted to ask you further about that manuscript you knew about in the market bazaar... that day we met at the tailor...?"

There was silence. She looked at Sam who was clearly within hearing.

"Very well...Come then, of course, we would be delighted..."

"At noon then" said Amanda finally before hanging up resolutely.

Sam handed her a pen for a signature then turned over the package that contained visa and passport. Amanda walked out to the lobby and found the car waiting at the entrance; she got in, gave him the address and sat back, her eyes shut with relief as it pulled smoothly away.

The house amounted to a walled compound in the upper section of the city with a barred gate that led into the courtyard. The fact that the car stood waiting just outside the gate was not lost on the residents inside, and once Amanda emerged, she was greeted at the steps of a veranda. It was porch that wrapped gracefully around the villa swathed in grape vines and tropical green. Around the corner, was Sophia?

"My dear Ms. Wells..." began the professor ushering her into a room of seated guests "allow me to introduce you to my brother...my sister in law... my two nephews..." She alone wore a bright silk dress in deference to Western culture, but all others wore tan or black garb. The women were nodding and smiling shyly.

Amanda wondered if the man Saoud would be there. Not in person, evidently. But Sophia the girl was, now in the background and waiting her turn to shake hands. Amanda made sure to give her long and definitive eye contact while her Aunt flustered with offering drinks from servants waiting on the veranda.

Under the full force of a strong-willed Lebanese woman, Amanda was beginning to wilt. But not before she asked for the girl's help on the manuscript. And it was - understandably for security reasons, kept in the library of the Embassy building.

Seeing panic almost rob the professor of her composure she added softly "I'll make some digital images for her if you'd like...?"

"Of course..." said the professor, getting the full impact of an Amanda's resolve.

"We'll work on it together for a few hours today, and perhaps she could come back tomorrow?"

The girl was seated in Amanda apartment with a drink of lemonade in her hand. The place inspired her, she said and felt liberated to talk about her culture and her world of women and men.

"Does that suite you Sophia?" asked Amanda
"Absolutely!" she said defensively. "Saud is a good man. He is my uncle and will take care of me".
"Then who am I to argue with you?" replied Amanda. "Now, shall we get to work? I have the manuscript here with me. Can you read it?"
"Yes" she said, laying her hands over a document she recognized.
The hours passed quickly. Ice cream was laid on. Later, they would continue.
"Would Saturday afternoon be alright...Yes? I'll send the car for her then..."
She would call the aunt.

Amanda climbed back into the car, satisfied for the moment. Yet as she thought about it, there was edginess to the professor's pitch of voice bordering on panic, not entirely matched by her imploring eyes.
Clearly she was nervous.
There were hospitality invitations for the night. Amanda wanted none of them.

Amanda took a taxi and wandered down the Cornish, bought an ice-cream and walked.
So much had happened since that damned manuscript had come into her life.
Across the street was a restaurant where she and Trevor had eaten al fresco. She strolled along the promenade contemplating the effect that the pouch had had on her - from the first day of terrorized victimization to the new realities of life. She paused and looked out across the Mediterranean Sea glittering in diamonds, once a

dreamy new arrival with an exciting job, now feeling like a soul touched by the ancients.

She walked further down. She remembered Trevor, and his crazy night swim!

Oh God let him live... The idea that her actions might have put him in harm's way was irreconcilable.

The memory of that night in water warmly surging around them within a rocky lagoon - together locked in their private venturing-embrace, and it brought joy.

She was standing there with tears in her eyes.

She went home directly, and rather than call it a day, went instead to the dark roof top terrace of the building. She sat back in a deck chair, and watched stars drift across a heaven where God surely lived, and for whom so many had given their lives here in the Holy Land.

That's when it came to her. She sat up. Unbelievably clear, it now fell into place. She went inside and wrote down in her notes: The items of the Phoenician script was less a matter of owner, as to title to a location. Not only that, but its resources, without limit, the family of the patriarchs who must have handed it down as an inheritance. The inheritance, evidently, now belonged to the girl! As did the proceeds from its resources...

That's what the Uncle Saoud wanted! Once he married her, he would have it as inheritance by new law...

After that, it would be only a matter of time before he disposed of her. As he had her previous legatees, through the female line of inheritors; the mother, brother...

Amanda was rested and prepared for the day.

This was the day of the exchange. Casualties of an ambush ...to be re-routed directly onto a flight to Europe, as medical patients - without political ramifications...

She carried a small backpack of extra clothes and few emergency essentials. She checked her wrist watch for time, put the white package with the manuscript watched the time.

She went down to the Security desk and asked if Yusuf was around. Yes, he would be in at three o'clock. There was a later Airport run he had to make. The car she had ordered was waiting.

She checked her messages, and her heart skipped a beat. One asked for her to report to the office. Trevor's senior advisor was replaced, according to the message from the Ambassador, by a Mr. Wilkins. He wished her see her.

What to do? Did they suspect anything? Wasn't this the same man who quizzed her about Trevor at the Fashion Show? Was he not with the Ambassador that night?

What if he were...? Come to think of it, had he been officially introduced to the staff? Was he on staff, an Attaché, an inspector or something?

Was he legitimate? She couldn't believe she was asking herself these questions! She, a staffer...?

Then again, a staffer who had come into the country like a naïve idiot and made a total fool of herself on her first months... Someone without a long history, or understanding of much in these parts...

Yet, the questions lingered. *What if he...* If his intentions were less than. No! Surely not. That would implicate the Ambassador himself. Private profit was always a dalliance with which loyal staff could be tempted...Or pressure. Or coercion. God knows...But something was definitely not right. Besides, too late now.

Proceed, she decided.

Proceed, by God, and don't look back.

* *

"There you are Miss Wells!" called out Mr. Wilkins "Wait! I've been trying to reach you for hours!"

She had seen him through the glass partition wall of the Security Desk before rounding the corner to the front Lobby of the Embassy Entrance. Thick brass rimmed revolving doors revolved, and she pushed hard. Then outside she popped. Those indoor words were easily figured out, if left unfinished.

Normally, she could turn around and respond. She would pause, and explain. She could tell all.

Instead, something within her instinctively leaped at her throat for flight. Whatever she saw in there - just inside that building to which she had dedicated herself 24/7, a place she had considered a safe haven, was now threatening danger. She lifted her arm to hail a passing taxi.

She did not know the man. *She did not trust the man.* Trust had not been officially extended to him. He was an unknown. He had not been introduced by anyone in authority...

"Taxi!" she was panicking. It screeched. The vehicle was still rocking when she opened the rear door and slammed it shut, a bus blocking visibility to the Entrance, a shield.

"...to the Airport" she said "quickly, please!"

It had barely stopped, and the youth at the wheel took his job seriously to recognize an Embassy party being late for a plane. He pounced on the accelerator, and left the curb with a lurch.

Amanda opened her makeup compact. She moved it around her, seeing in the rear window of the cab. The man Wilkins was hailing a taxi and waving up security from the doors of the Embassy. Amanda's cab made a U turn and raced down the other lane of the Cornish beyond the median strip of plantings that divided the two highways. They were one cab in traffic passing fast, not particularly distinguishable by anyone. Good, they had swept by without notice. Or so she thought.

Wilkins suddenly pointed to her cab while he entered another taxi, and clearly gave his instructions to pursue, even as a staff car from the Embassy came around the corner as per his request. But he turned it down!

That, by Amanda's standards and protocols was unusual. He did not want to report his *cause for pursuit,* evidently. This was unofficial activity. He wanted to give chase in a damned taxi!

Hell, the man was working for himself, she decided. She made a sudden decision.

"Please, to the Convent of the Catholic Orphanage, now!" she asked the driver.

The driver looked back. Making good speed for a late plane-to-catch was one thing, but to change direction was another? He was clearly puzzled. She opened her wallet and presented him a bill of money. It had the right effect. He made a sharp turn into the heart of the city. At the next light just turning amber. *Good!*

She looked out the rear window. She waited to see the pursuing cab go sailing past. It almost did, then streaked on two wheels through a red light and turned right also.

 The color in her face drained. This was no Embassy protocol. My God. *Think fast!*

They moved from the Avenue de Paris section of the Corniche to the Luxury Apartment complex of the Four Seasons Tower and into Beirut Central. Everywhere, construction projects impeded their progress with traffic detours, barriers, banners, scaffolding, signage upgrades for Soldier, and the development company responsible, established by the Lebanese Prime Minister. The streets quickly changed. Beirut touted had seen its share of armed conflict, bombing, and shelling, first by the Syrian then by the Israelis

Amanda waved the driver on. And on. Not really knowing where she should go. He kept looking back at her, clearly flustered as his options flew by, his obligation to a rider sending him further into districts he knew he should not go...

"Madam..." he said, to no avail.

Amanda was fixed on peering out the rear cab window, watching for a pursuer.

The cab driver stopped. She turned. Had they arrived yet? What was the destination that she had achieved?

It was silent. She looked ahead, an empty city block, a downtown highway flanked by tall buildings of commerce and culture like any other capital, but absolutely void of humans. *No man's land*. She looked at the driver's face. It was blank, pained, and apologetic - but not for the reasons of the here and now! Rather, for reasons of a past fraught with anguish...

"The Green Line" he said. Just like that. In one of those human to human moments of understanding. Neither she, nor he, could say more. He had taken her as far as civilization had allowed, that line that separated west and east Beirut since 1982. Its story seemed inscribed on the silent walls of the buildings themselves, beautifully designed and built, but redolent with the marks of violence since the collapse of the Ottoman Empire following World War I when placed under the French Mandate. Then again in 1943 when it received its independence and flourished as a Capital city showing regional intellectual, tourism and banking from the Parisian Gulf oil boom.

Amanda looked around, this was a place fallen victim in 1975 to the Lebanese Civil War, dividing the city with Muslims on the western side, Christians on the eastern side. Even after 60,000 casualties, more followed: A Syrian siege of Achrafiyeh bombed the eastern quarter Christian militias defeated the Syrian elite forces in what would become a modern day Hundred Days War.

Later, in the Lebanon War, Western Beirut would come under siege by Israeli troops, such that even French and US barracks were attacked by suicide bombers.

Amanda felt as if she were in a free fall, a dead-end of sorts, peering down the alleys of desolation before her. "I'm sorry" she said "I'm trying to get away from someone...*As if he didn't know*. How much, err...how much do I owe you?"

"For you Madam, I take no more..." She paid and jumped out. He swerved and left.

As if just on queue, a slow car turned the corner behind her and she knew who it was. She did not run.

"Well, Miss Wells!" he said, his face mounted like cold steel armor. "You gave us quite a fright...Or, should I say *flight*. Perhaps, as member of the staff you have something to hide. Um?"

He was not only up to her, but remarkably, in company of an Armed Guard who stepped out his vehicle. How in the world he managed such a feat, if he had pursued her all this time, she could not understand. Unless of course, he had collaborated with authorities to intercept her and fix a point to merge with them? That meant further reinforcements were on their way... *What had he conjured up, about her?*

This was dangerous turf, with a highly sensitized police force responding to any acts of discord let alone potential threat...My God, he was treating her like the enemy! This man was no longer a friend, but a rogue who had inserted himself in the world she lived in, a world of strict security, protocols, conventions and safety for its staff. He had motives beyond his bounds. He was a private individual with motives that threatened her. He was an assailant.

"Is there something perhaps that you are hiding for us, Ms. Wells?" he bantered, the other circling to the flanks.

Something within her panicked, like a lion cornered. Not good. She was alone. Where, *where* to go? She turned, her leather pouch firmly affixed to her side, and Amanda vaulted into a dead run. She must have startled them, taking off down the Green Line. She ducked suddenly into a side alley where surely nobody went. Especially those in authority.

Where she emerged, finally, she was not sure. It seemed like a canyon of tall walls flanking her, a city of desertion. Then she turned.

Adjacent was a construction site where perhaps new beginnings were to emerge for the district. She crossed the fenced boundary, and stepped into the workmen's site now closed down for the day. She paused, moved slowly, and then waited for any signs of her assailants. Close to the cement pillars where rebar still poked out, she could peek out. Mounds of mortar and sand and mixing dregs still trailed at the ground level, she rested there.

For an hour she perched behind grey load-bearing bulkheads. From the sand and gravel mounds, the smell of the sea permeating still, damp, drying, grains about to be formed into something firm and stable, like a promise of new building materials having cinderblock and stone shapes. The sun passed overhead, her guard lowering, and it left bright spots and long shadows between tall girds and intended finished spaces. Amanda looked up, her mind wandering into the look that some architect must have envisioned; highly polished marble, glass walls and chrome. Fresh uses for a damaged neighborhood - blueprint lines marked with design and function - monetized by venture capital and hope for a new city. Never easy, always a risky, but greatly needed, she concluded.

She leaned back again a wall of freshly stacked cinderblock: Such thoughts came easily to someone from the West. Less so for those who had suffered so much and for so long - often forgotten or trapped in the crossfire of territorial claims and religious wars. *Would the world ever learn to live peaceably together?*

She felt stiff, yet in the strange silence of the site, somewhat safer from any pursuer. She moved from her hideout to another set of columns and watched carefully. No movement, anywhere. OK. So the coast was clear. She picked her hands off the dusty ground and started to brush them off when she heard a sound. Behind her.

She turned. Angling herself to recede further into cinderblocks, a safe wall from which she could peer out. Then she saw him. She froze.

A Lebanese youth was aiming an AK 47 Rifle at her.

* *

Twenty Six

She accepted the lamb kebabs, humus and pita bread with thanks. Hot tea followed, and a baklava on a chipped white china saucer.

The family was destitute, they said. Refugees from Syria hiding in the building at night, and existing on the fringes for fuel and food. The mother, grandmother and infant were tightly wound up in Muslim clothing, the men militant fighters.

"You can't be safe here, surely?" asked Amanda.

"No. We are not. But at the end of the day, it's the Muslims who feed us" said the youth nodding to the West side of the Green Line "...and the Christians who shelter us" nodding to the East side. They know we are here. And we're on a day to day existence.

"You speak English well" observed Amanda.

"My father...He was an American trained doctor." He averted his eyes. He need say no more.

The women were staring at her. She had been honest with them about being chased by someone on her staff that she did not recognize. Her problems seemed far away, but they understood, nodding only. The infant cried weakly.

They invited Amanda to sit with them and eat a meal, apologizing for their condition. The daughter gave her a shawl for her shoulders. But it was the youth who spoke, his rifle never far away.

"You are safe here, for the night, if you wish it..." he said.

"No" she said. "But thank you for your hospitality. I have a better idea!"

She dug into her bag, reached for her cell phone. Finally she looked up. It was all arranged.

The next day, Amanda showed up with a yellow school bus and drove them all to the Orphanage where the Sisters took them in.

Amanda waited in the front room of the Orphanage as she had once before with Sister Margaret. The great oak table seemed a little whiter in color, as if bleached or something. Or perhaps it was just the passage of time that did that to oak under the daily caressing of the sun. Like people, she mused.

The door opened. It was the Mother Superior who walked in. She folded her hands calmly.

"You did well, my dear" she said finally "We have a pipeline to a nearby Red Cross camp. The children are borderline healthy, and the women are dehydrated. The boy is fine...if broken hearted" she added. "How about you?"

Amanda looked up, smiled, her thoughts barely focused.   "They...err...They   have   Trevor MacDonnell" she said.

"I heard..."

Amanda looked down at her hands spread open on the wooden surface of the great oak table. "I don't know if I'm even doing the right thing anymore! The people I trusted...hell, I have NO credibility at all in this place!"

The Sister turned slightly "So. It's not so unusual to cry wolf in error. But not everybody does it on the end of a jetty with their hand stuck to a manuscript!" she added, her hands opening somewhat.

The effect was good. Amanda smiled. She took a deep breath.

Okay!

"The boy said he wants to go back to his village and look for their family. He said he wants to ask about *your man*, missing"

"Is that wise?"

"The poor fellow may get himself shot even before he reaches his village. It's hard to say. But of one thing we can be certain" she took a step forward "He shall never forget the kindness that you showed to his family by bringing them here for safety."

"What war *is this?*" asked Amanda.

"We do not involve ourselves with sectarian fighting. Only God's work of charity and love to all men..." She took a step back "Now. What are your plans? It is not good for you to hide here. You must report to your government immediately, and explain everything. A *misunderstanding*, perhaps?"

Amanda looked down at her cell phone and read the response she was waiting for "Right!"

"How can we help, otherwise?"

"Can you give me a ride to the AUB? I'll stay with Bill and Diane for a couple of days, and send a message to the Embassy Staff Administrator. .."

The Mother Superior nodded. "Can Sister Madeline take you in the truck? I have some

vegetables to be   picked up at the market…Be ready in half an hour, yes?"
She closed the door softly.

* *

Jacques was sitting in his hot tent in the south central desert. The sun bleached everything, the sand eroded everything and the wind leveled everything, as far as he was concerned.
He had just taken a shower, of sorts. A few clothes, hanging outside his tent between two trees would dry in ten minutes from dry gusts that blew relentlessly. He put them there to have a more frequent change of shirts for this god-awful perspiration in this god-awful climate.
"Dr. Jacques!" sang out a woman across the camp compound "We need your diagnosis if you would Dr. Jacques!" she added with the theatrical German intonations of the Indiana Jones movies.

He would have preferred to lay down on his cot for the next day or so, and leave it at that. But no. They wanted their labor out of any human they could get these archeologists. He got up, grabbed a shirt which he pulled over his shorts, put on his straw Panama beach hat stepped outside.
"Unless it's the Holy Grail itself, then I'm not interested!" he shouted back, his act.
Sandra Bellingham was a University of Pennsylvania graduate student working on a summer dig. She was pretty, white bloused and never sweaty. She appealed to him. Plus, she was knowledgeable.

"OK" she said "It's a campfire date for tonight, and we'll talk. But first, here!" she said, handing him a trowel. "Dig!"

"I did find something yesterday!" he whined

"A Bronze Age pig's tooth is not entirely a discovery, but neither is it chicken feed. So, not bad for a disco-boy!" she said, settling into a hot pit in the ground squared off with string grids and two students drawing on clipboards.

Those at the sieve giggled. Yep, he sure made a fool of himself with a few tunes, tequilas and twirls on the desert dirt dance floor with the girls last night! Worse, he made a late night sauna shower from a pierced water bag up a tree...

Luckily for him, there was plenty of cereal, yogurt and tea served at breakfast. And aspirins. All this for a little information from the world's leading authority on Phoenician scripts, and any ancient legacy titles to land ownership. He shrugged. It was done. They laughed, besides. Only the looks of admonishment that followed him all morning made it abundantly clear that this was no summer camp for teenagers; no military barracks on leave, and no unprofessional archaeological dig!

Still, he had made a faux pas. *Get the info and get out, that's it.*

"The word is written in several ways, with several meanings" she explained. "*Father/leader of a king; my father/leader*, a king was probably the most common reference amongst Philistine kings. The Biblical narrative implies a sort of crown prince, especially supported in the Haggada when "Benmelech" son of Abiomelech changes his name to Abimelech when becomes king...Also, *my father is MLK*, reference to a Canaanite deity named Moloch who demands child sacrificing for appeasement – something for which the God of Abraham specifically admonishes the children of Israel to put away in the Biblical texts."

"So, is there a connection to Sarah receiving any legacy from him as a Priestess, which she might pass on?"

"Well, Yes. And No. In that early references show the word Abimelech as prominent amongst the Philistines, perhaps king of Gerar, and king over this polytheistic society, it is no unlikely that the Biblical narrative is accurate with regards to the Sarah incident. Scholars argue for two counts: First, the town here which was known as a Philistine "lodging place" community features in two of the three patriarchal wife-sister narratives in Genesis, during the Middle Bronze period, and secondly, that Sarah's gifts, if you suggest she is the Priestess who received a legacy then passed it off to her handmaiden, if, if, if...again, then she might, I repeat *might* have conceivably handed it off to her handmaiden to keep. Entirely speculative of course, but if it had lasting value to a ...a Hagar, perhaps. Or handed down to a later wife by Abraham after Sarah dies...we don't know exactly. .."She looked at him apologetically "We can't be sure"

"Was it legitimate to offer any deed of gifts relating to land grants etc...?"

"Apparently so. Abimelech is shown trying to do right by Abraham's God, implying possible allegiance some scholars say: We *do* see the name appear later down through Biblical history, like

Abimelech in the book of Judges proclaimed king after the death of his father Gideon; then the son of Abiathat, a high priest in the time of David in First Chronicles and Second Samuel. So, he might have aligned himself with the Children of Israel as a family with inheritance rights."

"What about *here*?"

"Here, archaeologically, we see the king of Gath, or Aschish, referred to as Abimlech in the title of Psalm 34. It was most likely the valley of Gerar mentioned in the Book of Genesis, but back then it was a large city in southern Canaan covering some 40 acres. See, over there, there's a rampart clearly associated with the Philistine plain."

"You're doing good work!"

"Thank you! I have a lot to write up this season. Everyone here is very excited about what we're finding. We'd like to prove the scriptures, of course, but that's everyone's dream. God's Word and our world seem to meet only rarely, I suppose. Historically, we do have connections. We do know that according to Genesis 20, Abraham lived here after living between Kadesh and Shur in western Sinai, and that the King of Gerar took his wife then returned her for 1000 shekels of silver. Possibly offering more, in the way of deeded lands and gifts. We can only speculate... "

"So, how does the title gifts survive through time, in real legitimate terms, today?"

"Legalistically, I don't know, given the sovereign history of territorial conquests since then. But spiritually, they mean a lot. They might even mean more than real boundaries in terms of commerce. See, on each document is a reference to God. If no God is acknowledge, then no document is ratified. So, if anything was executed sans God's endorsement over the passage of history, then they are non-binding, and their legacy claims of legitimate becomes contestable."

"How about these, then?" pointed Jacques, referring to what he had procured in the markets of Jaffa.

"References do exist of such exchanges. They were avid marketing accountants, back then!" she laughed "Look at the Amarna Tablets. Or the Tuthmoisid Period, when such exchanges of value are referenced in later ancient Egyptian letters when cataloging conquests of Canaanite cities, like a loot list. Also found monumental inscriptions, and other unknown un-catalogued scripts and documents..."

"Like this one?"

She looked at his scroll. "Possibly! Without provenance it's hard to say...But there is much that has gone undocumented about the ancient world. Who knows?" She got up. For Sandra Bellingham the conversation was over, Jacques knew. Here was that imaginary line between the documented world of the scholarly, and the undocumented world of antiquities dealers. And unless contested before a court, the two never met.

Jacques understood. It was a treasure for the antiquities markets; the scholarly communities, and the governments related to its culture. But it had more significance, and Jacques was getting the picture.

"In terms of commerce, it may have a great deal of meaning to one of the Mediterranean's key ports, and its rights of usage and protections..."

He nodded.

"It might mean some bartering or diplomatic negotiating, let alone an understanding of its commercial contracting."

Still, he got what he came for.

Confirmation that what he had *was corroborating evidence of a parallel scripts that proved one thing.*

The item in the possession of Amanda Wells was real.

He would assign a man to do the work. *He could get his hands on it now!*

* *

Amanda found Sophia waiting at the gate. No need to rouse the whole brigade thought Amanda as she opened the window and invited the girl in with a wave to the family standing on the steps.

The car pulled away, and Amanda asked the driver to return to the Embassy. This relaxed the girl visibly, and slowly Amanda asked her a few questions about her interest in history, her knowledge of ancient languages and her heritage, all of which she was happy to answer.

As they approached the Embassy, Amanda leaned forward

"Could you drop us at the corner? We'll walk around" she said, implying that that they would take the garage entrance to the building.

They began to walk up the sloped street across from the Embassy and the AUB. Amanda was moving at a leisurely pace, and Sophia, who had a head scarf, looked furtively about. Amanda had the distinct impression she would have preferred just now to retreat behind the safety of the shadows. But then she stopped suddenly, and all anxiety drained from her face.

Just inside the gated entrance of the AUB she saw Emmanuel Yani leaning against a shiny Mercedes, smoking. She wanted to run, her breath caught in her throat, and she looked pleadingly at Amanda who nodded.

She flew across the street, and the guards seeing Amanda behind her allowed her to pass. Emmanuel looked up, his dark hair tumbling down his forehead. He too would have like to run to her. Instead he waited, allowing them both to approach. Then he opened the rear door and invited them both inside.

He jumped into the driver's seat and pulled up to the hospital parking lot and turned to face Sophia, she kissing and leaning over the seat with happiness and surprise.

"Come with me" he said, getting out and striding into the Emergency room doorway. She followed. Amanda held back.

They turned into his office and shut the door. A few minutes later Amanda knocked on the door. Time was getting close.

Emmanuel opened the door.

"You were followed!" he said roughly. The overhead hospital speakers were growling "Dr.

Yani. Please come to Surgery immediately. Dr. Yani..."

"I've got to go. Put these on her!" he said planting some hospital whites on Amanda and flying out the door. The girl was weeping.

"Sophia. It's for your own good..."

She said calmly "He ...he...told me..!" her scarf now a handkerchief for tears, "Saud is...is..." the reality was sinking in. She could hardly utter the words: She was being sent to a Syrian terrorist camp by her new husband to be trained as a ...suicide bomber.

"He killed my mother...and my brother!"

The expression on her face was disbelief. Why me? It was a horrible question in her eyes. Yet even as she was asking, the answer was obvious. For money! He had the power to do so once she was married.

"May he die in the pit of hell!" she said suddenly in English.

"Spoken like any good Christian!" said Amanda, laughing at the joke. "Now really, Sophia. Pull yourself together."

"My aunt...does she ...?"

Amanda felt compelled to take her into her arms and give her a hug.

The response was another flood of tears.

She nodded disconsolately.

"This is the manuscript that your aunt probably put on me at the souk. It frightened me half to... It is *yours* By right! Take it... You'll be going through from London to BWI where Lizzie -- remember Lizzie? --where Lizzie will be meeting you in the morning!"

"But I want to give it away!" she stamped her leg.

"No. You won't. It'll be a keepsake piece for your family.   I don't really know what it will reveal, exactly. But it is yours by inheritance."

The girl looked up.

"I do know that someone appealed to me for help. If I have helped, then I'm satisfied! So, if it has survived all these years it is important for you to know what it says. And then *you* make your decisions. Do you understand?"

The girl smiled gamely.

"Now. We must make this work, OK?"

Sophia shed her clothes in record time then stopped suddenly "will you tell my aunt...?"

Amanda looked at her squarely. "She will know that you are safe. And she knows you love her more than anything. Now hurry!"

Emmanuel Yani was back "All ready?" Sophia smiled her brave face dry and clean.

He turned to Amanda "Passport?"

"She's got it!" replied Amanda, and with rattling efficiency she replaced everything back into the bag. He acknowledged.

"It's time! Lufthansa leaves in half an hour: We have special medical privilege from the tarmac into the rear cargo hold with pressurized cabin space. Now let's go!"

She followed the two of them down the hall.

He marched them into the surgery room where another door led to the operating theater number 3. He scrubbed, and without seeing anyone around he then ushered them in through the door.

Yusuf was immediately recognized by Amanda. He was pushing a gurney, rigged with fluids feeding a patient. She knew who the patient was. He looked dead.

Another patient was in a wheelchair. Together they proceeded towards the exit and a waiting ambulance.

Trevor's eyes were closed. His face was ashen and hardly recognizable. But he was alive. Amanda remained steady. .

As they approached the ambulance, a change took place. The girl replaced the nurse in the wheelchair, Yani took the wheelchair into the ambulance.

"The others?" asked Amanda

"Dead" said Yusuf.

The doors were about to shut. Yani lurched forward "Wait..." he said "Thank you!" He nodded towards the patient "And...I'll stay with him in London."

Amanda looked into the face of youth grown old with the realization that he had been alienated from his own. The girl sat across from him, weeping in a sightless stupor that Amanda realized was a condition induced by sedation.

Amanda turned back to spot the approaching search lights.

 "Good luck" she managed to say as the door slammed shut and she imagined that she saw him take Sophie's hand in his own.

Police sirens shredded the cover of night runways. It was the authorities come to collect their patients at the Hospital. They went inside to present themselves as the Ambulance pulled away as a routine call. In it were their subjects of interest.

Hopefully, by the time the policy identified who was where, the patients would have driven on the airport runway tarmac, loaded onboard the jet Aircraft. And it would be airborne... The engines were already warming up and revving.

She felt an arm firmly steer her into the shadows. She followed, numb.

Yusuf walked Amanda towards the waiting car and opened a door for her. She could have walked home. He waited, the door still open.

"Miss Amanda, please..." he whispered.

She got in.

"There is a saying here in the Mediterranean..." began Yusuf from behind the steering wheel...

She sat in the rear seat of the vehicle, responding barely, weeping, not really knowing.

"It's not safe for you in the city for a while. Especially when they discover the girl has gone...Embassy or no! The war is spreading." He turned to her "...You can stay with my family for a few weeks I call my Anna to prepare...till things settle down...I will circulate rumors that the girl has flown to Paris... They will not panic then, and...they eventually, they will lose interest... she is only a girl!"

Amanda knew who "they" were.

"What happened to Trevor, Yusuf?" He drove, not answering. Then he stopped and said

"At least, Miss Amanda, he is alive!" And with that he drove on in silence.

* *

Less than two weeks later, two men were dropped by air lift. They were in full military desert combat gear. They scurried behind a sand hill and waited, watching the road travelled by many.

To the naked eye, they were invisible in the sand dune.

Two hours passed.

"We have visual contact" said the communications lead into his speaker.

"Confirm!"

"Affirmative. Positive identification is confirmed. Execute commission" came the electronic reply to his headpiece.

"Copy. Affirmative mission to execute. Commencing now."

The car approaching on the open road was moving at approximately 80 mph. They focused their sights, computing speed, distance and power.

It was an easy target.

The explosion was immediate, deadly and clean. The fireball hung in midair, as if suspended by a desert mirage, then dissipated. The Gibraltar BMW tags vaporized. ATZAR.

"Mission executed. Request for extraction. Over"

* *

They walked down the beach, the sun blazing down and waves roaring through a haze of brightness. Sea spray and squealing children in the surf playing came and went with far away sounds.

The two of them had taken a picnic, fresh fruit and pita sandwiches. A small beach umbrella made a small oasis where Amanda and Jim made a day of it. They both needed it, not the hot sun and dry heat that throbbed like a silent alarm, nor the gritty food, or residue of suntan lotion in their skin caked in sand, but the sea roaring in their ears dwarfed any of the world's problems.

"Funny, this place, isn't it?" said Amanda "So much has happened here that fill the record, yet so little is resolved. You would think that time or destiny would make a place more sage, don't you think?"

"I do" said Jim, settling down for a nap and pulling his hat over his eyes.

"What I can't understand..." continued Amanda, her mouth full of pita bread "Is why things don't get resolved in these parts...I mean, is a case of rogue European wannabe's that take root and ruin their country over a period of generations, colonists perhaps?"

"Could be" said Jim

"Then, why don't the locals reorganize themselves?"

"I have no idea!"

"You don't know much for an intelligence officer, do you?" she teased.

"Maybe not, but this I do know. You love him, don't you?"

The question totally startled her. With her head already shaking in denial, she knew she was totally without defense.

"I do" she said.

"And now...?"

"I don't know...Maybe one gets over these things, and you move on?"

"Well, that's the essence of overseas service. You experience things, sometimes great earth shattering things, but you move on!"

"Yes"   she said, putting away the lunch picnic basket and rearranging her own towel in the shade under their beach umbrella.

She would move on, she decided. Just like that. No looking back. No reliving that damned incident on the beach. No Ambassador's nonsense – thank God he was now recalled!

No regrets.

But had she done the right thing? This was the question that lurks just beneath the surface of everyone serving overseas. Minute by minute. Day by day. Response by response. Your role?

Their role? The official role?

"Do you remember the TV movies series Star Track?" said Jim suddenly from under his cap.

She looked at him, not snoozing at all. He got up on one elbow.

"I know what you're thinking. Did you do the right thing...Right?"

She nodded, squinting in the haze.

"You did! You were given one hell of a challenge. And you passed it. But you did the right thing. Only, you have to move on...That's all. Besides,

Trevor is somewhere else in his world...You should forget him, and focus on guys like me...!"

"Right" said Amanda.

But her thoughts never changed. Everyone who comes here leaves a part of their heart here, surely?

And Trevor. Forever in her heart, she decided.

How do you change that?

She was introduced to Trevor's replacement the next month. Somehow, it was all strange and she yearned to turn the routines back to the familiar.

Most remarkable of all was that not even the Ambassador acknowledged much in the weeks following. In fact, he was absent for of the time and it was rumored that he was not coming back. The *Chargé D'Affairs* took over the Embassy staff functions. .

 The days turned into drab weeks.

Amanda hastened for her moment of mission departure.

Still, she hoped for news of Trevor. Such intelligence missions could remain clandestine. It was generally held that he was dead. His name remained absent from all bulletins.

Gone.

She returned to her routine. Her place was her sanctuary. On the wall calendar, she was crossing out the months remaining for her tour, then the weeks.

Even the seasons changed. Deep in her heart she remained numb. She spent the weekends jogging at the beach, but she felt a loneliness, even abandonment.

Two weeks later, news come through that stunned her. Nothing eventful. Just a bulletin of personnel notifications.

It was announced that new post was created for a division at the Home Office at London. The Acting Director was to be Trevor McDonnell.

She could hardly believe it. She read it many times. Unwilling to draw attention, she said nothing. But the thought filled her with joy.

The sea and the salt and the sun surrounded her like an island in the Mediterranean from which there was no escape. It had overwhelmed her with its traumatic demands and bewitching environment.

But she'd had enough.

 She decided not to leave the Embassy premises unless absolutely necessary, and she threw herself into her work during the day, books by night – even if meant sharing pizza with her crazy neighbor Jim, on occasion.

Finally she realized that her tour would soon be over. Only two more months!

Less than a week later, she received a letter.

It was an invitation from the Laird of Glen Bruce for the official opening of the Fishing and Boating season at Bruce castle in Scotland. At the bottom was a handwritten inscription. "I'll meet you at Holgate on the Thames on June 2$^{nd.}$ For Dinner...
..."

"And, pack that little black swimsuit"

She stared. Trevor would be there?

In the sun-bleached brightness of the Mediterranean world, nothing could have been more refreshing.

Trevor. London!

The vision of the crisp green colors of London. She held the card. It all seemed a million years away. Only later could she believe the sensations that began to surface. She felt as if she were living with encrusted emotions. She was going to survive!

June 2nd. *What...?*

She put her hand to her mouth, calculating incredulously. Was it possible that he was aware her tour of duty in Beirut ended May 31?

Throughout the days, and well into the evening, her thoughts focused a little more clearly. She giggled.

That damned swimsuit... for some waterfront festivities in Scotland?

That was just like Trevor, to invite her to the party with him as a former colleague. Perhaps he had a girlfriend by now? She wondered.

It wasn't until later, actually almost a month later, that she noticed. Below his handwriting was the inscription that suddenly made itself clear. Something she had clearly missed.

He was not just an invitee. He was not a guest.

She paused suddenly.

Trevor MacDonnell was the titular host.

He was the Laird of Glen-Bruce.

* *

END